*Where*

*I'm*

*Home*

*For Charlotte*

## Acknowledgements

Firstly, I would like to thank my wonderful beta-readers and editor, Sarah, Elyse, Torie, and Caitlin, without whom this novel would not be what it is. I could not have done this without any of you, and I am so lucky to work with a team of people who love the characters as much as I do.

I would like to thank Deborah Bradseth for her hard work on the cover art for the book. You make this process so comfortable and easy, even when I cannot always articulate what it is I want until I see it on the page, and I am so grateful for that.

I would also like to give a massive shout out to Jeremy McLean at Points of Sail Publishing, not just for all the formatting work on both *Where I'm Home* and *All That Compels the Heart*, but for all the times I have had questions and needed support during the publishing process. This whole process is so much easier because of your experience as an author, and I appreciate you sharing your wisdom with me.

And last, but certainly not the least by any means, I would like to thank all of the fans of *All That Compels the Heart*. I could not have anticipated how well-received this series would be, and it is because of each and every one of you that this series did not end on that massive cliffhanger in the first book.

Any resemblance to persons living or dead is purely coincidental.

Copyright © 2020. All rights reserved.

# Table of Contents

Prologue .................................................................................. 1
Chapter One ........................................................................... 8
Chapter Two .......................................................................... 14
Chapter Three ....................................................................... 20
Chapter Four ......................................................................... 28
Chapter Five .......................................................................... 35
Chapter Six ............................................................................ 48
Chapter Seven ....................................................................... 79
Chapter Eight ........................................................................ 87
Chapter Nine ......................................................................... 98
Chapter Ten .......................................................................... 111
Chapter Eleven ..................................................................... 123
Chapter Twelve .................................................................... 135
Chapter Thirteen .................................................................. 149
Chapter Fourteen ................................................................. 155
Chapter Fifteen .................................................................... 175
Chapter Sixteen .................................................................... 187
Chapter Seventeen ............................................................... 197
Chapter Eighteen ................................................................. 215
Chapter Nineteen ................................................................ 231
Chapter Twenty ................................................................... 241
Chapter Twenty-One ........................................................... 254
Chapter Twenty-Two ........................................................... 265
Chapter Twenty-Three ......................................................... 277
Chapter Twenty-Four ........................................................... 287
Chapter Twenty-Five ........................................................... 294
Chapter Twenty-Six ............................................................. 304
Chapter Twenty-Seven ........................................................ 312
Chapter Twenty-Eight ......................................................... 320
Chapter Twenty-Nine .......................................................... 334
Epilogue ............................................................................... 339

## Prologue

All the roads not taken stretched before him, the choices he had made that had led him here to this moment. What he had thought were once broad boulevards leading him to one central point – Aoife O'Reilly – had instead turned out to be a warren of back alleys down a path of disappointment. As he watched her plane fly away, he could feel the eyes of a security guard trained on him. His hazel eyes were not unkind; he just had a job to do, and what he really wanted right now was for Michael to leave without causing a scene.

"Ah, for Jesus' sake, man, sure, and you're not going to make this any more difficult than it needs to be?"

The guard was attempting to be reasonable with him, humorous even, but there was an undercurrent of seriousness in his tone as well. He didn't want to have to remove him, but he would if he was forced to. The two of them had been doing this little dance for a few moments now, but it was time for one of them to make a decision.

Sizing up the guard, Michael thought about his options for a split second. The older man was probably in his mid-forties with light brown hair that looked like it was starting to thin out. He was shorter than Michael by several inches, but had a stockiness to him that told Michael that his height probably wouldn't give him an advantage in a tussle; the guard could probably tackle him to the ground and keep him there if needed. There were faint lines around the edges of his hazel eyes as he narrowed them, waiting for Michael's response. Not really wanting to get locked up in airport security for the rest of the day for assault, Michael forcibly relaxed his posture, and felt the other man instinctively do the same.

"Alright, I'm going." He held his hands up, a show of good faith that he meant him no trouble.

The security guard's face relaxed, and he uncrossed his arms, the unconscious gesture of deterrence no longer needed.

"Sure, and I'm grateful to ye. I don't get paid enough to deal with love-struck fools." He gave Michael a sympathetic look. "Sorry."

Michael shrugged, taking no offense. He knew that this must be exactly how he seemed right now.

"If you're looking for advice from a man who's been married to the love of his life for twenty years now, I'd tell ye to go back to the Aer Lingus counter and get yerself a ticket for the next flight out."

"Does she drive ye up the feckin' wall, your wife?" Michael ran his long fingers through his dark hair, his go-to sign of frustration or worry. Thinking about Aoife made him feel both lately.

"Every single day." A huge grin came over his face. "And her cooking's shite, but you didn't hear that from me. And I'm pretty sure her father still hates me as much as the day she first brought me home to meet him, but I wouldn't have it any other way."

Michael smiled and then looked at him curiously. "And what makes ye think that she's the love of my life?"

He nodded to the now empty runway.

"The look on your face. It's the same one I had the day I met my wife."

"Fair play." Michael nodded to the guard and turned to go.

Although his heart told him that if he just stood there a little longer he'd see her coming back through the gate, glad to see him, his head reminded him, cruelly, that this wasn't true. He could stand there until the sun had set, and all the flights had come and gone, and she still wouldn't walk back up that breezeway. She'd made that pretty damn clear by leaving in the first place.

"Best of luck to ye, son. Oh, and don't forget to credit me in your wedding speech when ye finally convince her to marry ye."

The guard winked at him and moved on with his rounds, whistling a tune as he went. His duty to protect the airport from the likes of Michael fulfilled.

The journey from the terminal back towards the car park was all a bit of a blur for Michael as he struggled against the reality settling in. He tried to focus on the illuminated signs overhead, lighting his way. All the while, the guard's words ran through his mind: all he had to do was get a ticket and hop on the next flight to New York City. Simple as that. Except that it wasn't as simple as that; with him and Aoife, it never was. It was always just such a goddamn mess.

Who was to say that if he got on that flight and showed up at her flat in New York, that she would even let him in? She'd closed herself off to him even before leaving Ireland, pushing him away before they had really started something. Sure, there had been his father's heart attack to use as an excuse, but it had been just that: an excuse for her to slip away without giving him a choice in whether he should stay or go with her. Whether or not she realized it, she'd decided what he would do before she'd even told him about the writing opportunity in New York, and so he'd felt cornered when she eventually told him. When he felt cornered, he always got stubborn and dug his heels in; she knew that. He'd reacted exactly the way she'd imagined he would, which had made it easier for her to go.

Now he had a choice. He could continue his way back to the car park, head back home and forget about her completely, or he could get himself a ticket on the next flight out and make a grand gesture and risk everything. He put his hands in his pocket and cursed when he realized he'd left his wallet in the car.

"Shit." Well, that was that, then. Also, he didn't have his passport with him. It was back home in Ballyclara. "Jaysus feckin' Christ!"

A few travellers on their way through the terminal gave him a few stares, clearly wondering if he was some kind of madman they should be concerned about.

"Not mad!" he wanted to shout at them. "Just a love-struck fool." Well, maybe that did make him mad, after all.

He made his way past the duty-free shops selling magazines, and booze, and perfumes, and everything else under the sun. Nearby were the cafes and fast-food vendors, people queuing up for that last bit of greasy food before being subjected to the congealed mess airlines liked to pretend was food. The heady scent of grease, fried food, and perfume all mingled and overpowered his senses.

Who was to say that if the universe had provided him with his wallet and passport right this second, and he went to New York, that things between him and Aoife would be any different? It wasn't like the two of them had had a straightforward relationship with each other since they first met nearly a year ago. In fact, they'd spent most of that time arguing with each other, trying to avoid their feelings. It wasn't like they had a good foundation for this relationship to find its footing and take hold.

Still, a large part of him wanted to buy that ticket to LaGuardia Airport, hail a cab to her place, beat on the door until she opened it and scoop her into his arms in the biggest, longest kiss until the two of them couldn't breathe, just like it happened in the movies. He would apologize for being an eejit and for ever letting her leave in the first place, and would promise to move to New York with her, or that they would somehow make it work long distance.

It was then he realized he had no idea where she was staying in New York. He hadn't thought to ask her. He was sure she'd left an address with her best friends, Bex and Millie, and that he could have asked one of them for it, if he'd known how to contact them. Although he'd met her friends, it wasn't as if they'd moved to the phase of dating where he had the official "be interrogated by the friends" dinner and gotten to know them. Anyways, he was pretty sure they had seriously mixed feelings about him, given his and Aoife's track record. When it came right down to it, it could hardly be said that the two of them had dated. They had skirted around the whole dating phase and moved straight into the "moving in with each other," and "meeting her family" phases, all to disastrous consequences. Was it any wonder their relationship had imploded? Had they ever stood a chance in the first place?

A sudden well of emotions bubbled inside him and he had to step out of the flow of traffic moving through the terminal to lean against the wall. He let its sturdiness support him while he paused a moment to catch his breath. He was well aware that he was attracting more stares now from the people walking past him, and he wondered if he might get another visit from the security guard again. But no one approached him and, after a moment, he re-joined the crowd, fighting against the anxiety that threatened to drown him. He continued to move forward in a bit of a daze, only brought back to the present when the moving sidewalk he'd just got on brought him to the end of the line and nearly tripped him up.

"You alright, mate?" A firm grip clasped his upper arm, preventing him from stumbling forward. It took him a half-second to realize that he recognized the voice and looked right up into the face of his best friend, Brendan McCaffrey. The faint laugh lines around Brendan's light-brown eyes made him look more serious than normal.

"Michael?" Brendan looked at him expectantly, concern now creeping into his voice.

He found he couldn't respond.

"Here."

Brendan guided him to one side, his grip on Michael's arm still firm. A golf cart carrying some elderly and disabled passengers whirred by them, ruffling his dark hair. He shivered slightly from the cool breeze it made when it passed and was brought back to the present.

"What happened?"

He saw Brendan glance around, trying to see if he could find Aoife in the crowd of faces.

"She's gone."

There wasn't anything else to say, was there?

He searched Brendan's face, hoping to... what? Hoping to find some hint of denial? Brendan had been his best mate since primary school, not because he was good at taking liberties with the truth, but because he told it to him straight. He might not like it on most occasions – or *any* occasion, for that matter – but it was always what he needed.

Brendan nodded slightly and cast his eyes to the floor.

"By the time I got to the gate, it was too late. Her plane was already taking off."

A sad look came across Brendan's face, and his lips tightened with disappointment. Michael knew he liked Aoife, that he'd come to think of her as a good friend. The news that she'd left had been distressing for him, too. Neither of them knew what to say.

"C'mon, mate; let's go home."

Brendan transferred his hand to Michael's shoulder and guided him back to the car, neither of them saying another word the whole ride back to Ballyclara.

## Chapter One

*New York City, USA*
*Three Years Later*

Aoife's office phone rang loudly beside her, disturbing the quiet that had settled over the room. She pushed aside the stack of papers on her mahogany desk to reach it. The caller ID read "Gina," the name of her new assistant, the fourth one to take over from her best friend, Millie, after she'd heartlessly abandoned her for a career in modelling and left her to fend for herself and find a new assistant. Ok, so that description of events might have been a tad over-the-top, but Aoife clearly still felt a hint of annoyance at having to train someone to get used to her working style all over again. She sighed and picked up the receiver.

"Aoife?"

## Where I'm Home

Gina's American accent struggled a bit with her name, still trying to reconcile the spelling with the pronunciation of it. She'd long ago accepted that, anywhere outside of Ireland, her name confused the hell out of people and there was no sense in getting worked up about it. She tried to hold back another sigh from escaping her lungs, lest she sound annoyed.

"What can I help you with, Gina?"

She tried to keep her tone as friendly as possible. It *was* her first week, after all, and she was still getting used to things. She didn't want to scare her away so soon if she could help it. It was just that she and Millie had a shorthand after so many years of friendship, and she was finding it was more difficult to train a new person than she'd expected, hence the reason she'd gone through so many assistants since Millie had left. Perhaps she was being unfair; Millie was one of her best friends after all, and just because she had gone off to Italy for her modelling career did not mean that Aoife should take out her abandonment issues out on poor Gina.

"I know you said you didn't want to be disturbed this afternoon, and you wanted me to hold your calls, but there's this young man on the phone who says it's urgent that he speak to you."

"Who is it?"

She wasn't expecting anyone to call her today. In fact, she had specifically arranged her schedule so she could get herself caught up on all of her work this afternoon. She had promised Colin she wouldn't bring work home this weekend so that they could take Miriam to the zoo – she was feeling guilty for spending so much time working on the weekends, which was supposed to be family time. To assuage her parental guilt, she'd promised Miriam they could do whatever she wanted this weekend to make up for it, and she wanted to keep that promise.

She wondered if it could be Colin who was calling, but Gina had fawned enough over him this week when he picked Aoife up that she would have assumed she'd know his voice by now. Not that Aoife could blame her; he had that effect on people. He was warm, generous, charming, handsome, and exceptionally unable to recognize any of these traits in himself. It all worked together to make one perfectly modest person who failed to notice most of the attention directed towards him, which endeared him to her all the more. However, Gina had said it was a *young* man. Colin was in his early thirties and didn't have what Aoife would describe as a "young" man's voice.

"I don't know. He didn't say." Gina's voice sounded worried, like she couldn't believe that she'd forgotten to ask something as simple as the name of the person calling.

"It's alright. Transfer him over."

Not wanting to make the poor girl feel terrible, she figured that there was no harm in breaking her rule about not taking calls today, just this once. The odds were good that Gina would accidentally drop the line during the transfer anyways.

There was a brief pause, and then her phone rang again.

*Shit.* She'd kind of been counting on Gina dropping the call.

She didn't immediately recognize the number on the caller ID, but she did recognize the area code as coming from Ireland. Her heart leapt in her throat. Who could be calling her from Ireland? Surely no one in her family, unless it was her cousin, Connor, but then she'd know his number.

*Maybe he got a new mobile?*

It was plausible enough, she supposed, even though she knew he'd just gone and upgraded his mobile the other week. He was the only person from Ireland she heard from on a regular basis, unless you counted Mara and her son, Rory. While they almost always chatted whenever Connor initiated a phone conversation, tagging on their news for her as a last-minute update before hanging up. They never called her just to talk to her on her own.

She couldn't really blame them for it. When she'd left Ireland, she'd left behind Mara's brother, Michael, too. Even though she'd been too polite to bring it up with her in the three years since Aoife had come to New York, she knew Mara still held a bit of resentment towards her for it. If Mara wasn't currently dating Connor, Aoife doubted she'd hear from either her or Rory.

The number of people from Ballyclara that would have reason to call her was a small circle of friends: Sinead and Dermot Flanagan, Mara and Michael's parents; Brendan and Molly McCaffrey, Michael's best friends; Karen and Jimmy, the young couple that Mara had sort of taken under her wing; and Father Patrick, the kindly village priest. And Michael. And let's face it, hell had a better chance of freezing over than Michael calling her. Still, she found her heart jumping a bit at the thought.

Mustering up whatever courage she could find, she gently cleared her throat before answering. "Aoife O'Reilly speaking."

The conversation was brief, but it left her reeling. She hung up the receiver with a heaviness in her heart. Swivelling her leather chair to face the floor-to-ceiling windows of her office, she got up and rested her forehead against the cool pane of glass. Clouds hung low over Manhattan, matching her grey mood. New Yorkers hurried about their day, rushing to and fro with even more gusto than normal, worried the skies could open up at any moment and drop a deluge on them. Everything in this city moved so quickly; it was still a little overwhelming to her even after living here for a few years. She pinched the bridge of her nose where it met her forehead, the skin crinkling like crushed silk.

When she opened her eyes, it was to see the first pitter-patter of rain against the window. She smoothed down her green jumper and matching plaid skirt, glad now that she had worn something warmer on this cool, early summer day, despite the earlier forecast that it would be warm and sunny. Growing up in Ireland, she had learned to always be prepared for any type of weather, because it could change at any given moment, much like life.

With a heaviness she hadn't felt in quite some time, she sat down in her chair and swivelled back towards her desk. Taking a steadying breath, she picked up the receiver.

"Gina? Could you cancel all of my appointments for next week, please?"

"Sure."

She could tell that her attempt to keep her tone neutral had not entirely worked and her assistant definitely knew something was wrong.

"Should I reschedule them for another time?"

"Um, yes. Try rescheduling them for the week after next, please."

She glanced at her desktop calendar, mentally running through who would be annoyed with her for shifting their meeting, and who wouldn't put up a fuss. She might have to make a few calls herself to smooth a few ruffled feathers, but there was nothing urgent coming up that she couldn't handle while she was away.

"Ok." She heard Gina clicking her pen and writing down her instructions. "Is there anything else you need?"

"Yes, can you book Colin, Miriam, and I onto a flight to Dublin? The sooner, the better. Tonight would be best, in fact. Tomorrow morning at the very latest."

"Dublin? Are you going home?"

She thought the words over a moment. Ireland was where she was from, where she'd been born, but was it home?

"Yes, I am."

## Chapter Two

The day was typically Irish: a mixed bag of everything. It had started out rainy and dreary, but this had eventually tapered off into a slight drizzle. Michael was grateful for this; at least now they wouldn't have to walk to church in the pouring rain. A little rain was considered good luck, but a deluge would be simply awful. He wouldn't normally have considered himself a superstitious person; he didn't believe that seeing the bride before the wedding would doom a marriage, for example, but on a day like today, he wanted as much to go right as it possibly could.

"Ready to go?" Ailish asked, looking up from the mirror where she was fixing the stud of her pearl earring.

He held up the ends of his navy-blue tie towards her in response, looking a little helpless. He knew how to tie his own tie; of course, he did. He'd been doing it for years on his own. It was that he couldn't seem to keep his hands steady enough today. Every attempt had resulted in him becoming frustrated and throwing the bloody thing down on the dresser in front of him.

"Here, let me." She smirked a little in amusement and deftly achieved in seconds what he'd been trying to do for the last several minutes.

"There." She patted his chest, fixing it into place. He caught her hand and kissed her palm lightly, eliciting a musical laugh as his lips tickled her skin.

"Thank you." It wasn't only for helping him with the tie; it was for all the moments in the last three years that she'd been there for him.

They'd met when his father, Dermot, was staying in the hospital three years ago after his heart attack. She'd been working at the front desk of the hospital, the person who guided people to the right floor or answered any other enquiries they might have. That day at the airport, the day Aoife had left, Michael had asked Brendan on the drive home to take him back to the hospital. He and Dermot had always been close, and in that moment, he needed to talk to his father. When he had walked through the front doors, however, he'd suddenly felt his courage waning. Dermot had tasked him with going to the airport and bringing Aoife back. Now he had to find a way to tell his father that he'd failed in that mission.

He hadn't realized at the time that he'd been standing in the middle of the lobby – probably looking a right eejit – when a light, slightly musical voice with a Cork accent asked, "Can I help you?"

He'd looked and realized the petite brunette sitting behind the reception desk had been talking to him.

"Can I help you?" she repeated, her algae-green eyes staring straight at him.

"Oh! Uh, no, I'm afraid ye can't." His words had

tumbled out, as he remembered that the one person who could help him right now was probably halfway across the Atlantic Ocean.

"Only, it looks as if ye might need someone to talk to." There was a note of concern in the young woman's voice. "Come, let's get you some tea, eh? Only I was about to go on my break, and it looks like you could use a cuppa, too."

And just like that, he found himself being guided towards the hospital cafeteria and talking to Ailish. She had an easy and comforting way about her that made him feel safe. She took charge of the conversation at first, telling him how she was a student at the university, hoping to major in hospitality. This job was her way of finding some experience in customer service, but she really loved it because it meant she got to help people who were facing some of the worst times in their lives, and she got to make things a little easier for them. At least, that was what she'd hoped.

Ailish was friendly, outgoing, and a talker for sure, which was good for him because it meant that he didn't have to contribute much to the conversation beyond an occasional nod of the head or grunt in agreement with something she'd said. It was as if she'd been able to read his mind and known exactly what it was he'd needed in that moment. She hadn't put any pressure on him to open up to her, which he'd greatly appreciated.

"Oh, look at the time!" she'd suddenly exclaimed, standing up and drinking down the last of her tea. "I'm late getting back again. I'll see you tomorrow. If I don't get fired, that is. And, if I do happen to get fired, here's my number. In case you need to talk. Seriously, give us a ring any time. And I promise not to do all the talking next time."

She'd hastily scribbled her number down on the

back of her receipt for him and slid it across the table. He still had that receipt in a fold in his wallet.

As it had turned out, Ailish had not been fired – her boss, it seemed, couldn't resist her ray-of-sunshine attitude either – and that one cup of tea slowly became a regular occurrence. Michael began to feel like a new person; not in any radical, definable way, but he felt the difference between the man he'd been when he'd been with Aoife, and how he was with Ailish. Aoife had challenged and intrigued him; Ailish made him feel relaxed and content.

On the day of Dermot's release from the hospital, he had felt a pang of loss he hadn't been expecting, knowing it was going to be the last time he would have an excuse to come in and see her. As if reading his mind once again, when he came to the reception desk to say hi, she'd asked, "Would you like to maybe go out sometime?"

He'd completely surprised himself by saying, "Yeah, I'd like that."

One date had turned into several and had evolved into bringing her home to Ballyclara to meet his folks. Although Dermot had not been able to completely hide his disappointment that Aoife was not coming back, both he and Sinead seemed glad to see their son happy again and did their best to give Ailish a warm welcome. Mara had taken a bit more convincing; with her dating Aoife's cousin, Connor, Mara still felt a sense of loyalty to Aoife.

Michael knew she still kept up with what Aoife was doing; he'd come across her stash of celebrity gossip magazines she would hastily stow from view when he'd come over to visit one time. On the front covers were little photos of Aoife attending club openings and glitzy fundraisers, or fashion shows. He couldn't help but notice that she never seemed to attend them with a new boyfriend; usually she was in a group shot, either with her best friends, Bex and Millie, or with people he didn't recognize. He tried not to read too much into the photos, especially the fact that she didn't appear to be dating anyone else.

Of course, this was all easier said than done, especially when Aoife's cousin, Connor, returned to Ireland. He and Mara had struck up an interest in one another on one of his visits to Ballyclara to see Aoife before shipping out on another military tour. The two of them had kept in touch the whole time he was away, interest giving way to genuine feelings for one another. Now that the two of them were making a serious attempt at having a relationship, the temptation was always there for Michael to ask how Aoife was every time Connor visited. He knew he should tell them it was fine to talk about her, that he was happy with Ailish, but he had to admit that it was easier to put that whole chapter of his life behind him when he didn't have to hear her name mentioned all the time.

And so, little by little, Ailish became a part of the fabric of his daily life in Ballyclara as he tried to rid the ghost of Aoife from all their familiar haunts. He and Brendan offered Ailish some work at their pub, *O'Leary's*, on the weekends when she wasn't doing work for uni or at the hospital, even though he and Brendan had only been able to afford to pay her a pittance of what she made at there. She never seemed to mind, though, nor did she mind the commute between her place in Cork and his place in Ballyclara. As she spent more time in Ballyclara, Michael introduced Ailish to all the places that had been special to him and Aoife: the church, the pub, the waterfall just outside of town, until Aoife faded into the background, even if she was never entirely gone from his memory. Eventually, there just didn't seem to be a

## Where I'm Home

need for her to go back to Cork all the time. It started with a drawer with her stuff, then a closet, and now they were practically living together. He knew that was the next step everyone expected from him.

He had to admit that it had been so important to him that Ailish had been here every day with him, especially these last few months. As Dermot's health began fading again, they'd all known that this time he wouldn't be bouncing back like before. In his usual way, he hadn't wanted anyone to make a fuss over him. He'd insisted Michael focus on the pub and his contracting business with Brendan, and on Ailish. He'd demanded Mara spend time in Dublin with Connor and not wait at home for him to die.

Those last few months had been the hardest in his life, more difficult than losing anyone else he'd ever loved. He didn't think he would have made it through them without Ailish always by his side, not just a rock for him to lean on, but a feckin' boulder propping him up when he felt like he was about to go over the edge of a cliff.

"Ready?" she asked him again, bringing him back to the present. She smiled up at him with that same sweet smile that had charmed him since the moment they'd met. He knew he'd been a wreck of a person to be around when they'd first met, and he certainly hadn't been any easier to live with in the time since; his failed engagement to Eliza and his failed whatever-the-hell-it-was he'd had with Aoife had taught him that. But Ailish made him want to change, to have things work out differently this time.

"Let's go," he said, taking her hand.

## Chapter Three

Fog clung to the tops of the Wicklow Mountains in an eerie fashion. As if at any moment, something dark and sinister might emerge from their murky shadows and descend upon the tiny village. In a way it had, for Death had come to Ballyclara.

The air was still and heavy, but cool, as Michael and Ailish walked up the path from his cottage to meet his sister, his nephew, Rory, and Connor at his parents' cottage. He shrugged off a chill as they drew closer to Aldridge Manor. The old rectory had once been owned by the local lord and then gifted to the Catholic Church, and then had been bought by Aoife. As a child, he'd always thought – dreamed, more like – that he'd live in it one day. Of course, it was only a dream for a man who owned to businesses and still found it difficult to pay his bills every month.

## Where I'm Home

In the three years since Aoife had left for America, Aldridge Manor had been abandoned yet again. She'd hired a realtor to sell it for her, but she'd made it clear that any potential buyers would need to be vetted first through Michael's parents, Sinead and Dermot Flanagan, since they knew more about the property than anyone else. She knew she could trust them to make sure the place was sold only to someone who was worthy of it.

In all the time she'd been gone, the place had had only one offer made on it, but this had been quickly quashed by Sinead. When the man had shown up at the cottage on the instruction of the realtor, he'd not been given the same kind of welcome as Aoife had been given. He'd not been offered a seat in the front room, nor even a cup of tea. She'd made him stand there awkwardly in the kitchen, fidgeting with his business suit, while she'd bustled about as if she couldn't give him the time of day. When he'd tried to ask Dermot questions about the property and its upkeep, Sinead had been monosyllabic with her responses, making it clear that she was the one to impress, not her husband. When he'd finally put his briefcase on the table and opened it up to write down a bidding offer on a piece of paper, she'd snapped it out of his hand. She'd eyed him with suspicion for a moment, then pronounced that his offer was too low, and she couldn't possibly accept on Miss O'Reilly's behalf, even though it had been more than Aoife had asked for. The buyer had apologized, fearing he had caused some offence and quickly offered to double his price, but Sinead would hear none of it. She hurried him out of the cottage on the pretence of having to go down to the shops and rushed him back to his car. When the fancy realtor Aoife had hired had called inquiring about the potential buyer, Sinead had feigned ignorance, saying that she'd not seen anyone come through with a reasonable offer on the place.

After hanging up the phone, even though Dermot hadn't done so much as raise an eyebrow in her direction, Sinead had said snippily:

"Don't ye be judging me, Dermot Flanagan! It's true; that man's offer wasn't half what the place is worth. It isn't lying if he didn't come up with something reasonable."

She'd genuflected though, just in case this counted as blasphemy.

"Perhaps it's less that the offer wasn't reasonable than it simply wasn't the right type of person," Dermot had agreed quietly, going back to the paper he'd been pretending to read.

"Quite right," his wife had agreed with him.

It wasn't as if he hadn't been hoping as much as any other person in the village that Aoife would return from New York, and they could put all this nonsense of selling the manor house behind them. Mara and Karen had been going every week to keep up the gardens, "in case any potential buyers came along," but everyone knew they were doing it because they hoped Aoife would come back to it. No one had wanted to admit that, that day wasn't going to come, but slowly, Mara and Karen had stopped going back to Aldridge Manor, and the gardens were now in the same ruinous state as when Aoife had bought the place. It was sad to see the old house looking so abandoned as he and Ailish drew closer to it, but he put the thought from his mind. There were more important things to focus on today.

When Michael and Ailish approached the Flanagans' cottage, they could see Connor and Rory were already standing by the gate to Mara's cottage, dressed in their Sunday best, along with Brendan and his son, Desmond McCaffrey, who was also Michael's godson.

## Where I'm Home

"They're inside helping your mother to get ready." After thirty-odd years of friendship, Brendan hadn't even needed Michael to ask a question before responding to it.

"I should go in and check on them," Ailish said, rubbing Michael's arm lovingly before heading for the cottage.

The five of them stood there in silence, not sure what to say to one another. Michael took the momentary reprieve to light a cigarette. He'd been trying to cut down on his smoking habit since meeting Ailish; not because she'd pressured him into it, but, he supposed, Dermot's health scare with his heart had made him rethink his own health and that maybe he should cut back on the smoking and drinking a wee bit.

As he puffed away silently, he noticed Des had a protective arm wrapped around Rory, holding him up. Rory's cheeks were damp, and he wiped at them with the back of his hand, but making an effort to seem like he was bearing up. Michael walked over to the lads and folded them both into a tight embrace. He did his best to give them a reassuring smile, fighting back his own tears. He was happy that his nephew was the best of friends with Brendan's son; everyone needed someone to lean on in times of trouble, and he couldn't think of anyone better for Rory to have than Des. He let them both go and hastily stamped out his cigarette into the dirt path, giving Ailish a guilty look as she reappeared with Mara, Molly, and Sinead.

It was so strange to see his mother without his father. Dermot had always been a quiet, mild-mannered man, but he had arguably been the lynchpin of the entire Flanagan family. Now that he was gone, it left a gaping hole in their family tapestry. Although perfectly coiffed, he noticed the corners of his mother's eyes were a little damp, and that she was fidgeting with one of his father's handkerchiefs in her hands.

"Hello Mam."

He pulled her into a hug and was surprised to find how small and frail she felt. Sinead had always been a force to reckon with; to suddenly find her vulnerable was jarring for him. He suddenly wondered how much longer he and Mara would have their mother around before the two of them were made orphans. She patted his back lightly and he let her go, both of them trying to compose themselves; not that the others were faring any differently. There wasn't a dry eye among them.

The mood was broken by the sound of tires coming up the lane, and they saw the hearse slowly approaching, followed by most of the couple of hundred residents of Ballyclara. More than a few seemed the worse for wear, probably because of the wake held in Dermot's honour last night at the pub that had lasted well into the wee hours of the morning. The Flanagans fell into step behind the hearse and made their way with the whole village to the little parish church up the lane.

There weren't enough pews to seat everyone, so a fair number of people had to stand in the back. Not that anyone minded. Dermot was as much a fixture of Ballyclara as his son's pub, or the fountain in the village square, or the church they were standing in. His death had rocked the entire village, and there was not one of them who wouldn't be there to give him a proper send-off.

And a proper send-off it was. Des and Brendan performed a heart-breaking rendition "Be Still" by The Fray. As he listened to father and son singing in perfect harmony, Michael couldn't help but notice how Des had a voice just like his father.

If there had somehow been a dry eye in the church

after Des and Brendan, there surely wasn't anyone left who wasn't moved after Mara's reading Mary Elizabeth Frye's poem "Do Not Stand at My Grave and Weep." The poem so moved him, Michael had had serious fears he wasn't going to get through his eulogy. As Connor stepped forward to help a sobbing Mara down from the pulpit, Ailish took his hand and squeezed it reassuringly. As he rose from his place in the family's pew to go to the pulpit, he gave her a light kiss on the temple, grateful she was here.

"Da would be so happy to see you all here today, even if he'd have told you that you needn't have bothered with making such a fuss over him," he addressed everyone gathered in the church. A few faint smiles appeared on the lips of those gathered in the pews before him. He paused a moment, looking down at the notes he'd stayed up most of the night making, then looked out at his friends and family.

"You don't need me to stand up here to tell you what a good man my father was. You all know it through the way he was always there to help a friend in need, in the way he loved his family," Michael smiled at his mother, sister, and nephew. "He wasn't a good man because he went around telling everyone so, in fact, I don't think there was ever a time he could take a compliment without getting at least a little embarrassed. No, he was a good man because of the things he did, how he greeted everyone in kind, no matter where they came from. He was rarely one to judge another person, rarely ever saying an unkind thing about anyone, even if they'd wronged him.

"Da, we all were so blessed to have ye in our lives, being that shining example of unconditional love and kindness, and the world is a poorer place now without you." He took a steadying breath and stepped down from the pulpit, giving way to Father Patrick.

"Thank you, Michael and Mara. Such beautiful words," Father Patrick said, momentarily taking back leadership of the ceremony. He then delivered the Eucharist before saying a few final words before they proceeded with the Committal.

"I'd like to take a few moments now to follow up on the words of Dermot's son, Michael, and open the room to anyone who would like to share a little story or memory of Dermot Flanagan."

There was hardly a pause before people rose from their pews, eager to share with Dermot's nearest and dearest how he had touched their lives, whether it was helping them on their farm, or helping to carry their shopping for them, the happy regular you could count on to be down at the pub and give you a laugh, to times when he sat with them during the darkest moments during their lives, his kind words a salve when they couldn't see the way forward. There was laughter, there were tears, and then a lull descended upon the church.

"Thank you all for sharing. If any of you were too shy to share a story or memory, or if you think of any others, please feel free to continue them down at the pub after the service. For now, I'd like to conclude this part of the service with a song chosen by Dermot himself."

The familiar sound of Monty Python's "Always Look on the Bright Side of Life," played over the church's little stereo system, giving them all a little chuckle, for it was just like Dermot to want the final words of his funeral to be about looking at the brighter side of life than focusing on the sadness of his passing.

Father Patrick gestured to the pallbearers to come to the front of the church and bear the coffin outside to the little to the little graveyard adjacent the church, to its final resting place.

## Where I'm Home

"In sure and certain hope of the resurrection to eternal life through our Lord Jesus Christ, we commend to Almighty God our brother, Dermot, and we commit his body to its resting place." Father Patrick paused a moment, looking out over the crowd at something behind Michael. He noticed the priest's hesitation, but as he'd quickly recovered and resumed the service as if nothing had happened, Michael pushed the momentary falter from his mind.

With the service concluded, Father Patrick, Michael, Mara, Connor, Rory, and Sinead formed a little line near the church, facing the long string of mourners, thanking them for their kind words. As the mourners made their way down to the pub, Ailish motioned to him that she was going to follow them down.

"I'm just going to go and help Molly and some of the others put out the food and such for the reception. I'll see you down there in a bit?"

"Thanks." He gave her a quick kiss and interlaced his fingers in hers. She squeezed his hand affectionately before letting their hands drift apart as she turned to meet up with Eliza Kennedy and her family and they made their way down to the village.

The crowd of mourners had thinned out now. Michael headed back towards the cemetery to find Father Patrick – who had gotten separated from the family by a group of parishioners – to thank him for the lovely service and then walk down to the pub with his family, when he heard a familiar voice come from behind him, a voice he had not heard for a very long time.

## Chapter Four

"Hello Michael."

No matter how much time had passed between them, he would recognize that voice anywhere. He couldn't count the number of times he'd rehearsed in his head what he would say the next time he saw her. He'd been practising ever since he'd watched her plane take off for New York.

Michael wasn't sure what he'd been expecting to feel in this moment, but perhaps the biggest shock for him wasn't in seeing Aoife for the first time in three years; it was that seeing her again felt nothing like he'd imagined. After all the daydreams of running off to New York after her, and all the time and anxiety spent planning what he would say to her over the last three years, he now felt little more than mild surprise at seeing her standing in front of him again. Perhaps it was the shock.

## Where I'm Home

She was dressed in a smart, but plain black dress that fell just above the knee, and a thin black jacket with three-quarter length sleeves. She wore a black fascinator over her auburn hair with a tiny black veil perched upon it. A half-smile formed on her mouth, twisting it into a partly grim look. He could never presume to know what she was thinking most of the time, but this time especially, he couldn't tell what was going on behind those sapphire-blue eyes. Of course, he should have known his sister would have told her about Dermot's passing, but he certainly hadn't expected her to come all the way from New York for the funeral.

He returned her smile, looking around for his sister, mother, nephew – anyone really – to get him out of this situation, but none of them had noticed the intruder amongst them. With only the slightest hesitation, he stepped around his father's grave and came to stand before her.

"Thank you for coming."

His voice was hoarser than he would have liked, his throat tight with emotion and the cold, damp air around them. She shivered slightly in her light jacket, feeling the same chill as him. Instinct, and a lifetime of having good manners drilled into him by his mother, made him move to take off his suit jacket to drape it around her shoulders when another man came to her side and did that very thing.

"Here, babe. It's getting cold out again."

He was a handsome man, well-tailored. He was tall; only an inch or so shorter than Michael himself. His hair was jet black, and his eyes dark brown, like peat soil. His features were of Asian descent, but his accent was American; somewhere from the west coast, if he had to guess. His dress shirt was fitted around his arms and torso, showing off an athletic frame, and the grip from the handshake he proffered enhanced the fact that his athleticism wasn't just imagined.

"Hi, I'm Colin. I wish we were meeting under different circumstances. So sorry for your loss."

A small sliver of something – anger, regret, jealousy – formed in Michael's stomach as he shook Colin's hand in greeting.

"Michael Flanagan. Thank you for being here."

Suddenly feeling extremely awkward, Michael did not know what else to say to the man whom Aoife had clearly chosen to move on with. Before Aoife could confirm his fears about why Colin was here at his father's funeral, a little voice said, "I'm hungry. When are we going to eat?"

Michael looked down at a young girl peeking around Colin's leg. She was dressed in a pretty black dress with a lace frill around the skirt and pearl buttons down the front, paired with a short velvet jacket over her arms.

"We're going to go soon, love," Aoife reassured the little girl as she came over and nestled her face in Aoife's skirt, looking up at Michael with curiosity. Aoife lovingly put a hand on her shoulder and smoothed her long black hair.

Michael couldn't help but see the maternal gesture, and immediately felt a pang in his heart so intense that it took him off-guard for a moment. He wasn't going to say that he'd hoped even just a little in the last three years that maybe, just maybe, Aoife had been unhappy without him or pined for him just a little, but seeing her standing here before him with her family made him realize that somewhere deep down that was exactly what he'd been hoping for. Well, now he didn't need to ask her what she'd been up to in the time since she'd been gone; it was plain for all to see. Before he could say anything, his own family came to his side.

"Aoife, Colin." Connor kissed his cousin's cheek in greeting, sounding slightly surprised to see her as he shook Colin's hand with a familiarity that could only come with knowing someone for awhile.

*Bastard.* Of course, her cousin would've known that she'd moved on with someone else.

It wasn't that Michael was angry with Connor for knowing about Colin; it was that he'd not said a damned thing to him about it. Of course, there had been the virtual moratorium on mentioning anything about her, but this was one of those times you ignored that and gave a man some warning so he could move on from his ex, because clearly *she* had.

"Connor!" The little girl standing by Aoife stretched arms towards him, begging to be picked up.

"Hello Miriam," he greeted her, obliging her by scooping her up into his arms.

"I didn't think the three of you would be here," Mara said, hugging Aoife and Colin, looking apologetically over Aoife's shoulder at Michael and making a gesture to show that she was just as surprised as him to find her here.

So, if Mara hadn't been the one to tell Aoife about Dermot's passing, then who? Connor? Even though he'd been happy to see Aoife and Colin, he'd seemed genuinely surprised to see them too. So, who would want to bring Aoife back here and mess up the carefully crafted life he'd built in her absence?

"We probably wouldn't have if Rory hadn't called," Aoife answered Mara's implied question.

His nephew hunched his shoulders a bit at having

had his secret revealed, but didn't bow his head in fear, daring his mother and uncle to say that he'd been wrong to call her. Michael involuntarily narrowed his eyes, but didn't say anything. The lad hadn't meant any harm by it, after all. It wasn't Rory's fault that Michael had his hang ups over seeing Aoife again. He'd just been trying to let her know about the passing of someone he knew had meant a great deal to her.

"My God, how you've grown up," Aoife said, giving Rory a once over. "You've shot up like a bean sprout. I suppose Des is just the same."

Rory blushed a bit.

"Come down to the pub and see him for yerself," Mara said to her. "There's a reception for Da and I'm sure everyone will want to see ye. Mam will be especially pleased."

"Oh, I'm not sure…" Aoife looked like she wanted to be anywhere else right now and Michael couldn't help but feel a momentary pleasure at seeing her squirm under the scrutiny he'd had to live with the last three years. That way, the joy of living in a place as small as Ballyclara: nothing escaped the notice of your neighbours.

As if speaking of Sinead had brought her forth, she exclaimed, "Aoife? Is that you? Christ, but it's so good to see ye, love."

"Hello, Sinead." Aoife hugged his mother lightly and kissed her cheek. "I'm so sorry to hear about Dermot."

Michael saw tears forming at the corners of Aoife's eyes and her voice caught in her throat a little. "He'll be sorely missed."

Sinead said nothing in return, but gripped her hand and tried to smile through the tears she was fighting back.

"And who's this?" she asked, trying to distract herself from crying yet again.

"This is Colin," Aoife introduced her partner, "and this is Miriam."

"Oh, isn't she a dear?" Sinead smiled up at the little girl in Connor's arms, and then raised an eyebrow in Aoife's direction. "Well, we have much catching up to do, don't we?"

A faint blush rose in Aoife's cheeks. Michael could tell that she was not looking forward to the interrogation to come.

"Can we eat now?" Miriam took the moment of silence that fell on the crowd to loudly whisper to Connor, who smiled up at her.

"Alright, monkey, let's get you something to eat then, shall we?" he said, leading the group down towards the pub.

"Sure, and it's yourself," Father Patrick greeted Aoife.

"Colin, I'd like you to meet Father Patrick," she said, introducing him to the priest.

"I've heard so many things about you," Colin smiled at him.

"Only good things, I hope," the priest replied, winking at him.

"Are you going with us to the pub?" Miriam asked him. Aoife gave her a parental look which warned her not to bother the old man.

"I am child, I am," he smiled at her.

"Father Patrick, I'd like you to meet Miriam."

"It's a pleasure to meet you, Miriam," he said, extending a hand to her.

"I apologize for her; she's off her schedule, what

with the overnight flight and coming straight here from the airport." Aoife looked apologetically at the priest.

"Oh, she's fine," he scoffed. "Now, I heard someone was hungry, and you know what? So am I!" He smiled at the little girl, eliciting a laugh from her. "Would you care to join me?"

She nodded eagerly.

"Well, what are we all waiting around for? Let's go!" With a spry step, Father Patrick bounded down the lane towards the pub, as if they were all his sheep and he was their shepherd, showing them the way.

<u>Chapter Five</u>

As the plane descended towards to Dublin Airport, she couldn't help but admire the sheer beauty of her home country. The sea of emerald-green fields were broken only by the grey stone walls dividing farmland, and the white sheep dotting the landscape until countryside gave way to the commercial and industrial landscapes of the city. She found herself both excited and unsettled about being home again. There was something indescribable about Ireland that pulled at her from across the Atlantic; however, it also gave her a profound sense of anxiety to face all that she'd left behind her.

She knew the thing she dreaded most about coming home was going to be the questions. Or rather, *the* question: why did she choose to leave Michael for New York? The answer, however selfish it may sound to others, was that she'd done it for herself. It had been an opportunity she'd wanted to take, and it was only after the years had passed that now she didn't feel the need to apologize for it. She regretted that Michael hadn't come with her, but she also knew he'd have hated it there: the noise, the busyness, the frantic energy of the city. It was the exact opposite of the quiet life he led in Ballyclara; everything he despised. Having him there with her would only have marred what had otherwise been a beautiful experience for her.

No, going to New York had been the right decision. It had given her an opportunity to learn more about the publishing industry that she wouldn't have otherwise had, and she'd needed to pursue that dream for herself. She knew that if she'd stayed in Ireland with him, she would have spent every day of the last three years wondering what could have been had she only made the decision to go. But she would have been lying had she said that letting go of what she'd left behind hadn't been the most difficult decision she'd ever made. Now that she was coming home, she wasn't sure how she felt about having to face the very ghosts she thought she'd put behind her.

Despite the long flight, and how tired they all would be because of the time change, Aoife knew they needed to get through the airport quickly if they had a hope of making it in time to Ballyclara for the funeral. She took a still-sleeping Miriam from Colin's arms, the little girl unconsciously burrowing her face into the crook between Aoife's neck and shoulder. Aoife smoothed down her hair, breathing in the floral scent of her shampoo. Miriam groaned at being shifted but didn't wake as she carried her through the terminal to customs, and on to get their luggage. The three of them headed out into the grey light of early morning to get a taxi to their hotel.

Her flat in Dublin had sold practically before she'd gotten on the plane to New York, and while she knew Connor would have no problem with them staying at his flat while he was in Ballyclara, it had just been easier to get a hotel and not have that feeling of obligation or of being a burden by staying with someone they knew. Besides, she'd wanted the freedom of being able to pack up and leave right away; she had no plans to stay here longer than was absolutely necessary. When they got up to their room, they quickly changed out of their travelling clothes and went downstairs to pick up the car Gina had hired for them and drove down to Ballyclara.

By the time they arrived, the picturesque village was practically deserted; she knew where they would all be. She passed by the pub and the fountain in the centre of the village, and turned up the lane towards the church, passing by Michael and Mara's cottages, barely taking them in, trying not to think of the memories she'd made in this place. She turned off the road on the left, pulling into the drive of Aldridge Manor. There would be nowhere to park along the narrow lane by the church, so parking here and walking the rest of the way would be their best bet to get there on time.

"C'mon, we're going to be late," she said to Colin as he picked up Miriam from the back seat. She'd woken up sometime on the ride down and was now looking around silently, half sucking her thumb, just taking in all the unfamiliar sights, sounds, and smells. Aoife felt sorry that she had upended their planned weekend of going to the zoo, and wished to be back in New York right now, but she knew she had to be here for this. Dermot had been so kind to her when she lived here, and she felt in her bones that she needed to pay her respects to him.

More than that, there was a feeling deep inside her that she needed to be in Ballyclara itself, to see these people again who'd had such an impact on her life, even if it was going to be awkward as hell. Without them, she wouldn't have the life she had now.

The air felt cooler and damper here than it had in Dublin, as if it had been raining recently, even though the ground beneath their feet was no longer wet. They arrived at the church just in time to see them carrying Dermot's coffin to the graveyard beside the church. The Flanagans had decided to bury Dermot near the top of the gently sloping hill behind the parish church, giving him a view of the village below. The trees around the graveyard were silent, the only sounds coming from the quiet chatter of those gathered near the grave, and the occasional rustle of the wind through the trees.

The three of them hung back a bit and stood near the edge of the crowd, but still trying to blend in. The last thing she wanted to do was to draw attention from the solemnity of the occasion. As everyone faced the gravesite, the only person who saw them arrive was Father Patrick. She could see from the way his eyes widened slightly, and the slight pause he gave in conducting the rituals that he'd been surprised to see her but, ever the professional, he carried on with the rest of the service with the respect Dermot deserved. As the service drew to a close, she moved aside, trying to get out of the way of the others headed back towards the village, where she knew there was going to be a reception down at the pub Michael and Brendan owned.

"Hello Aoife."

The voice beside her immediately filled her with dread. Of all the people she thought she'd have to face again, Eliza Kennedy was the one she could have done without. Michael's ex-fiancée, the woman whom Aoife had unintentionally replaced in his affections, stood before her and she instinctively looked for a way out. The last thing she wanted was to hear the litany of names Eliza was probably going to call her – not all of them undeserved – and avoid having a huge fight at Dermot's funeral.

"I didn't think we would be seeing you here today."

To Aoife's surprise, Eliza's tone was more curious than interrogative. Turning to greet her, Aoife pasted on her best fake smile, hoping to seem unfazed.

"Eliza!" she said with far more enthusiasm than she felt. She drew a few looks from those passing by and reminded herself to tone it down a bit. This *was* a funeral, after all.

As Aoife got up the courage to look Eliza in the eye, the first thing she noticed was that she was enormously pregnant. She found herself temporarily dumbstruck at this revelation, mixed with a strange sense of happiness for the other woman. Michael had told her all about how he and Eliza had struggled with the miscarriages they'd suffered through, the toll it had taken on their relationship, leading to Eliza's affair with another man, and Michael eventually finding his way to Aoife. To see her pregnant again made Aoife feel inexplicably happy for her. The two of them had, unsurprisingly, never gotten on with each other. How could they when, from Eliza's point of view, Aoife had been the other woman in her already collapsing relationship? It had been fairly obvious that her engagement to Michael wasn't going to last, no matter how much Eliza might have tried to pretend – especially after her affair was revealed – but her inability to accept responsibility for her own part in her relationship's demise had led her to resent Aoife, and Michael's affections for her.

"Oh wow!" was all Aoife could think to say.

"I know," she said, putting a hand over her bulging stomach.

"I'm so happy for you." Despite what some people might think, she meant every word.

"This is my husband, Tom," Eliza said, gesturing to the man standing beside her. "And this is our eldest, William." A little blonde-haired boy, a little younger than Miriam, who looked just like his mother, peeked out from behind her skirts, looking up at her shyly.

"Hello there," she crouched down to smile at him, but he hid his face and she stood up again so as not to crowd him.

"This is Colin and Miriam," she introduced her own family, and she could see Eliza's eyes light up like a Christmas tree, like she'd just landed on the juiciest bit of gossip that Ballyclara had heard in a long time. Aoife O'Reilly had a new man, and a child to boot! Aoife felt the anxiety she'd been having earlier return.

"Pleasure to meet you." Colin politely shook hands with them both.

Before Eliza could respond to this revelation, her husband turned and said, "We should be heading down to the pub," in a crisp, clear English accent. From the look on his face, Aoife could tell he was just as anxious about being here as she was.

"Yes, dear, we should. Well, Aoife, it was good to see you again. Maybe we will see you at the pub later?"

"Um…" Even though Aoife had known there would likely have been a reception afterwards, she hadn't actually planned on going. She'd only planned to come here from the funeral and get back to Dublin as quickly

## Where I'm Home

as possible so they could hop on a flight and be back in New York and get back to her life of pretending Ballyclara didn't exist.

"Oh, do say you'll come down. Everyone will want to see you again. I'm sure you and Michael have a lot of catching up to do." She gave Aoife a sugary sweet smile in farewell before joining the crowd of mourners heading down to the pub, proving that the petty side of her Aoife had seen more than a little of was still in there somewhere.

"So that's Eliza, huh?" Colin smiled politely at her retreating form.

"Yep."

"Well, she wasn't half as bad as I thought she was going to be from how you described her. I thought she'd be much more of a… witch." He looked down at Miriam, amending what he was going to say.

"I guess marriage and motherhood really can change a person," Aoife replied idly, her eyes inadvertently settling on the one person she wanted to see even less than Eliza Kennedy.

He had his back turned to her, talking to Eliza's mother. She could have just turned away, given her sympathies to Mara and Sinead, and left with Colin and Miriam for Dublin, but she knew she wouldn't do that. She left Colin behind with Miriam as she walked towards where he was standing. After all this time, she was still inexplicably drawn to him.

"Hello Michael."

His back stiffened immediately at the sound of her voice, and he turned around slowly, gazing at her like he couldn't quite believe she was really here and wasn't just some figment of his imagination. She was surprised to find him completely unchanged since the last time she'd seen him; the same muscular build from years of building work, the same dark hair, the same intense blue eyes that were currently boring a hole through her.

"Thank you for coming." His voice was hoarse, tight with emotion. She couldn't blame him. She'd found it difficult enough to keep her own voice steady when she'd greeted him.

She shivered slightly under his intense stare. Curiously, his eyes softened at this, a strange look coming over her face before Colin stepped in and draped his suit jacket around her shoulders. She saw Michael's gaze harden as he noticed Colin.

"Here, babe. It's getting cold out." She glanced over her shoulder and gave him a small smile as she pulled the suit jacket around her, breathing in the scent of his aftershave and trying to ground herself again.

"Hi, I'm Colin. I wish we were meeting under different circumstances. So sorry for your loss," he said, shaking Michael's hand. It didn't matter to Colin that Michael was her ex; he still treated him with the same respect he gave to everyone. She loved him for that.

For someone who had once thought to make her living off the written word, it seemed a touch amusing to Aoife in this moment that she had absolutely no idea what to say. What *did* one say when introducing one's ex-boyfriend to one's current boyfriend? She'd not really been in this situation before, so she just stood there, awkwardly. She was saved by the impeccable timing of Miriam, who stated loudly and boldly, "I'm hungry. When are we going to eat?"

"We're going soon, love."

Miriam came over and wrapped her arms possessively around Aoife's left leg, looking up at Michael, probably wondering who this stranger was. Aoife smoothed her long, black hair off her face and rubbed her shoulder reassuringly. She watched as Michael's eyes widened in surprise, but he didn't have a chance to ask the question clearly on his mind before the rest of the Flanagans joined them.

"Aoife, Colin." Connor kissed his cousin's cheek and shook Colin's hand in greeting. He looked surprised to see them both here, and perhaps a little guilty that he hadn't made the call himself to let her know about Dermot's passing.

She couldn't blame him; it was a tough decision to make. On the one hand, Connor and Mara knew how much Dermot had meant to her; but on the other hand, the thought of Michael and Aoife being in the same space together was something they'd obviously been trying to avoid. Whenever she'd spoken with either Connor or Mara over the last three years, they'd always been careful not to mention Michael's name, as if bringing him up might cause her some pain. She was grateful to them, even if handling her with kid gloves after she had moved on with her life was somewhat over the top.

"Connor!" Miriam, happy to finally find someone familiar, stretched her little arms up at him, begging to be picked up.

"Hello Miriam," he said, obliging her.

"I didn't think the three of you would be here," Mara said, hugging Aoife and Colin. Her voice sounded uncertain whether having left her and Michael to talk to one another without a chaperone had been a good idea. Aoife tried not to roll her eyes. She and Michael had been talking for five minutes and the world hadn't ended. They were both a little more mature now; they could totally get through one awkward conversation without blowing up at one another.

"We probably wouldn't have if Rory hadn't called." She nodded towards Mara's son, who hunched his shoulders at the sound of his name, clearly a bit embarrassed about having been called out, but to his credit, he didn't bow his head in fear. Instead, it was as if he wanted to dare them to make a scene over having done what he felt they should have done themselves.

"My God, how you've grown up. You've shot up like a bean sprout. I suppose Des is just the same." Aoife tried to lighten the mood, hoping to avoid any blowback from his family.

Rory, with all his gangly pre-teen embarrassment, blushed a bright red.

"Come down to the pub and see Des for yerself," Mara said to her. "There's a wake for Da and I'm sure everyone will want to see ye. Mam, especially, will be thrilled." Aoife could hear a bit of reluctance in her voice, but she was trying to be polite.

"Oh, I'm not sure…" This was all getting a little out of hand, more than she had bargained for.

She glanced at Michael, wondering how he felt about all of this. She noticed he had a bit of a smug look on his face, and she felt her nostrils flare in annoyance. Of course, he'd like to see her squirming under the societal pressure to avoid offending anyone in his family, since they'd just lost their patriarch and all. The bastard.

As if Mara mentioning Sinead had brought her forth, she exclaimed, "Aoife? Is that you? It's so good to see ye, love."

"Hello, Sinead."

She hugged the older woman tightly, having missed her dearly over the last three years. The first thing she noticed was how much frailer she felt when she hugged her, and how she'd seemed to age several years in the span of only a few. Grief would do that to a person, she supposed.

"I'm so sorry to hear about Dermot."

There was so much more she wanted to say; how Dermot had been like the father she'd always wanted, how she'd cried so hard in Colin's arms that night after going home from the office and having to tell him why she needed to go back to Ireland straight away, even though she'd silently vowed never to return. Of course, ever the gentleman, he'd insisted that he and Miriam would join her to support and comfort her. She wanted to tell Sinead how desperately sad she was that Dermot would never get to meet Colin, to see how well her life had turned out. She knew he would have been happy for her. She wanted to say all this and so much more; she just didn't know how to get the words out. They all seemed to jumble up on the tip of her tongue, and she was afraid if she opened her mouth again, they'd all come tumbling out in a mess.

She coughed slightly, trying to clear her throat of the emotions building up inside her. She could tell that Sinead wanted to say something in return, but was fighting to keep her own emotions in check, so she simply gripped her hand and gave it a squeeze.

"And who's this?" she finally asked, changing topics.

"This is Colin, and this is Miriam."

"Oh, isn't she a dear?" Sinead smiled up at the little girl, and then gave Aoife a look that made her blush slightly. She knew what she was thinking about what she'd been up to since she'd been gone. "Well, we have much catching up to do, don't we?"

As Aoife let an awkward silence descend, Miriam repeated her earlier question.

"Can we eat now?"

She'd whispered the question to Connor, but loudly enough she knew Colin and Aoife would hear her. She gave them both a look, as if to ask if she was being rude. The poor thing had just flown halfway around the world with little notice, had been thrown into a situation she was too young to understand just yet, with a bunch of people she didn't know, and she hadn't made a fuss once. Aoife gave her a look but then smiled at her, thanking her lucky stars she'd been blessed that Miriam had her father's easy-going temperament.

"Alright, monkey, let's go and get you something to eat then, shall we?" Connor said, leading the group down towards the pub. They'd only made it a few feet when Father Patrick joined the group, causing them to pause for a moment.

"Sure, and it's yourself."

She grinned widely at him, happy to see the old priest once again. He'd been such a fount of wisdom for her when she was living here, always knowing the right thing to say at exactly the right moment.

"Father Patrick." She hugged him tightly in greeting.

"Colin, I'd like you to meet Father Patrick," she said, introducing him proudly to the priest.

"I've heard so many things about you," Colin smiled at him warmly, shaking his hand.

"Only good things, I hope," the priest replied, winking at him, seemingly unfazed by the changes in Aoife's life since he'd last seen her.

"Are you going with us to the pub?" Miriam asked him. Aoife widened her eyes at her, as if to say, "Ok, we get the point."

"I am child, I am," he smiled at her. Aoife's gaze

softened as she saw how warmly he welcomed her. Of course, she wouldn't expect anything less from him, but it was still nice to see.

"Father Patrick, I'd like you to meet Miriam."

"Pleasure to meet you, Miriam," he said, extending a hand to her, his face lighting up again.

"I apologize for her; she's off her schedule, what with the overnight flight and coming straight here from the airport." She gave him an apologetic look.

"Oh, she's fine," he scoffed at her. "Now, I heard someone was hungry, and you know what? So am I!" He smiled at the little girl, eliciting a laugh from her. "Would you care to join me?"

Miriam nodded eagerly.

"Well, what are we all waiting around for? Let's go!"

Aoife couldn't help but notice how spry he still was, even at his age. He was fairly bounding down the hill faster than the rest of them. She took a much slower gait, trepidation about being suddenly thrown to the rest of the village making her feel anxious again.

*Buckle up*, she told herself, *It's going to be a bumpy ride.*

Chapter Six

They walked down to the pub, mostly in silence, everyone lost in their own thoughts. The only exceptions were Miriam, Father Patrick and Connor, who were chatting amiable with Miriam about what animals she was supposed to be seeing at the zoo this weekend, but Daddy had said they had to come here instead, and that they would go to the zoo next weekend.

"Well, we have a wonderful zoo in Dublin, don't we, Aoife? We went there loads of times as kids. You should take her there."

Aoife shot him a quick glare because she knew exactly what he was doing: now that she'd finally come back to Ireland, he was trying to get her to stick around longer. Ever since she'd left, he'd been trying to get her to come back home so he could have her around again. Even though he'd been proud of her career in publishing, she knew there was still a part of him that had hoped she would come back to Ballyclara and settle down with Michael. Connor liked Colin, but if it came right down to it, she was pretty sure he would be Team Michael all the way. But, if he couldn't get Aoife to live here with Michael, he'd damn sure try to convince her to move here with Colin and Miriam.

She and Connor hadn't had the traditional upbringing that Michael and Mara had enjoyed with Dermot and Sinead. Now that it seemed like Connor was finally establishing that stable family life he'd always wanted when they'd been growing up, she knew all he wanted was for her to be right there with him to enjoy every minute. But in his desire to have her here with him and the rest of the Flanagans, he was unintentionally negating the great life she had in New York. The life she knew that he knew she would want to get back to straight away, and he was using Miriam to convince her to go against that carefully laid plan.

Even knowing what Connor was up to, she couldn't help her resolve melting when she saw Miriam's face light up with excitement.

"Can we? Can we, please? I want to see the n'aminals," Miriam adorably stumbled over her words in her excitement.

*Damn you, Connor!*

"Let's wait and see," Colin told her, taking Aoife's hand as they walked down the lane and briefly kissed her knuckles. He was excellent at ensuring both he and Aoife were on the same page when it came to making promises to Miriam. The two of them made a great team together.

Miriam grinned toothily at them because she knew that when Daddy said "maybe," this usually meant "yes."

Aoife rolled her eyes at Connor, as if to say,

"Great, look at the situation you've put me in." He shrugged his shoulders unapologetically, clearly happy that his little plan might be working.

All too soon for Aoife's liking, they approached the village square. Ballyclara was a small place; only a few hundred inhabitants, or so at most. It looked like nothing had changed since she was last here. A creek ran around most of the village, forming a natural boundary line that was crossable by a little stone bridge on the far side of the village. A fountain and a stone cross stood in the village centre, and all roads seemed to radiate out from this focal point. The post office and corner store were still there, as was O'Sullivan's bakery, Byrne's hardware shop, and the lawyers' office, Drummond & Drummond, who had helped her with buying Aldridge Manor.

On the opposite side of the square from the post office stood a building Aoife knew all too well: *O'Leary's*, the pub owned by Michael and his best friend, Brendan McCaffrey. The two of them had bought it from old Mrs. O'Leary when her husband had passed, and ran it together with Brendan's wife, Molly, who worked in the kitchen. It was a rustic, two-storey, red-brick building, mid-seventeenth or mid-eighteenth century like Aldridge Manor, and among some of the oldest buildings in Ballyclara.

It still looked just as well-kept as the day she'd left town; clearly, business was good. A flower box hung below each window on the front of the building, filled with brightly coloured flowers, and the little garden near the car park was also in full bloom, making the place look picture perfect. The car park, normally empty, was now full of villagers who couldn't all fit inside. The strains of a fiddle and a piano floated towards them; Brendan and his band had gotten the celebration started.

## Where I'm Home

The inside of the pub, normally a little dark, was lit as much as possible, and it was packed with what looked to be every single person in Ballyclara, and possibly the surrounding villages as well. Almost immediately, Father Patrick and Sinead were stopped to talk to a group of people who seemed not to have made it to the service but had come up for the wake. Connor handed Miriam over to Colin as he and Mara were pulled in the opposite direction to talk to another group of people. Suddenly, Aoife found herself in the middle of a packed room, but it might as well have been empty except for her and Michael, for that seemed to be all she could focus on. Her eyes searched the room for someone, *anyone*, she knew she could talk to when her eyes latched onto Molly McCaffrey laying trays of food out on a buffet table that had been set up near the bar. As she started gravitating in that direction, Brendan jumped down from the little stage at the front.

"Hello stranger." He smiled and pulled her into a hug.

She was grateful for him; she'd always liked Brendan, right from the day she met him here in this pub. She felt a wave of guilt for not having reached out to him or Molly after she'd moved to New York. She hadn't heard from either of them in the last three years, either, but it was not like she'd expected to. They were Michael's closest friends, after all; she'd fully expected them to stay on his side after their break-up, but she'd have been lying had she'd said she hadn't missed them both.

"Hello yourself." She hugged him back.

"Now where on God's green Earth have ye been?" He gave her a slightly accusatory look at not having stayed in touch, but it was softened by the grin on his face.

Same old Brendan. Not one to judge others, but definitely not one to hold back his opinions, either.

"Well, that's a funny story. So, you remember that little publishing deal I got?"

"Uh, yeah, I seem to remember something about. Not like it was a big deal or anything," he teased her.

"Well, turns out that I'm better at running a publishing house than writing for one, so I kind of stayed on and started my own business."

"Well, look at you," he said admiringly. "I'm happy for ye."

"Thanks." She felt a sense of relief that his conversation was going better than she'd feared it would.

A quizzical expression then came across his face. "And ye couldn't have come back home and started your own publishing house here?"

"Well…" Aoife looked over at Colin and Miriam, who were standing slightly behind her. "Let's just say I found a good reason to stay in New York. Brendan, I'd like you to meet my family, Colin and Miriam."

The same fleeting look of surprise that had been on Michael's face at the cemetery now crossed Brendan's face before he reached out a hand to Colin and gave him a firm handshake.

"Welcome to Ballyclara!" If he had any other thoughts on the fact that Aoife had moved on, he wasn't going to let on in front of her new boyfriend.

"It's great to finally come here. Aoife talks about all of you so much. I feel like I already know everyone."

This was exactly the thing to pique Brendan's curiosity. "So, she hasn't forgotten all about us, then?"

Aoife's cheeks flushed bright red.

"I… of course not…" she stammered, trying to find the right way to explain things to him when he noticed someone behind her. He took her by the shoulders and turned her around to face his wife, Molly McCaffrey.

If Aoife thought Brendan seemed surprisingly supportive of her being here, the same could definitely not be said about his wife.

"Molly, come and look who it is."

She looked up at the sound of her husband's voice, and her face immediately went pale and blank at the sight of Aoife standing there next to him. Trying and failing to bring her face to a neutral expression, Molly nodded in Aoife's direction and offered a curt, "Hello," then promptly turned on her heel and walked back towards the kitchen, not giving her former friend a second glance.

"It was nice to see you, Aoife, and nice to meet you, Colin, Miriam. Now, if you'll excuse me, I think I'm needed in the kitchen."

Brendan's tone was slightly apologetic for his wife, and he hurried after her. The frosty reception served as a reminder that it hadn't only been Michael she'd hurt when she'd left. Aoife was about to turn towards Colin and suggest they leave when she heard another familiar voice.

"Aoife."

"Jimmy!"

She beamed up at the face of Jimmy Connolly. When last she'd seen him, he'd been a lad of eighteen, a new husband and about to become a new father. He seemed to have grown into himself a bit more over the last three years; no longer was he the tall, gangly late teen with arms and legs slightly too long for his body. He still wasn't exactly what Aoife would call handsome, but his smile was still as sincere and infectious as ever.

"And Karen!" she said, turning towards Jimmy's

wife. Karen's green eyes sparkled at seeing her again, and her beautiful smile widened.

"Don't tell me this is little Molly? Oh my, look how you've grown!" She crouched down to the little girl's level, hoping Molly's namesake might give her a better reception than the older one had done.

The last time she'd seen little Molly – other than in the Christmas cards she and Karen exchanged – was when she'd just been a baby. Now she was a girl of nearly four years old, but since she'd inherited both her parents' height and thin frames, she looked easily tall enough to be more like five or six years old.

"Aren't you going to be a tall one?" she said, noticing how her face went as red as the hair she'd inherited from her mother. "I don't suppose you remember me, do you? You were only a wee one the last time I saw you, after all."

"This is little Miss Molly Mae. We call her Mae now, to tell her apart from her namesake. It was something Jimmy started calling her, and it just stuck. And this must be your wee Miriam." Karen smiled at Miriam, who was now standing by her father, holding his hand, and watching all the interactions going on around her.

"Miriam, this is Karen, Jimmy, and their daughter, Mae. Why don't you go and say hi?" Aoife asked her, encouraging her to come over and introduce herself. She happily obliged, standing by Aoife and stuck out her little hand to Mae. "Hi."

Mae looked a little hesitant for half a second, the green eyes she'd inherited from her mother giving Miriam a once over, but it seemed she approved of what she saw, for she gave Miriam a winning smile, so like her father.

"Hi!" And just like that, the two girls were fast

friends.

"Do you two want to come with us and get some of this delicious food?" Rory asked the girls, coming over to them with Desmond McCaffrey at his side. Mae and Miriam looked up at their respective parents, who nodded for them to go with the boys, and they scampered over to the buffet table where the boys helped them get some plates of food.

"She's lovely," Karen said, watching the two girls as they chatted amiably to Rory and Des, picking a table near the musicians, making sure they were always in sight of their parents.

"Thanks," Colin said, smiling proudly at his daughter.

"Where are my manners?" Aoife exclaimed. "This is Colin."

"That much we figured out from your Christmas card photos," Jimmy said laughingly, shaking Colin's hand. "It's nice to finally meet ye in person, Colin. I'm Jimmy, and this is my wife, Karen."

"I've heard lots about the both of you." Colin smiled at the two of them.

"Come on, let's grab a booth and catch up before I get pulled away again." Mara came up behind Aoife, took her by the arm and started pulling her, Colin, Karen, and Jimmy towards a booth where Brendan and Connor were currently sitting with drinks already on the table. Aoife noted that Molly hadn't joined them. As if reading her thoughts, Brendan shrugged and looked apologetic again; clearly their conversation earlier hadn't been enough to convince Molly to forgive Aoife just yet.

As they settled into the booth, she saw Michael standing next to a petite, young brunette, who smiled adoringly at him, and gave him a kiss on the cheek. As if drawn by her gaze, he glanced over at her and Colin sitting beside his sister, a look of disapproval crossing his face.

*Well, to hell with whatever Michael thinks.*

She wasn't going to abandon her friends just because he didn't like her being there, even if this was his father's funeral. He got some leeway from her based on the circumstances, but she wasn't going to cower from him just because he might not like her being around. It wasn't like she was going to be here for much longer anyways.

"Who's that with Michael?" she asked before she had a chance to stop herself. It was none of her business, after all; she was clearly just being nosy, a quality she despised in others, let alone in herself.

"That is Ailish," Mara replied, "Michael's girlfriend."

"Oh, good Lord." Aoife nearly spluttered over her pint as she'd tried to take a drink. Ailish looked to be at least ten years younger than Michael, making her younger than Aoife herself by at least a few years.

"I know," Mara said, picking up on her train of thought. "I thought the same thing at first, but after you meet her, you'll get to like her, I promise."

Aoife shot her a look. There was no way in hell she was going to meet Michael's new girlfriend, of all people. It had been awkward enough introducing him to Colin, and for her to see Eliza again back at the cemetery.

"She's nothing like Eliza," Mara said hurriedly, as if that was what Aoife was worried about, and not the fact that Aoife had no interest in meeting any of Michael's new girlfriends, whether they were as snobbish as Eliza Kennedy, or not.

She didn't have time to discuss the matter further

before the very topic of their conversation was walking towards them, arm in arm with Michael, who looked like he would rather be just about anywhere else than have to face introducing his ex-girlfriend to his new one.

*Welcome to the club*, she thought dryly.

"Aoife, let me introduce you to – " Mara had said when Ailish jumped in, holding her hand out in greeting.

"Hi, I'm Ailish." Realizing what she had done, she immediately apologized. "Sorry Mara. It's only that you can imagine my surprise when Aoife O'Reilly of all people shows up in Ballyclara. I've heard so much about you."

*Oh, sweet Jesus.*

Dread filled Aoife, wondering exactly what Michael had told his new girlfriend about her. She arched an eyebrow in Michael's direction, as if to say, "Oh really?" but his face remained neutral, giving her no hints.

"Nothing too awful, I hope," she said with one of her unfailingly polite smiles, the one she reserved for public appearances she had no desire to be at. While she might have failed to say an unkind word about the residents of Ballyclare, she couldn't guarantee that no one had said anything unkind about her when she wasn't here.

"Oh, of course!" Ailish replied, genuinely shocked at the implication that anyone would think anything terrible about her, which surprised Aoife more than she'd realized. "I loved your novel, by the way. I don't know why, but I always thought when I was reading it you could have been writing about Ballyclara. Dare I ask if you'll be writing another one?"

It was a question Aoife loathed. Her first book had been modestly successful, earning her a spot on a few bestseller lists and earning her a modicum of acclaim. But when her editor had asked her if she was planning to write another one, she'd frozen up. It wasn't that she didn't love writing. She'd loved the time she'd spent writing here in Ballyclara, but the beginning of her literary career had been the final chapter in her life in Ireland, and there was something about the pursuit of writing that seemed less fun now. And if it wasn't fun anymore, what was the point? Eventually, her editor had stopped asking about a possible follow-up, and she'd been left wondering what to do with her life.

For a time, she'd pondered going to work for her family's pub chain, *O'Reilly's*, but she'd dismissed idea that pretty quickly. As much as she'd loved her grandfather, the chain of pubs he'd started was nothing like the dream he'd once envisioned, and she knew she wouldn't fit into his company in its current state any more than she fit into her own family. Connor, for his part, had tried to convince her to join him at the company after he left the military, but for all his charming attempts, it just wasn't for her. It was then that she'd struck upon the idea of opening her own publishing house and becoming an editor. She still loved being around other writers, poets, playwrights; she knew this was the field she wanted to be in, and she wanted to create opportunities for other writers who might not normally be picked up by the larger publishing houses.

It wasn't like she didn't have the experience; she'd worked in publishing her entire career to date. Sure, she didn't exactly have the desired background on the business side of things, but having been around her grandfather's company her whole life, it wasn't like she was a total novice, either. What she didn't know about running a business, she could learn, which is exactly what she did. She took online and night courses in business management, and what she couldn't do on her own, she could hire others who had the necessary skills. Within the year, she had a business plan, and she took the remaining money she'd inherited from her grandfather to start her own publishing house.

"Probably not for a little while, yet," Colin answered for her.

Rather than being annoyed with him for speaking on her behalf, she was grateful to him. They'd often discussed her career goals and whether she would return to writing, and he knew better than anyone how much she hated getting asked this very question. As a poet, it was something he knew all too well; as soon as he finished one collection, people were always on him for another. It was exhausting at times.

"Well, I suppose you probably don't have much time for writing now, what with being an editor with your own publishing house to run. It must be all so exciting living in New York, surrounded by so many literary folks such as yourself. I imagine you must host such great soirees with the most interesting people."

By now, Ailish had sat down beside her and was looking her directly in the eye, eager to hear all about the glamourous life she thought Aoife led. She wondered if Ailish would be as impressed if she knew that most nights, she and Colin considered it a special evening if they could sit in with a pizza and a couple of beers and get through an entire episode of a show on the telly without any interruptions from Miriam or work.

Ailish had an endearing quality about her that made Aoife want to like her, but she also found it kind of awkward that the young woman had done so much research on her boyfriend's ex. Like, who did that, other than crazy stalkers and/or jealous, possessive types?

Somehow, Ailish didn't strike her as either, but then again, she'd only just met the girl five minutes ago and knew nothing about her, and she *did* seem like she'd memorized Aoife's entire Wikipedia page.

Despite her best charms, there was something about Ailish that grated on Aoife's nerves, almost as much as Eliza had the day she'd first met her, but in a different way. Eliza had been an elitist snob through and through, a stuck-up little madam with pretty much everything about her being just as fake as her nails. Ailish was the opposite; she was beautiful, for sure. She had a petite frame, but she was sturdy rather than delicate. Even though she didn't look like she was the kind of woman to spend time at the gym, Aoife would bet that she was nearly as strong as most men. Her face was pleasantly round, her nose delicate, but well-suited for her face, and her glittering blue eyes were the colour of a sunny, cloudless summer sky. Michael obviously still liked his beautiful women. This observation wasn't mere self-aggrandizing flattery; one had only to look at both Eliza and Ailish to know he dated beautiful women. And while Aoife wouldn't have placed herself in the same class as either of them, she was reasonably confident with her own appearance to not sell herself too short.

What bothered her about Ailish wasn't how good she looked; it was that she seemed so goddamn *nice*. Whereas Eliza had been petty and self-interested, Ailish was warm, friendly, and open with people, always with a ready smile on her face. Her eyes seemed to light up with intense interest for everyone she spoke to, like she was truly fascinated by what they had to say. Not that she did not contribute to the conversation; she offered opinions or comments at regular intervals, but she did not dominate the conversation the way Aoife sometimes did, or making it all about herself, the way Eliza often did. She seemed perfectly even-tempered, hardly the sort to offer more than a stern word or comment to someone, unlike Aoife, who'd had zero problems in the past having more than one shouting match with Michael if he'd put her in a foul mood.

"Ailish, by the way; nice to meet you."

She reached over Aoife to shake Colin's hand and give him a warm, friendly smile.

"Colin," he said, returning her handshake, offering one of his own charming smiles.

"Oh, I know all about you," Ailish said.

Colin's eyes widened in surprise, clearly not expecting Ailish to have done research on him as well.

"I've read all of your poems. You're so talented. I wish I had a way with words the way you do. The way you see the world… I just can't describe it. It's magical."

"You're a poet?" Michael asked, speaking up for the first time since he and Ailish had joined the group. Aoife noticed he seemed surprised at this. No doubt he'd been expecting him to say something stereotypical like that he worked in IT development or in business.

"Is that how the two of you met? Through work?" Ailish kept her gaze on Colin, her friendly smile unwavering, encouraging him to elaborate.

"And here I thought you knew everything about us," Aoife muttered, not quite under her breath as she took a drink of her Guinness. Her tone was more sarcastic than she'd intended, and she felt Colin's hand on her upper thigh, a gentle reminder to be kind. She was trying to be nice to her, but she still wanted to find something to hate about the new woman Michael was dating. It had been so easy to hate Eliza with her territorial, possessive, insecure nature; why couldn't Ailish make it easier for her to do the same with her? Why did she have to seem like a good person?

*This would all have been so much easier if I'd come back and found Michael and Eliza had gotten back together.*

It *would* have been easier for Aoife to be less jealous if he'd gone back to his ex. She could easily keep on disliking Eliza, content that Michael would miserable the rest of his life, and be content to move on with Colin. But seeing Michael with someone like Ailish made her inexplicably jealous of what they had. She should be happy with Colin, she knew; she'd lucked out when she'd found him, but she couldn't help the nagging jealousy that wanted to rear its ugly head at seeing Michael happy without her.

*What the hell am I thinking?* she chastised herself. It wasn't like she was competing for Michael's affections anymore. The two of them had both moved on. Still, she couldn't help but feeling that, while she could have easily beaten Eliza in a competition for Michael's heart, she wasn't so sure she liked her odds against Ailish.

"Yes, we met through work. We met at Aoife's office, in fact," Colin replied, smiling at her, remembering the first time they'd met.

༄༅༄

*New York City*
*Three Years Ago (or thereabouts)*

Aoife looked at the stack of submissions from authors across the country and around the world, all of whom were hoping to be published. It was daunting, looking at that pile, but it also gave her a sense of profound purpose to be able to help some of them pursue their passion.

"Here's another stack." Millie plonked down more papers in front of her.

"But I haven't even gotten through this pile yet!"

"Better to have more submissions than you need than not enough, right?"

Aoife grumbled something akin to an affirmation. It was flattering to have this many authors wanting to work with her, but also a little overwhelming at the same time. She lay her head down on her desk and gave a defeated sigh.

"Oh, come now, it's not that bad. I'll put on a pot of tea and we'll go through these together."

Aoife gave her a smile of gratitude and tackled the pile nearest to her.

Several cups of tea later, they'd organized her office into something resembling a system. Their pile of rejections was noticeably larger than their maybes and their yes pile, but that was to be expected. They were nearing the end of their unread pile when Mille leaned forward and excitedly waved the manuscript she was holding in front of Aoife's face, trying to get her attention.

"Oh my gosh, you *have* to read this one!" she exclaimed, practically shoving the manuscript into Aoife's hands.

"Ok…"

Aoife took the papers from her, reorganizing them and starting to read. She hadn't even finished the first page when she looked up at Millie, a mixture of emotions on her face.

"I know, right?" Millie asked, a huge smile forming on her lips.

"This is... wow. I don't even think there's words appropriate enough to describe it. I mean, I want to cry, I want to smile... Who is this guy?"

Millie picked up the cover sheet. "His name is Colin Lee. He lives here in New York. Let's see, what else..."

"I want you to set up a meeting with him ASAP."

"Done!" Millie shouted, clapping her hands together.

"Alright let's... oh my God, it's eight-thirty at night!" Aoife swivelled around in her chair, looking at the glittering light of New York City against the black night. Turning back to Millie, she said, "Let's leave the rest of these for tomorrow and head home. I don't want to read another thing tonight and just leave things on a high note."

Aoife spent the rest of the night tossing and turning in bed, thinking about the poems she'd read. She'd brought home the rest of the work Colin had submitted and was reading them well into the wee hours of the night. His words had moved her in such a way she'd never felt before when reading another writer's work. He was still on her mind two days later when they'd been able to set up a meeting face-to-face.

She knew he'd arrived in the office even before she saw him. All three of the women working in the office, single or otherwise, simultaneously left their desks to fawn over the handsome Asian-American poet as soon as he'd stepped off the elevator.

"Oh. My. God," she'd heard Millie say loudly in her thick London accent. Aoife's "office door" at the time was little more than a sliding barn door to separate her workspace from the rest of the open-concept warehouse space she rented, so it was pretty easy for her to hear everything going on in the main work area.

Aoife appeared at the door to see what the fuss was about. The first thing she noticed was his smile as he held his hand out to shake hers. He had a firm grasp, confident, but not overpowering, but it was his smile that drew her in and had the rather unusual effect of making her insides go all mushy.

"Miss O'Reilly, I presume?" he asked as Millie and Aoife both just gawped at him for half a beat.

"Oh, yes! Uh… please call me Aoife," she stammered.

"Colin Lee," he said, introducing himself, seeming not to notice her making a total eejit of herself. "Aoife… that's quite a pretty name. I don't think I've heard it before."

"It's Irish for Eva. I'm Millie, by the way. Her assistant," Millie replied, a little too loudly considering she was practically standing only inches away from him.

If Colin felt awkward about the moment, though, he didn't show it. "Nice to meet you, Millie," he said, taking her hand and giving it a shake as well, not skipping a beat.

"Uh, Mille, why don't you let go of Mr. Lee's hand and bring us some tea?" Aoife asked, trying to save the poor guy.

As if just remembering where she was right that second, Millie reluctantly relinquished Colin's hand and smiled at him, looking slightly embarrassed.

"Or would you prefer coffee?" Aoife asked him.

"No, tea's great, thanks. Shall we?" He gestured to her office.

"Right, yes. Please, come in."

Aoife tried to settle herself behind her desk, hoping she looked far more professional than she felt right now. She let him get settled in the chair opposite her, smoothing down his open-collared shirt and khaki pants, and they'd just begun exchanging personal histories with each other when Millie came in with a tea tray and set it carefully on Aoife's desk between them, standing just close enough to Colin to rub shoulders with him as she set the tray down.

"I wasn't sure what you want in your tea, so I brought you a little of everything. Oh, and also these little chocolate-covered biscuits from this amazing café around the corner. I suppose you Americans would call them cookies…"

"Thanks Millie. That's great."

Aoife raised her eyebrows slightly and nodded in the direction of the door, urging her friend to leave before she killed the entire vibe she had going here. Millie looked at her quizzically for a second and then clued into what Aoife was trying to convey.

"Right, I'll just leave you two to talk business. If you need anything, I'll be right over here. At my desk. Just on the other side of the door."

"Thanks Millie; make sure to close it all the way, please." Aoife tried not to sound annoyed at Millie's deliberate attempts to stick around longer. When she finally closed the door behind her, Aoife turned to Colin. "Sorry about that."

"Nah, don't worry about it. She's really nice. Eager to please, it seems." He gave her one of those winning smiles again, and she felt all traces of annoyance at Millie flee her mind.

"Yeah, she's pretty great. A handful at times, but a superb friend."

"A helluva dresser too. Does she always dress like that?"

He was, of course, referring to the white and navy striped corset top with feathers coming out of the bust area and the royal blue tulle skirt Millie was wearing today.

"Oh, that's nothing. You should have seen her during our undergrad. Let's just say we never had a problem finding her in a crowd."

Aoife smiled as she remembered some of Millie's more colourful outfits and hairdos.

"You two knew each other before you worked together?"

"Yeah, we went to uni together, along with our friend, Bex. She's an American, like you. We all ended up rooming together through our undergrad years."

"Where did you go to school?" he asked, taking the liberty of expertly pouring them both a cup of tea.

"Harvard."

"Impressive! Milk? Or do you prefer sugar?"

"Um, a bit of both for me, please. Thanks."

She took the cup and saucer from him and they both settled back into their chairs, letting a silence settle on the room. It was a comfortable silence, though, which she thought odd considering she hardly knew anything about this guy and had only met him a few moments ago. She observed him over the rim of her cup as she took a sip and noticed how he, too, seemed perfectly at ease in her company. She set her cup and saucer down, reluctantly turning towards the business at hand and picking up the collection of poems he had submitted.

"So, I read your poems the other night, and I have to say, I was completely moved by them."

The two of them settled into an easy conversation about Colin's work, where he got his inspirations, his backstory, and so on. Long after the tea had been drunk, and the sun had set on the horizon, their conversation drew to a close.

"Well, thank you for having me in today, Aoife. This could not have gone any better if I'd planned it. And to think I was nervous when I came in here."

"Nervous? No way! You didn't seem nervous at all. Besides, I don't think I'm that scary, am I?"

"No, quite the opposite, actually." Colin looked nervous now and looked briefly down at the floor before saying, "In fact I think you're quite beautiful and I've been trying to both talk myself in and out of asking you out tonight because it would probably seem incredibly unprofessional of me, but I also kind of feel like I don't want to miss out on the chance to see you again."

If Aoife had had any tea left in her cup, she would have splurted it all over the desk in front of her. As it was, she simply sat there, mouth slightly agape, before she realized she probably looked a right eejit and closed it again.

"I'm sorry," Colin stammered, the first time during the whole meeting that he seemed less than sure of himself. "I don't normally do this kind of thing, especially in a business meeting. It was wrong of me to say that."

"No!" Aoife half-shouted, before calmly saying, "No, it's ok. To tell the truth, I was thinking something very similar."

Colin's head whipped up and his eyes widened. "Really?"

"Yeah, I mean, like you said, I wasn't sure it would be entirely appropriate. In fact, I'm sure it's not appropriate at all and if you want to work with someone else to publish your work, I'd completely understand…"

"No, I want to work with you. You understand my work in a way I haven't found with anyone else yet. And,

I'd still kind of like to take you for a drink to celebrate signing with you and just see how things go from there?"

"Yeah," she smiled at him. "Yeah, that works for me."

"Great. How about I come and pick you up around dinner time?"

"That would be lovely." Aoife felt a blush rising in her cheeks as he gleamed at her.

"Alright then. I'll see you soon." He gave her one last smile and kissed her hand before heading back into the main office towards the elevator.

As soon as he passed through the elevator doors to head downstairs, Millie came racing into Aoife's office, squealing with delight. "Please tell me you asked him out."

"No, that would be terribly unprofessional. I'm going to be his editor, after all."

"Aoife! You can't just let a guy like that go! He's so lovely, and wonderful, and…"

"Handsome? Yeah, I couldn't tell you thought that at all," Aoife teased. "And who said anything about letting him go? After all, I may or may not have a date with him tonight."

Millie gasped and squealed again. "Wait, what?! I thought you said you didn't ask him out?"

"You know Millie, I know it's an old-fashioned concept, but a guy can ask a lady out."

"Pshaw!" Mille replied, giving Aoife's comment a dismissive wave. "Who has time to wait around for a guy to decide to ask a girl out when you can just ask him out yourself?"

"Well, I have all the patience in the world, and it looks like it paid off!"

"You do not!" Millie replied emphatically. It was

true; Aoife hardly had the right to call herself a patient person, since she had the patience of a bull racing towards a red flag. "Now, what are you going to wear tonight? We have to get you ready. There's so much to be done and not nearly enough time to do it all in."

Aoife didn't know whether she should be offended by this or scared at what Millie had planned for her. A prudent person would have felt both.

※

*Ballyclara*
*Present Day*

"And that's how we met," Colin said, finishing his account of their first meeting.

"Yes, he took me out that night for a picnic in Central Park and everything after that, as they say, is history." Aoife smiled at him, remembering how happy she'd been that night and every night since meeting him.

"Why don't you do nice things like take me out on a romantic picnic?" Mara asked Connor, punching him playfully in the arm.

"Hey! I do romantic things…"

"Yeah, like what?"

"I'm struggling to think of one off the top of my head under all this pressure," Connor replied, a slight smile tugging at the corner of his mouth, "But I'm sure I'll think of one." Before anyone could tease Connor further, Sinead came over to their table.

"Brendan, would you mind lending a hand to Mrs. Byrne? She is going to take some of this food over to theirs for me. We've no room at ours or Mara's, and

Molly says the freezer here is full as well," Sinead asked, coming over and interrupting their conversation.

"Sure," he replied, Karen and Jimmy standing up to let him out.

"I'll help," Jimmy said, standing up and joining him.

"Mara, the O'Sullivans wanted to meet Connor before they head home," Sinead said, turning to her daughter and her boyfriend. Mara rolled her eyes slightly, but she and Connor obeyed and also exited the booth behind Jimmy and Brendan, following Sinead's lead.

"Oh, and Ailish, Molly asked if you could help her in the kitchen, dear."

Ailish nodded and immediately stood up.

"It was nice to meet you both," she said to Aoife and Colin. "I hope I'll see you again before you leave for America."

Aoife smiled politely, planning on getting out of Ballyclara as soon as she could to avoid that happening.

"Mummy!" Mae and Miriam ran over to the table, beaming with excitement from a total sugar rush, for their faces and hands were completely covered in chocolate.

"Rory Flanagan and Desmond McCaffrey, have you been letting these two into the chocolate ice cream?" Karen shot a stern glare over her daughter's head at the two pre-teens, who both had the grace to look embarrassed.

"Come on, monkey, let's get you cleaned up," Colin said, hopping out of the booth as well and taking one of Miriam's sticky hands.

"I'll show you to the toilets," Karen said, nudging Mae in that direction.

"I can take her." Suddenly, Aoife noticed that, with

everyone else gone, she was going to be alone with Michael.

"It's alright, I got this." Colin kissed her lightly on the head and followed Karen to help Miriam wash up. She narrowed her eyes at his back, entirely sure he'd offered to take Miriam on purpose so she and Michael could talk. Aoife pouted.

Having no one else to hide behind, she looked across the booth at Michael, observing how he was avoiding her gaze and seemed to be looking for some excuse – anything – that could get him out of here. She realized then they were both were stuck in the exact predicament they'd both been trying to avoid since they'd laid eyes on each other earlier. He turned towards her then, but it wasn't to look at her. It was to look through her to something going on behind her near the kitchen.

"Sit yerself down. I've got it," Brendan said, popping up beside him suddenly and heading over to the kitchen door to help his wife with carrying some trays. Michael reluctantly did as he was told and took a long, slow drink from his pint, drawing out the silence as long as he could.

"You cut your hair," she opened the conversation before he tried to run away again. Someone had to be the grown-up here; it might as well as be her.

*You cut your hair? Stellar opening line there, Aoife.* She was deflecting from the bigger conversation they needed to have, but at least it was a start.

As she sat there observing him, she noticed that the slightly shorter hair seemed to be the only physical change about him; his hands were still calloused and rough from a life of constant manual labour, his physique still muscular and defined. But there something had changed about him, something she couldn't quite put her finger on. Although being around her obviously put him on edge, for the most part, he seemed more relaxed, comfortable, less like he was an animal ready to spring from a cage at any second, which had always made him seem a little imposing, even after she'd gotten to know him.

"You dyed yours." His voice trailed off as Karen and Colin emerged with Mae and Miriam looking much cleaner than before.

She gave a little sigh of relief that this conversation was going to be much shorter than she'd feared. That is, until they were stopped by some of the well-wishers who, no doubt, were wondering who they'd come here with. Everyone knew everyone in Ballyclara, so newcomers were a treat. Colin gave her an apologetic glance, and she smiled back, trying not to look as uncomfortable as she felt. She wasn't sure who she was trying to reassure more: him or herself.

Miriam was chatting animatedly to the elderly couple that had stopped to talk to them, and her smile widened, proud of how adaptable she was, even at her young age. She turned her attention back to Michael, noticing the dark look he'd had before at the graveyard had returned.

*So, the caged animal is still in there somewhere.*

She puzzled over it for half a second, but then realized what he was thinking, what she'd unconsciously let him think this whole time: that Miriam was her daughter with Colin. Somewhere deep down, she knew some selfish part of her had wanted him to think about it, to see how he'd react to seeing the family that might not be hers biologically, but was hers, nonetheless. She guessed this was her answer. Although she hadn't corrected him before, she knew he'd find out eventually. She might as well put an end to her spiteful charade now.

"You're terrible at math, Michael Flanagan. Miriam isn't my daughter." She looked him straight in the eye, making sure he knew that she knew what he'd been thinking.

He was obviously taken by surprise by her abruptness and nearly choked on his sip of Guinness. He cleared his throat and tried to compose himself to appear nonchalant, as if this was not exactly what he'd been thinking this whole time.

"I met Colin when Miriam was two years old. His wife had passed away the year before."

She didn't get the chance to say anything more before the very topic of their conversation returned.

"All cleaned up?" she asked Miriam, who gave her a big hug and hopped up into the booth beside her.

"Mmhmm." Miriam was distracted by a plate of sweets Brendan was carrying back to the kitchen. Seeing the look on Miriam's face, Brendan stopped and held out the tray to her.

"I think that's enough for one day. We're going to be peeling you off the car roof on the way home." Aoife softened her refusal to let her have more sweets with a little smile.

"Oh, go on, one little sweet isn't going to hurt her." Brendan winked at Miriam as if to tell her to go ahead anyways.

"You aren't planning to head back so soon, are ye? You only just got here." Brendan gave Aoife a puppy-dog look, clearly hoping it would convince her to stay.

She rolled her eyes at him and watched as Miriam snuck in a sugar cookie, stuffing it all in her mouth, ensuring Aoife wouldn't be taking it away from her.

"You say that because you don't have to deal with

the sugar hangover and jet lag she's going to have later. And yes, we should be heading back. We got in early and came straight from the hotel. Jet lag is going to hit all of us soon, I think." She brushed Miriam's long hair off her shoulder and tucked it behind her ear. "This one will need her sleep, for if she's cranky, none of us are going to be getting any sleep. Nothing can make hell look more appealing, quite like a cranky toddler."

"This one? Not a chance! She's perfect, aren't you?" Connor asked Miriam, coming back to the booth and scooping her up into his arms again, making her giggle.

"Says the one who doesn't have to sleep in the same hotel room with her after all the sugar she's just had," Colin retorted good-naturedly.

"Well, how long are you staying in Ireland for? Tell me you plan on sticking around for a little while, at least." Connor perfectly imitated Brendan's earlier puppy-dog look.

Brendan pointed at him as if to say, "See?"

"Just until tomorrow, I'm afraid."

Both Brendan's and Connor's faces dropped a bit in disappointment.

"Now, we need to get this one back to the hotel if we have a hope of her staying on any kind of sleep schedule," Colin insisted.

"Oh, but ye can't be driving all the way back to Dublin now, surely?" Sinead asked, returning with Mara.

*All the way to Dublin.* It was barely an hour and a half's commute from Ballyclara to Dublin, not to mention that it was still the middle of the afternoon. Back in New York, it could take her an hour to go only a few blocks, depending on the traffic. It was the little things like this that reminded her how assimilated she'd become to her American lifestyle.

"It's not that bad," Colin echoed her unspoken thoughts.

"You should have told us ye were coming and we would've had the house ready for you," Sinead chastised lightly. "It's sitting there, waiting for you to come home."

*Home.*

Had Aoife ever thought of Aldridge Manor and Ballyclara as home? She thought that at one time she had, but now she wasn't so sure. She'd spent so little time here when all was considered. But in the end, was it the amount of time one spent in a place that made it a home? Or was it the way the place made you feel?

"You must stay overnight, at least. We haven't seen you in three years; we have so much to catch up on. You wouldn't deny an old widow a request on the day of her husband's funeral now, would you?"

Mara looked at her mother, mouth agape, like she couldn't believe she'd just played that card.

"We couldn't impose on any of you."

Aoife tried to take a polite tact, side-stepping the blatantly manipulative question, seeing that this was quickly turning into another predicament she didn't want to be in. She'd just about managed the awkwardness with Michael as best she could; she didn't need to create more complications by staying in Ballyclara longer. This was devolving into far more than she'd bargained for. She'd wanted to be here for Dermot's funeral, and she'd done that. She'd not signed on to spend more time in Ballyclara than was absolutely necessary.

However, her well-bred manners wouldn't let her be impolite when Brendan said, "Why don't you take the room upstairs? We've not got any lodgers at the moment."

Aoife wondered what Molly and Michael would think of that. One look at Michael's face and she knew she had her answer.

"That's very kind of you, but…"

"Are you sure you wouldn't prefer to stay at the Old Rectory?" Sinead asked, referring to Aldridge Manor by its local nickname. "Mara, Karen, and I could go up and open it up, still get it ready. You wouldn't have a whole lot in the way of furniture, but your bed is still there, and we could rustle up clean sheets for it, I'm sure. And you can come over to ours for your tea, since the electric's been shut off at the big house."

Aoife couldn't help but hear the tinge of hope in Sinead's voice, and it gave her a pang of guilt. She knew it would thrill the Flanagans to have her here again, and she should spend some time with them.

*Well, almost all the Flanagans.* She noted that Michael's expression hadn't lightened at his mother's suggestion.

Colin looked at her and shrugged, indicating that he'd go along with whatever she decided. She knew he truly wouldn't care where they stayed in Ireland. He wasn't bothered by her past here; he'd made that clear to her before they'd flown out for Dermot's funeral. He knew from what she'd told him of her time in Ballyclara how much this place, and its people, meant to her. He wasn't going to let either of their pasts haunt them, which was just one of the many reasons she loved him. Spending one more day in Ballyclara wasn't going to wreck their relationship.

"Sure. We can stay for one night. But just for one night, mind. There's no reason to open up the house again. We'll stay here at the pub." Although it wasn't exactly what Sinead had hoped, she grinned widely and winked at Aoife.

"Right, I'll go back and get our things from the car, shall I?" Colin asked her. "And I should try to put this one down for a nap for at least a bit," he said, ruffling Miriam's hair.

"But I'm not tired!" she complained, while stifling a yawn.

"Uh-huh." Colin raised his eyebrow at her.

"Well, this place is about to get noisy, so she'll not get any rest here," Brendan warned.

"Here, let's go up to my place. She can take a nap on Rory's bed," Mara offered, as Colin scooped Miriam up into his arms, and he and Aoife followed her out of the pub, promising Sinead they'd be back soon.

## Chapter Seven

"Well, that went as well as could be expected." Michael and Brendan watched as Aoife, Miriam, and Colin walked out of the pub.

Michael rolled his eyes. "It was a feckin' disaster."

He turned on his heel and headed straight for the kitchen, his face a dark thundercloud of emotions. Brendan followed him, bracing himself for the storm to come.

Instead of finding his best friend tossing pans around or breaking the dishes as he'd half-expected, he found him resting against the counter, his body tense with pent-up emotions but otherwise remaining calm. Molly observed him carefully from the corner of her eye, just in case he planned on exploding and taking it out on her kitchen. One thing both of them had to admit, though, was that Michael had calmed down considerably in the last three years. He was still the most stubborn person in the world, except for perhaps Aoife herself, but he'd learned to keep it under wraps somewhat better since he'd been with Ailish. It had been quite a disconcerting thing for Brendan at first, as he'd become used to Michael's temperamental outbursts, but he had to admit that he kind of liked this change. However, he doubted that this new, relatively Zen version of Michael had taken into account Aoife's return.

"I've got to get out of here." Michael loosened his tie from his throat and tossed it onto a counter, leaving the back door swinging in his wake before Brendan could get a word in.

"Leave him be," Molly chastised, guessing his intention before he did it. "He'll tell you about it when he's ready."

Brendan knew his wife to be the font of all wisdom, but he couldn't help but want to go after his friend. As if today wasn't going to be hard enough with losing his father, throwing Aoife into the mix had only been a recipe for disaster. He sighed, watching Michael's retreating form, but did not follow him. He had to sort this out on his own, and Brendan just had to accept that there was very little he could do about it.

෴

As they exited the pub, Aoife caught a bit of movement out of the corner of her eye, watching as Michael stormed out of the pub and disappeared down a path before the others could see him.

"Colin? Why don't you and Miriam go on up to Mara's cottage? I'll meet you there soon."

"Where are you going?" He searched her face,

trying to assess if anything was wrong, other than the fact that she'd just seen her ex and was trying to work through everything she was feeling. She smiled at him.

"I just need to take a walk, is all. Today has been a lot to process. I won't be long, I promise."

He seemed satisfied that nothing was wrong and nodded to her, before turning around to let Mara lead the way to her place.

At first, Aoife had just started walking with no particular destination in mind. She had just wanted to find somewhere quiet, somewhere she wasn't likely to be disturbed while she took a moment to think. She hadn't really even been paying attention to which direction she was going in until she was standing in front of the clearing with the waterfall Michael had taken her to when they were first getting to know one another.

*Shit.*

She hadn't planned on coming here at all. This was Michael's place, his special place where he came to think, to get away from everything and everyone. She immediately felt like an intruder. It made it all the worse when she noticed he was sitting on a rock only a few yards in front of her, his back turned away. His shirt was open at the collar, his tie long gone. His hair was mussed up, like he'd been running his fingers through it.

Maybe the sound of the waterfall had masked the sound of her arrival and she could just slip behind the treeline quietly before he turned in this direction and saw her...

"Aoife?"

*No such luck.*

"Michael." She turned on her heel to face him.

"Did ye crawl through the woods in those heels?" he asked, looking down at her attire.

"Of course not. I took the easy route, like a sensible person," she retorted. She'd been so annoyed with him the first time he'd brought her up here, making her traipse through the trail in the old forest, only to find out later that there was a much easier route along the road that they could have taken. She softened her tone, reminding herself that today had been difficult for him, and she wasn't likely making it easier by being in the one place he'd probably come to escape her.

"I'm sorry. I didn't mean to intrude. I'll leave." She turned away, intending to leave him to whatever contemplation about her he'd come here to do.

*Well, you certainly flatter yourself, don't you?*

She wasn't sure how she knew he'd come here to think about her – after all, he could easily have come up here to process his father's passing – but something in her bones knew he was here because of her. As she was deciding whether it would be rude to leave him here to his thinking, or if it was worse if she stayed, he spoke up.

"Don't go."

She was surprised by this, and it must have shown all over her face. He shrugged.

"There's only so many places to go in Ballyclara, and it would seem fate is determined that you and I should be left alone together today. Might as well not fight it."

She acquiesced and walked over to a rock near him, still keeping some distance between them. The roar of the waterfall behind them filled the silence. The day had turned pleasant now; the early morning's rain clouds had dispersed into fluffy cumulus ones floating lazily across the sky. After what seemed like an interminable amount of time, Michael spoke again.

"When do you leave for America?"

## Where I'm Home

She knew he'd heard Colin back in the pub when he'd answered this question; he was just stalling, skirting the question he really wanted to ask her.

"Tomorrow."

"He's lucky to have you." This comment threw her off almost as much as the way he'd said it. His voice was soft and tinged with something... regret, perhaps? She wasn't entirely sure she'd been meant to hear what he'd said.

"And Ailish is lucky to have you."

"Did ye not think I'd find someone else?"

His question surprised her a bit. She must have let a little more sarcasm into her voice than she'd intended.

"It's been three years, Aoife, and it's not like you didn't move on yourself."

Of course, she knew he would've moved on. Despite his stubborn ill-temper, he was a good man with a kind heart, and the woman who ended up with him would be lucky indeed.

"No, of course not. I knew you would find someone else." She picked off a leaf that had fallen onto her dress and twirled it in her hands.

"Yeah, well, it's not like I could sit around waiting for you to come back, could I?" he asked, his tone defensive. His whole body was tense, and he sprang from the rock he'd been sitting on.

"I can't do this right now," he said suddenly and stalked off towards the village, leaving her there just staring at his departing form.

☙❧

"God-damned bloody truck! You useless piece of

shit!"

Michael slammed the steering wheel of his truck. It just stood there, silent and as pig-headed as its owner. After leaving Aoife at the waterfall, he'd come back home, hoping to just drive around for a bit, do something to clear his head before the small town of Ballyclara's borders hemmed him in and made him feel like he was confined, as if he was in a prison. Before he ended up screaming his head off or snapping at someone in an effort to get out all the emotions inside himself right now.

He'd been hoping to get some peace up at the waterfall, his one place to go to in order to escape it all. But *she* had been there. He could blame her, say he was furious right now because she'd taken over the village again, taken over his place of quiet and solitude – somewhere even Ailish didn't know about – but he knew he wasn't upset with Aoife. Not really, anyways. He was angry at his reaction to her return, how it made him feel.

What right had she to be happy that he had moved on from her? Why wasn't she more upset about him and Ailish being together? Why wouldn't she tell him why she'd left? Why did he still care so much?

He and his father had been working on the 1950's Thames pickup truck for as long as he could remember. It had always, inevitably, needed something fixed. It had become something for him and Dermot to do together, giving them something to bond over. When his sister, Mara, had given birth to her son, Rory, and he had grown old enough, the father-son time had expanded to include him too.

It was difficult, of course, not to think of the one time that he'd been working on it that had nearly ended in disaster. This time three years ago, when Dermot had nearly died and Michael thought he was going to lose his father. It was difficult not to think of how he'd sat here in the drive, holding onto his father, willing him to stay alive until the ambulance could come and take him to the hospital. His whole life had fallen apart then, and he wasn't entirely sure that he'd found all the pieces to put it back together again.

"You god-damned piece of shit!" he yelled at the vehicle again. He got out of the driver's seat, rolled up the shirtsleeves of his dress shirt as he went around to the front of the truck and lifted the hood. Steam billowed out, and he swiped at the air to clear it away.

"Shit!" he exclaimed again, hitting the fender with his shoe and running his fingers through his dark hair furiously. He wasn't going anywhere anytime soon. When he was certain that the steam had all dissipated, he closed the hood and ambled up the steps of the cottage. Ailish was in the kitchen, putting away the food from the wake.

"Your mother insisted we take these," she greeted him as he came into the kitchen. If she'd observed what had happened outside from the kitchen window, she didn't mention it. He came up behind her, folded her into his arms, and placed a light kiss on top of her head. Her walnut-brown hair still smelled of the fruity-scented shampoo she used this morning, mixed in with the scent of fresh grass and flowers.

"I didn't have the heart to tell her we had more than enough in the freezer as it is. I've tried arranging the casserole dishes in there three times now, and even with Molly and I trying to use up as many of the dishes at the wake today as we could, and storing as many leftovers in the pub's fridge, I still can't make everything fit. I fear that some of this is probably going to go to waste."

"Leave it for now."

He took her hand and lead her towards the staircase. She arched an eyebrow at him, wondering if this was really what he wanted right now. He gave her hand a little squeeze. It had been the worst day of his life, and it had not been made easier by Aoife's return. He simply wanted to lie in Ailish's arms, forget about the world outside for a moment, and just be here.

When they reached the bedroom, he kissed her gently, moving her towards the bed. She paused a moment. "Are you sure?"

He kissed her again, this time with more intention, and she did not protest. She took off her dress, as he removed his own clothes. She lay back on the bed in her underwear and he lay down beside her, holding her face between his hands, kissing her lightly. He closed his eyes, trying to slip away to some far-off place where it was just her and him together, but was interrupted by Aoife's face flashing behind his closed eyelids. The image gave him a jolt, and he rolled quickly onto his back, staring at the ceiling, but still seeing Aoife's face.

"What's wrong?"

"Nothing," he answered immediately, but it was obvious that something was not right. "It's been a long day and I'm tired. I think we should just go to sleep."

She didn't protest, only smiled gently at him. He knew that she knew he wasn't telling her the whole truth, but she didn't want to press him any further on the topic tonight. Grateful, he kissed her lightly and turned over on his side, facing away from her, hoping that the taunting image of Aoife would leave him alone.

## Chapter Eight

"You know, we could really use your skills here at the Dublin office. If you were so inclined, of course." Connor said it off-handedly as he took a bite of biscuit laden with beef stew, but Aoife knew him too well. He was going to try to make any play he could in the short amount of time he had to get her to stay here longer.

After her encounter with Michael earlier today, she'd made her way back down to Mara's cottage where she found her, Connor, Rory, and Colin setting the table for dinner. Miriam had just woken from her nap and was looking bleary-eyed at the food on the table, but the delicious scent seemed to wake her up. They'd left the wake to wind down on its own, knowing it would likely go on late into the night, and Mara had said she'd had her fill of well-wishers for one day.

"Aoife! Just in time for a bite," she greeted her.

"You want me to eat again? I'm going to gain a stone from just one day back in Ireland at this rate."

"You could use a bit of fattening up. You're all skin and bones since you went to America. Don't tell me you're on one of those silly kale diets that are all the rage. You need proper food; ye can't live off lettuce alone."

*Easy for you to say*, Aoife thought, enviously admiring Mara's toned figure. It didn't come from stepping foot in a gym; that was purely from working all day as a landscape artist. Mara was constantly busy and moving, unlike Aoife, who had to work at keeping her figure the way it was by going to the gym at least three times a week.

She looked down at herself. She didn't think she'd changed that much in the last three years; she straightened her hair more often now, smoothing out the curls and waves, kept her hands manicured, the fingertips gone soft without any manual labour to do. She might be a bit thinner, but nothing compared to most New York women with their beauty and fitness regimes. But maybe she'd conformed to the pressures of certain beauty standards more than she'd realized.

"Hello, love. How was your nap?" she asked Miriam, bending down to give her a quick kiss on the top of her head and changing the topic.

"I'm hungry," Miriam replied, eyeing the bowl of biscuits Rory had just put on the table in front of her.

"Why am I not surprised?" She smiled down at Miriam and helped her into a chair, taking a biscuit and putting it on her plate before she hogged the whole bowl.

"How was your walk?" Colin asked, holding a chair out to her, inviting her to sit down.

"Fine." She wasn't exactly sure why, but a part of her told her not to mention that she'd seen Michael.

"Where did you go?" He ladled stew into a bowl

for her and they all sat down at the table.

"Just around."

It was during this moment of awkwardness that Connor took yet another opportunity to try and win her over to the idea of coming back to Ireland. "Or, if you would prefer, you could start in the New York office. Lord knows I could use someone there I could trust running the place."

"Except that I know nothing about running a company," Aoife reminded him.

"You own your own publishing house!"

"Yeah, but I have people who do the actual running of the place so that I can focus on working with our clients."

"I didn't have any experience when I first started." Connor dismissed her counter-argument with another wave of his biscuit, almost dripping stew onto the table. Mara slapped gently at his hand as some droplets came close to spraying her in the face.

"Stop talking with your hands while you're eating. And stop bullying Aoife into working with ye. If she doesn't want to, then she doesn't want to. She has her own business to run; she doesn't need you pressuring her and all. Sure, and she's plenty to do."

Connor acquiesced for the moment.

"Besides, it was easier for you. Not only did you go to school before assuming control of the company, you also had our grandparents' blessing," Aoife pointed out.

"So do you."

When she shot him a skeptical look, he hastily replied, "Ok, so maybe you don't exactly have Granny's approval, but since when have you ever wanted or needed her approval on anything?"

He was right, of course. She hadn't needed her grandmother's approval for how she lived her life in a very long time.

"If it was good enough for our grandfather to want you to be a part of his company, then it's good enough for me."

"For every excuse I give you, you are going to find a way to solve the issue, aren't you?"

"Yep." He smiled smugly at her.

"The answer is no, Connor." His gleeful smile faded and was replaced with a crestfallen look.

"C'mon, it can't be that surprising that I'd turn you down. I don't belong at *O'Reilly's* and neither do you, and you know that. I think you just haven't admitted it to yourself yet. You and I, we're not like the rest of them. It's time we stopped trying to fit into the way they see us and live the way we want to. The way we *should* be living, which is why I've got a counter-offer for you."

Connor paused, his mouthful of biscuit poised in the air, halfway between his bowl and his mouth. "I'm listening."

Today wasn't the first time that Connor had been trying to get her to join the family business. It was something he'd brought up on more than one occasion in his visits to her in New York over the last three years. She'd known that eventually she'd have to come up with her own idea on how the two of them could work together within the family business – without actually working for their grandmother – in order for him to back off. And on the flight over her, she thought she'd landed on the perfect compromise.

"We can both agree that neither of us belongs at a company like O'Reilly's; not like how they're running it now, so different from what Grandda wanted. So, I think you and I should buy Grandda's original pub and run it together, in exchange for some of our shares in O'Reilly's."

She stared across the dinner table and watched as a myriad of thoughts crossed Connor's mind as he mulled over this proposal. Everyone at the table paused what they were doing, as if afraid that if they so much as breathed, they would scare him off the thought. When Aoife could see he was giving it due consideration, she pressed on.

"The thing that Granny, our mothers, and Caitlin want most is a controlling interest in the company. So, we give them what they want by trading Grandda's original pub for it. We get to stick to his original vision for it, and the others get to run the rest of the chain separately, the way they want, with little interference from us. We wouldn't need to give up all of our shares; I don't think Grandda would have wanted that. But we would each give up just enough that we can still have a voice, but we wouldn't be able to interfere as much as if we keep our current shares."

After the room fell silent, Mara looked between Aoife and Connor.

"What do you think?"

"Do you think that Gran would actually give it up? Even if it doesn't fit into her vision of *O'Reilly's*, it's the one that started everything. It's the reason for everything her life has become," Connor replied, seemingly unconvinced by his cousin's proposal.

"I think if she had to give it just to me, then no, she wouldn't. But I think knowing it was safe under your management, I think she could let it go. It's the best compromise for all of us, really. You and I get to honour Grandda by continuing his legacy, and Gran gets to have you in charge of that vision, even if you aren't running the company in the way she originally envisioned. Also, it means you would be in Dublin a lot more than you are now, which will make her even happier."

"And it would make me happier not having you flying all over the world to God knows where all the time," Mara chimed in, giving Connor a pointed look.

Aoife hadn't spent all that much time around the two of them since they'd begun dating seriously, but despite Mara's easy-going nature, she knew all the work he did with *O'Reilly's* had to mean Connor wasn't home as often as he should be. Having him working only an hour's commute away would certainly mean he'd be home more often than he was now, or when he was working in the military.

"And it would mean you'd also be back in Dublin," Connor smiled.

"I was thinking I would be more of a silent partner," she was quick to clarify. She had no plans to return to Ireland, and she wanted this to be clear from the outset. Her life was in New York now, and she didn't want that to change.

Connor's mouth twisted into a bit of a grimace, but eventually nodded. She knew he wasn't exactly content with this, but it was as best a compromise as he was going to get for the moment.

"And you would be ok with giving up *O'Reilly's* to your mother? To Caitlin?"

"Yes."

She meant it. Her time in Ballyclara had taught her a valuable lesson: that she needed to learn to stand on her own two feet and make her own way in life, no matter what everyone else around her thought she should do. She needed to do what was right for her, not what was expected of her. She'd always known she would never be happy running her grandfather's company, even if it meant she would run it alongside Connor. What made her happy was running her publishing house, helping other artists like herself realize their dreams. It was her own way of carrying on her grandfather's dream. He had opened his first pub with the intention of it being a safe place for people in the neighbourhood to come to, to talk about their dreams and their fears, to feel like they were supported and loved like family, a place where they could escape the harsh reality of their lives for a time. By helping new writers and poets, she was giving them a safe place to show their work, a place where they could feel supported so that they could become their best selves. Now she was creating her own legacy, and she liked to think her grandfather would have been proud of her for it. She had no need to work in *O'Reilly's* in order to fulfil his dreams for her, but running his original pub with Connor would be a nice way to continue his legacy.

"You have a deal. As long as you promise to extend your stay in Ireland and work on this proposal with me and present it to Granny."

"We can work on it even if I'm in America, Connor. There's this handy tool called video chat…"

"Yeah, but it's not the same as having you right here beside me when I have a brilliant idea," he interjected.

"I have a publishing house to run," she reminded him.

"You've said before that you had people to run it for you. I'm sure you can leave it in their capable hands for a couple of weeks. Besides, you have this handy thing called video chat."

"A couple of weeks?!" she spluttered, almost

sending more droplets of stew onto the table. "How big do you expect this proposal to be?"

"We need it to be perfect."

She knew he was right. It had to be perfect so that Grainne O'Reilly could find no fault with it and turn them down.

Aoife inhaled slowly, mulling over it over. She looked over at Colin, who shrugged.

"I'd love to see more of Ireland, anyways."

Miriam grinned at her. "Does this mean we'll see the zoo Connor told me about?"

"I suppose it does." Aoife smiled at her. "Looks like you have a deal, Connor."

He licked drops of stew from his fingers and grinned at her like the Cheshire cat.

༄

Later that evening, Aoife and Colin walked back to Aldridge Manor to pick up the overnight bags they'd left in the boot of the car. As they approached the house, she admired the view before her.

The sun was beginning its slow descent below the mountains that stood guard over the little village nestled in the valley between. She never failed to be amazed at the wild beauty of the place; a stunning little hideaway from the hustle and bustle of Dublin, a tiny gem of a place that had – as of yet – gone mostly untouched by tourism and industry despite being so close to Glendalough. Aoife liked that it was still unscathed by the modern world, that it kept itself to itself and that the people there had not seemed to age or change a bit in the time since she'd last visited, almost as if the place was like the mythical Scottish village, Brigadoon.

"Are you sure you're alright with us staying in Ireland a little longer?"

Colin stopped and stood beside her.

"It's not like Ireland is the worst place to be," he said, smiling and gesturing to the very view she was admiring. "I mean, this place is beautiful."

"What about New York? Our lives are back there. Miriam's life is back there; her grandparents, and her friends, and her school."

"It's only for a week or two, Aoife. I think you're getting ahead of yourself, don't you? Or are we talking about staying here longer?" He cocked his head to the side, gazing at her.

"No, you're right. I'm just overthinking things."

"I mean, if you're talking about staying here longer, it's not like Ireland doesn't have excellent schools. Also, I can think of a million places worse than Ballyclara to raise Miriam. Dublin is only an hour away, and from there we can go anywhere in Europe. Don't you miss your friends and family? You haven't seen them in three years; I'm sure you miss being here. It sure seems that they've missed having you around."

She couldn't deny that everyone in Ballyclara seemed genuinely pleased to see her – Molly and Michael notwithstanding – but was that enough for her to move her whole life back across the Atlantic Ocean to a place she'd abandoned and thought never to see again? If Dermot hadn't died, would she even be here now?

Probably not.

"What about Miriam's life in New York? She wouldn't see her grandparents as often if we moved over here. And you would be further away from your parents, your home."

"My home is wherever you and Miriam are," he said, putting down the bags he was holding, pulled her in close to him and kissed her lightly on the lips.

"That was so corny," she said, laughing with him.

"And yet, you love me for it anyways," he said, smiling at her.

"Would you really move yourself and Miriam all the way to Ireland for me?" she asked, her tone suddenly serious and the smile fading from her face.

"Of course," Colin replied without hesitation. "We have everything we need here to make a good life for ourselves. There's a school here. You have a house already, so it's not like we would need to find a place to live. This place is wonderful for her to run around in and play, and meet children her own age. It's safer than New York, in any case. And there's a chance for her to see the world and have space to grow up in an environment where she would be close to family."

"But she wouldn't be close to your family."

"It's not like we can't go back to the States any time we want, Aoife. And before you say that your publishing house is in New York, you and I both know you could easily relocate it here."

"You're beginning to sound like Connor," she pouted.

"Is that such a bad thing? He's got good points, and he misses having you here. In case you hadn't noticed, he's made a good life for himself with Mara and Rory; family life suits him. I wouldn't be surprised if an engagement happens soon."

"You think so?" She looked up at him, watching the reflection of the setting sun lighting up his dark eyes, feeling the warmth of the last rays of sun warm her skin.

She hadn't given Connor's love life much thought.

She knew he'd made significant life changes over the last few years, and dating Mara had been one of them. She couldn't deny that Connor had seemed to fit in seamlessly into Ballyclara and that he'd seemed perfectly at ease in Mara's cottage with her and Rory, as if it was now his home. Even though he kept a flat in Dublin, she wouldn't be surprised if this *was* his home now. She liked Mara and Rory, but she'd never really thought of the possibility of them becoming part of her family until just now. And that would mean Michael would become part of her extended family, too. She wasn't sure how she felt about that.

"What's wrong? I thought you liked Mara and Connor together?"

"I do," she replied quickly. "I just caught a chill is all. Let's grab the bags and head back."

Colin nodded and walked with her to the car, dropping the subject and leaving her with the unsettling thought that her life was about to have some major changes in the near future.

Chapter Nine

"Careful. You keep looking at Aoife that way, someone might think you're still in love with her."

Michael turned his gaze over his shoulder briefly at the sound of Brendan coming through the kitchen doors, then looked back over at Aoife, Colin, and Miriam who were having a bite of breakfast after having been convinced by his sister's boyfriend to stay in Ballyclara longer. He liked Connor, but right now, he could wring his bloody neck.

Although Brendan had said it teasingly, Michael knew well enough that it was his way of asking him if it were true.

"Don't be daft."

He pretended to wipe at a spot on the bar that didn't exist. He could still feel Brendan's eyes on him but pretended not to notice. After last night, the last thing he wanted was any suspicion that he in any way thought about Aoife, or even noticed her, for that matter. He didn't need anyone getting any ideas into their fool heads.

*Or into your own.* Sometimes he hated his own subconscious.

It wasn't easy though, seeing the way she looked at Miriam, like a mother would, and he felt a pang of jealousy. The two of them had never talked about having children together; they hadn't been together long enough to even think of having that conversation. But seeing her now, how settled she was with her new life, he had a sudden wish that they'd found that kind of happiness together.

It wasn't as if he hadn't had his own experiences with fatherhood; he was as much of a father to his nephew, Rory, as anyone could be, and he and Eliza had had two of their own, although God had seen fit to take them home before they were born. Ever since, he'd put aside his dreams of fatherhood for fear that the sadness he felt for the children he'd lost would consume him. The only person who had made him want to try again had been Aoife.

"You mind the front for a bit. I'm going out back for a smoke."

"Mmhmm." Brendan said it like he knew exactly why he suddenly needed a smoke break, even though he was supposed to have quit. Michael ignored him, as per usual.

He went through the kitchen doors, to the back of the pub. Leaning against the solid stone wall, he breathed in the cool air around him, and pulled out a cigarette and his lighter from his pocket. He knew Ailish would smell it on him later and she would politely ignore it; she was like that. She made it known that she did not approve, but she also knew that quitting a lifelong habit did not happen overnight and she wouldn't nag him for sneaking a cheeky one here and there.

It was one of the many things he loved about her, along with her boldness, her surety that she knew exactly what she wanted from life. She may not be doing what she'd originally intended, but she wasn't whingeing about it; she simply got on with things and made the most of what she had. That kind of confidence had been what ultimately drew him to her, because he'd had no clue what he wanted.

Now that he thought about it, he'd always been drawn by confident women. That much had been clear when he'd first started dating Eliza, who'd had a whole life planned out for the two of them from the moment they met as children. He'd only been along for the ride. But things were different with Ailish; she wasn't there to tell him how he should change himself to fit into her life goals; he was welcome to join her on her journey if he wanted to, but if he didn't, she wasn't going to stick around and wait for him to catch up. She was much like Aoife in that respect, he supposed, although Aoife hadn't quite seemed to know what she'd wanted from life when he'd first met her. She'd only known enough that she hadn't wanted what she'd had at the time, and that she knew she wasn't going to find what she was looking for in Ballyclara.

*And that was the problem.*

He shook his head clear of the smoke around him and put out his cigarette. He needed to stop bringing up the past just because she was back here now. She was happy with her new man, and he was happy with Ailish. That was the end of it.

So why did he feel like everything was all topsy-turvy? Before he had too much time to dwell on it, he headed back inside.

He noticed that Aoife, Colin, and Miriam were still there, although now they'd been joined by his sister, his nephew, and Connor. He tried to ignore them and focused instead on Ailish, who'd also made an appearance.

"Hello, handsome," she greeted him with a kiss. She was almost a literal ray of sunshine this morning in her canary-yellow printed sundress and sandals. Just the vision he needed to brighten up his gloomy start to the day.

"You snuck out so early this morning. I didn't get to say good morning. I thought I would come down and see how you are. I thought you said you were going to take a few days off?"

He immediately felt guilty about how he'd let Aoife come between the two of them last night. Frustrated with himself, he'd left her there this morning, still sleeping, and had come in to open the pub. Brendan, in his quiet way, had just pretended like Michael had always been supposed to come in for shift and put him to work. He'd been grateful; he needed something for his hands to do to keep his mind from going idle more than he'd needed to sit around home thinking over how sad his life was right now.

"Michael? Did you hear me?"

Ailish's voice sounded far off, like it was coming from some disembodied entity on a faraway shore he couldn't quite hear. He looked back at her and saw her expectant look.

"I'm sorry, what?" He wiped at more imaginary spots on the bar, trying to avoid her hawk-like gaze.

"Where did your mind wander off to just now?"

she asked him. "I was asking how you were doing, and then your face turned funny for a second. I know you have a lot to deal with, but you know I'm always here for you, Michael. Whatever you need, just tell me."

She reached across the bar and took his hand, rubbing the inside of his palm with her thumb in a reassuring gesture. He put his rag down and put his other hand over both of hers.

"I know. And I'm so grateful to you, Ailish. I'm sorry I've not been giving you the attention I should have for the last few days."

"You don't need to put your attention on me, Michael," she told him. "I don't need you to be here for me, and I don't need to see you being strong and bearing up through this. What I need is to know that you will talk to me whenever you need to, to know that you know that I'm here for you and to know that you won't shut me out. We don't need to talk about things if you don't want to, but don't leave me out if you need to talk, either."

Her face was serious. He gave her a small smile and squeezed her hand.

"I do know that you're here for me, Ailish, and I'm sorry if I've made you feel like I've shut you out. It's the last thing I want you to feel."

He leaned across and gave her a quick kiss. "I promise I won't do it again."

"Good." She put her hand on the collar of his shirt and pulled him in for a longer kiss.

Happy she was appeased, he said, "You know, maybe you're right. I *should* take some time off. I think I'm going to check in on Mam and then go home. Care to join me?"

"Maybe in a bit. I said I'd lend Molly a hand with cleaning up a few things here from last night, and then

I'll join you at home."

"Go on, get out o' here," Brendan said to him, joining in on their conversation.

"You sure? What if it gets busy?"

Brendan rolled his eyes.

"Then I'll bring in Jimmy or Connor, or literally anyone in Ballyclara. Pulling pints and waiting tables isn't rocket science. I'm sure we can manage a few days without you being a mother hen and driving us all insane. And who knows? Maybe I'll convince Aoife to work behind the bar again. I mean, she was a roaring success the last time."

Brendan winked at him, as Michael remembered the weekend of Brendan and Molly's anniversary a few years ago when they'd had to take up Aoife's offer to help out with the pub so they wouldn't be short-staffed. Michael had thought it would be just about the worst idea at the time to bring in this upstart city girl with seemingly no experience to help during one of their busiest times, but it had turned out to be much more of a success than he could have imagined, and it had played a big part in bringing the two of them closer together.

Michael involuntarily smiled at the memory. "Cheers mate. Oh, and good luck with that plan, since she's leaving today."

"I'd care to wager a bet that we're going to be seeing a whole lot more of Aoife O'Reilly than you might think. Rumour has it she might be staying longer than originally intended."

Brendan smirked as Michael registered what he'd just told him.

"Now go on with ye before I change my mind and make you work out the rest of the shift," he said, practically pushing him towards the door.

"Here, I'll get it," Aoife said, taking the cheque from Brendan's hand before Connor could say otherwise and went up to the bar to pay.

"Michael seemed not himself. Anything the matter?" she overheard Molly ask Ailish, the three of them watching Michael's retreating form as he went home.

"No, not beyond the usual, I don't think... At least, I don't think so. He's been like that since..."

*Since I showed up in Ballyclara again.* That's what she and Molly knew Ailish was going to say, but hadn't wanted to, not with Aoife standing right in front of them. Whether she'd meant to or not, Aoife always seemed to put herself right in the middle of things.

"I was surprised to see him in here today," she said, boldly inviting herself into the conversation. If they were going to talk about her, she may as well join in.

"He wasn't supposed to be. He's gone up now to check in on Sinead." Ailish's bubbly mood from yesterday seemed to have dissipated into genuine concern.

"I'm sure it'll all be right in the end." Molly gave Ailish's shoulder a reassuring squeeze and headed back to the kitchen to prepare for the lunch crowd.

"Actually, Molly, I'd like to talk to you for a minute." Aoife didn't know what had made her suddenly so bold, but she knew that if she was going to be back in Ballyclara for any length of time, she needed to start mending some fences.

Molly pretended not to hear her and continued through to the kitchen. Aoife squared her shoulders and followed her. Molly was surprised at Aoife's persistence, but seemingly tried to pass it off as inconsequential by picking up a blue dishcloth as she started wiping down the counters. The sterile scent of surface cleaner hung in the air between them.

"Molly, stay still for a moment, would you?" Aoife's exasperation was apparent in her tone.

Molly continued to fidget with the dishcloth in her hands, but she stopped moving about the kitchen. She let out an enormous sigh of resignation but still wouldn't look at her.

"You've been avoiding me since I got back."

"That's not true," Molly started, but even she knew she was lying. "Ok, so maybe I have been, but are ye really surprised?"

"I am a bit, yeah." Aoife searched her face, trying to find out what she was thinking. "I didn't expect a parade or anything when I came back, but I would've expected more hostility from Michael than from you."

Molly tucked a sandy-blonde strand of hair behind her ear and took a moment before answering.

"It isn't just Michael you ran out on, Aoife. You left the rest of us behind, too. I know you had your reasons and opportunities you felt you couldn't miss out on, but it wasn't just him you left behind when you left here."

The realization of Molly's words stung her because they were true. She knew she'd hurt more than just Michael by leaving, but that realization hadn't truly sunk in until she was now confronted with it.

"Oh Molly, I'm so sorry."

She wanted to hug her, but wasn't sure how she would react just now. Molly was a sensible, no-nonsense, take-no-prisoners kind of woman. She wasn't unaffectionate, but she didn't exactly have the cuddliest personality either. "It wasn't how I wanted it to go. Everything seemed to happen so quickly, and I... I didn't know how to stay in touch after I left. I thought a clean break would be easier."

"Better for you." It wasn't a question.

"No, better for everyone," she blurted, but she saw the truth in Molly's words. "I don't know... maybe? Yeah. Thinking about it now, it must have seemed terribly selfish of me to do."

"Did it ever occur to ye the whole time you were here that maybe we were as invested in you as you were becoming in us? We opened our homes and our hearts to ye, Aoife. And then ye left us behind like we didn't matter anymore."

"That's not how I wanted it to be, I swear. I valued our friendship. I still do. It meant the world to me what you and Brendan have done for me, and all of Ballyclara, too. You don't know how much I've missed you all, how many times I wanted to pick up the phone and talk to all of you."

"So why didn't you, then?"

Aoife paused a moment, trying to give the question the thought it deserved. "Because every time I went to pick up the phone to tell you something, I worried that you and Brendan hated me for breaking up with Michael and leaving the way I did. I thought you might all hate me."

Something in the way Molly held herself seemed to soften and her posture seemed to relax ever so slightly. She put down the dishcloth on the countertop and folded her arms across the kitchen apron she was wearing, but her stance was more relaxed than defensive.

"Well, we weren't thrilled with how ye left, it's true, but we wouldn't hate ye, Aoife. We wish ye hadn't left, that maybe the two of you would have found some way to work it all out, but we wouldn't have hated you."

"Well, things seem to have worked out in the end, didn't they? Just maybe not how we thought they would."

Through the porthole windows of the kitchen doors, Aoife could see Ailish leaning against the bar, laughing at some joke Connor had made from the table where he, Colin, Mara, Miriam, and Rory were sitting. Brendan had paused what he was doing and seemed to join in on the conversation.

"She's good for him," she admitted, watching the casual manner with which the younger woman had inserted herself into life in Ballyclara.

"Well, he couldn't do much worse, could he? The only way was up," Molly said with a devilish grin on her face.

"Hey!" Aoife tapped her playfully on the arm.

"Things seem to have worked out for you too." Molly's tone was more serious as she nodded towards Colin and Miriam, who were having an animated chat with Karen, Jimmy, and Mae, who had just arrived and joined them. "Your man Colin seems a nice sort, and wee Miriam is dear. She and Mae seemed thick as thieves yesterday."

"I think she could charm even the coldest-hearted person in the world." Aoife beamed with pride. *Well, maybe except for Michael.*

"I'm glad you found them. I mean it," she said, seeing the surprised look Aoife gave her. "I might not like how ye left, but it seems that New York was good for ye."

"It has been good to me," she admitted. "But that doesn't mean that I've forgotten about this place and how kind it was to me before New York."

Molly narrowed her eyes, assessing her. "Alright, you're forgiven," and reached out and enfolded her in a quick hug. "I tried being mad at ye, but I can't do it anymore. I miss ye too much."

Aoife smiled and hugged her back. "But if anyone asks, I didn't let you off easy," Molly was clear. "I can't have people thinking I've gone soft now."

"Oh, I don't think there's any fear of that. I don't think anyone could describe you as being someone who typically goes soft on anyone."

"And don't ye forget it, if ye get any more fool ideas about running off and not keeping in touch again." Molly squeezed her tight before letting her go.

Aoife breathed a sigh of relief, glad that the air between them seemed to clear.

*One apology down, so many more to go.*

※

Back at the table, Aoife sat down in the space across from Connor that Colin had recently vacated so that he and Miriam could sit at a table with Jimmy, Karen, and Mae.

"Where's Mara and Rory?"

"They went back with Ailish to check in on Sinead. They'll have to think of what they're going to do with Dermot's stuff now. I'm going to head up there myself soon."

"If you need any help with the packing up, just let me know. I don't mind at all."

"I'm sure we'll be taking you up on that offer," he replied, adjusting the collar of his dark green shirt. "But in the meantime, I wanted to talk about this idea of yours.

I called Cait this morning and talked to her about it, and she thinks it's great."

Aoife stared at her cousin, temporarily speechless. "You didn't tell her the idea came from me, did you?"

To say Aoife and Caitlin, Connor's twin sister, did not get along was an understatement. They didn't full-on hate one another, at least not on Aoife's part, but they certainly had never agreed on much and just the mention that this idea had come from her would be enough for Caitlin to shoot it down.

"She wants us to put together the proposal, something we can bring to the family to look at. She'll look it over beforehand for us," Connor replied, deftly sidestepping the question.

"I knew it! You didn't tell her it was my idea."

"If it gets it approved, does it really matter to you that our family thinks the idea came from me?"

She considered the question. Of course, she would like them to know the idea had been hers, but it didn't really hurt her pride to have them think it came from him. It wasn't like Connor was stealing her idea because he wanted the credit; he was doing it because he believed in the idea and wanted it to succeed, which meant more to her than their family knowing she'd been behind the idea.

"No, I suppose it doesn't."

Connor smiled at her. "Good. Now, I'm going to go and check in on Sinead, but let's reconvene this afternoon and start working on this thing."

He stood up and put on the sunglasses he had previously put on top of his head, and ran his hand through his blonde hair, readjusting some stray locks.

As Aoife watched him walk through the doors out into the sunny day, she wondered how exactly it was that she'd gotten herself talked into extending what was supposed to be a two-day trip into what she knew would turn into a couple of weeks. She glanced down at her watch.

*Just about time that it would be considered respectable to contact New York*. She had calls to make and appointments to rearrange.

"I'm going to head back and make some calls," she said to Colin, coming over to his table.

"Ok," he said, getting up.

"No, you two stay here and enjoy yourselves. I'll only be a couple of hours and then we can get together for some lunch before Connor snatches me away to work on this proposal." He nodded to her and sat down again.

"I'll see you later, monkey," she said to Miriam before heading out. The little girl was so engrossed in the conversation she was having with Mae, she didn't even notice.

Aoife smiled at the two of them, appreciating the good fortune she'd had to find her and Colin and tried to put away any doubts she'd had over her to decision to go to New York.

## Chapter Ten

"When is Bex picking you up from the airport? I miss you!" Millie's British accent greeted her over the phone.

"Millie? Did I dial the wrong number? I thought I was calling Bex?"

"No, you have the right number," she heard Bex in the background.

"What are you doing in New York, Millie? I thought you were in Italy or God knows where?"

Millie had made an unexpected success of herself as a model not long after she'd started working as Aoife's assistant at the publishing house. Bex, their friend and Millie's former roommate, had been working so hard to put together her first ever photo-shoot for the clothing line she was designing, only to have her original model cancel at the last minute. Desperate for someone to stand in for her, she'd convinced Millie to do it for her.

To everyone's surprise, she was actually great at it, and Aoife and Bex both marvelled at how something Millie had done on a lark could turn out to be her new career. Now she spent most of the year in Italy or wherever she was sent out for photo-shoots. The lifestyle suited the flighty Millie just fine; she didn't have to stay in one place for very long, and she was never doing the same thing twice. Bex and Aoife had worried that the long hours, the standing around, and having to work to bring the aesthetic the designer and photographer wanted would be tiresome for her. They figured she would grow bored with it like with everything else she'd done, but instead, she seemed to thrive in the environment. She was happier than she'd ever been before, and the two of them were grateful she'd seemed to finally find something she enjoyed doing.

"I wanted to come to New York to surprise you, only to find out you weren't here at all!" Millie sounded put out.

"Can I have my phone back now?" Aoife heard Bex ask on the other end.

Millie, while loved by the other two, had little regard for personal space or property, especially when it came to Bex's things. The two of them had lived together in Dublin when Aoife had moved to Ballyclara, and it had been impossible to call Bex to talk to her by herself because Millie would simply answer her phone all the time.

"So, when are you coming back?" Millie asked again, ignoring her.

"Well, actually, I think you made a wasted trip. I don't think I'll be back for another couple of weeks."

Aoife heard a bit of a kerfuffle on the other end as

Bex attempted to wrestle her phone back and finally got on the line. Her tone was both curious and a little serious when she asked, "You're staying in Ireland?"

Even though she couldn't see her best friend and former college roommate, Aoife knew she had a concerned look on her face.

"Not indefinitely." That was certainly out of the question.

"How long are you planning to extend your stay for?"

"I'm not sure yet. Connor wants to talk about some business plans," she replied.

"Business plans? What kind of business plans? I thought you had no intentions of working for *O'Reilly's*?" Millie's voice floated over the speakerphone as Bex switched it over so they could both talk to her, knowing Mille would only take her phone again otherwise.

"I don't. We have a different idea in mind. We're thinking of buying Grandda's original pub from our grandmother and selling back some of our shares as part of the deal." She waited for her friends' responses, knowing they would probably have mixed reactions to this news.

"So, does this mean you *are* planning to stay in Ireland?" Millie asked cautiously. The implication, and worry, that this was going to turn into a permanent stay was apparent in her voice.

Aoife thought back to her conversation with Colin from the night before about how he'd be willing to move here if she wanted to, but thought it best not to mention that to either of them just now. Besides, that conversation had just been a hypothetical. Just because he was willing to move here didn't mean they needed to.

"I thought you didn't even want to go back to

Ireland?"

"I didn't say that I didn't want to come back to Ireland," Aoife tried to back-track on her previous statements even though she knew there was truth in them. "I'm only staying until we get the proposal done and approved. I intend to be a silent partner in this, so you don't need to worry about me moving away from New York," she reassured her. "Besides, Colin and Miriam have never been to Ireland before, so it made sense to stay a bit longer so the two of them can spend some time touring around."

"Oh really? Because I distinctly remember you saying, 'Millie, I never want to set foot back in Ireland again.'"

"I'm sure Aoife didn't say those exact words," Bex answered, trying to move past an inevitable she said/she said argument. "Where are the two of you staying? At Aldridge? Or with your folks?" she asked, changing the subject before Millie pushed it.

"Like hell I'm staying with my family," Aoife replied sharply. She didn't even want to see her family, let alone stay with them. She heard Bex chuckle at this response. Staying at Aldridge wasn't an option either, as far as she was concerned; she didn't want to be that close to Michael, if she could help it.

"In the flat above the pub."

"And how is Michael?" Millie's tone was piqued with curiosity, desperate for any little tidbit of information about Aoife's former flame. They all knew it was the last question she wanted to answer, but it was one which even the polite Bex would be curious to know the answer to.

She sighed and decided there was no getting around it, unless she hung up the phone right now, but that would only delay the inevitable. "It wasn't as bad as I expected. He has a new girlfriend now. A really nice woman named Ailish."

"Thank God you didn't say that he'd gone back to his ex. Eliza? That was her name, right?"

"I saw her at the funeral. She's married now and has a baby on the way. I was glad to see she's finally found someone to be happy with. Oh, and I'm pretty sure the guy she ended up marrying was the one she'd been having the affair with way back before Michael and I met."

"You're happy for that cow?!" Millie exclaimed. "My, how grown up we are."

"Well, let's not forget that things between Michael, Eliza, and I were a little complicated," she strove to be fair towards Eliza. "I wasn't exactly innocent when it came to her break-up with Michael."

"A little complicated? That's an understatement, but the fault for their break-up is squarely on the two of them. I mostly remember her being a possessive cow and he… well, he should have ended things with her a long time ago. He knew it wasn't going anywhere, and to string her along was cruel and he should not have come trying to start things with you before he had ended them with her."

Millie saw things as black and white when it came to Aoife's relationship with Michael, and there was no doubt in Aoife's mind who Millie thought was at fault for their break-up. She was a loyal friend, and Aoife's own indecisiveness and fear of attachment had clearly been glossed over in Millie's mind. She loved her for it, but she also knew that Millie was not the most impartial when it came to situations like this.

Bex, usually the voice of reason, tried to offer a

measured opinion. "Well, I think we can all agree that, whatever the circumstances, things probably worked out as best they could for everyone. You have Colin and Miriam, Eliza has her husband and her new baby, and Michael has his new girlfriend."

"She'll never be as good as Aoife, though. She will always be the one that got away from him." Millie was sometimes loyal to a fault.

"I think Ailish is good for him," Aoife countered.

"You've met her, then?"

"Yes, after the funeral, and she seemed really lovely," she said, trying to be kind. *Slightly stalkery, but otherwise harmless.* "I think she will be good for him. I'm glad to see him happy. Truly, I am."

Even to her ears, the words sounded slightly hollow. It wasn't that she didn't wish Michael all the happiness in the world. It was that she felt as she'd done when she'd first seen him and Ailish together: like she wished it was her standing beside him and not someone else. She knew it sounded selfish, but she also couldn't help but wish she'd been the one to make Michael happy. To reverse Millie's earlier statement, it wasn't necessarily her that had gotten away from Michael, but perhaps Michael who had gotten away from her. She couldn't help but feel a twinge of regret that perhaps she'd made the wrong choice in moving to New York. She hadn't regretted the decision once in the time she'd been there, but coming back to Ireland had stirred up some old feelings that she wished had remained in the past.

"Well, honey, you let us know when you're ready to come home and we'll be here waiting for you," Bex said, trying to draw a close to the conversation before it got too maudlin.

"Thanks, you two."

## Where I'm Home

"Better make sure that you come home soon before I head out again," Millie warned.

"Oh no, Colin, Miriam, and I will have to come to Italy so Miriam can visit her Auntie Millie," Aoife said with mock dramatization. "But seriously, I don't plan to stay here much longer. We are only checked into the hotel in Dublin until the end of next week, and as soon as Connor and I finish this proposal, I plan to leave Ireland for good. We will be home soon, I promise."

※

As it turned out, she wouldn't be keeping that promise.

Aoife and Connor did work on the proposal as she had intended, and she even took some time to take day trips around Ireland with Colin and Miriam. She loved showing the two of them her homeland. It was always such an adventure looking at the place where she'd grown up through the eyes of someone else, especially the eyes of a child. Everything seemed eminently more exciting to Miriam, which made it seem more exciting to her and Colin.

In typical fashion for Connor, as the time for them to return to New York drew closer, he wiled his way into getting her to return to Ballyclara. They'd stayed the day after the funeral with Connor and Mara, but they'd returned to their Dublin hotel soon after.

"It's more practical for Connor and I to work out of his office or his flat, since he has to be here for work this week anyways," she'd tried to reason with Mara and Sinead, who had been quite put-out by her quick departure.

"So long as you promise to come back here before you go to New York again," Sinead had said, reluctantly letting her go.

Aoife wasn't sure if it had been their idea or Connor's to hijack her plans to work on the proposal from his Dublin flat that day, but she suddenly found herself in the middle of telling him how she'd finally taken Miriam to Dublin Zoo in Phoenix Park the day before, when the surrounding scenery changed from cityscape to countryside.

"Aren't we going to your flat to work on the proposal?"

"We will work on the proposal," he said, "but I've just realized I forgot some documents we need at home in Ballyclara." It still felt weird to hear him calling Ballyclara home. She'd been so used to his Dublin flat being his Irish home-base when he'd been in the military, but now it was only where he stayed during the week if he couldn't work from Mara's cottage.

"What did you forget? I'm sure we can work around it until you get home tonight, and we can finish up tomorrow."

Even though she knew she'd promised to come back before she left for New York, some part of her was still hoping to avoid it if she could. It was more confusing being in Ballyclara, and she really had no desire to run into Michael again. The two of them still hadn't really talked to one another yet, not properly. A part of her was wondering if it wasn't maybe better to just leave things as they were. Did she really need to bring up her reasons for leaving him three years ago? Would that really bring either of them any peace? Both of them seemed perfectly content as they were, so why did she need to go and mess with that?

## Where I'm Home

*Is to being content all you want? Or do you want something more?* a voice inside her asked. She tried to ignore it.

"Don't worry; we can work on it just as easily at home as we can in Dublin."

She wasn't happy about him practically kidnapping her like this, but what was she going to do? Open the door and jump out onto the motorway?

"You know, there was a time when Dublin was home." She'd meant it only as an observation, thinking about how their lives had changed so much since their grandfather had passed away four years ago.

"And there was once a time when Ballyclara was home to you, too. You know, if it hadn't been for you moving down there, I would probably have never known the place existed. I would never have met Mara and Rory, and I wouldn't have the happy family I do now."

"So, what you're saying is that you owe all your good fortune to me?" she said smugly.

"I'd like to think I owe my good fortune to my own hard work, but sure, I suppose you played a small part." He grinned at her.

"Only a small part? I think you owe me way more credit than that, considering Mara is *way* out of your league. She's way too good for you. You were fortunate I introduced the two of you."

"I seem to remember a time when you weren't too happy about the two of us getting together."

Aoife thought back to when she'd moved down to Ballyclara and he'd come to stay with her before he got deployed on his last tour. She'd been wrapped up in her own drama at the time and projecting her own anxieties onto him and the relationship he'd been starting with Mara. She hadn't wanted her new friend to get her heart broken by her handsome cousin who, up until then, had never been in a stable relationship.

"Like I said, Mara's way too good for you, and I was worried you would hurt her. You were in the military at the time, and who knew if you'd get yourself blown to smithereens or not? And it's not like you've exactly been good at the whole long-distance relationship thing. How was I to know you weren't going to just sleep with her and then say you weren't interested anymore? I love you like a brother, Connor, but I didn't want to see her, or Rory get attached and have you treat them like your previous relationships."

She expected him to come back with some witty remark, or feign insult, but what he said completely surprised her.

"I'd never hurt her or Rory." His tone was serious and sincere.

Aoife glanced over at him and saw his normally smooth forehead was crinkled with fine lines, his greyish-blue eyes focused intently on the road in front of him. His whole body was tense, not at what she'd said, but at the idea of anyone hurting Mara or Rory. She realized for the first time that while she knew he cared deeply for Mara, it had never really dawned on her until now that he might actually *love* her. She'd always assumed that he'd eventually move on and find someone their family would approve of, which had been at the heart of her earlier comment. They both knew their family would not approve of Mara, so it had seemed inevitable that he would succumb to familial pressure and move on to someone else. She found herself pleased with the idea that she wasn't the only one who was balking at their family's preconceived notions of what they should do be doing with their lives.

"I can see that now." She saw his shoulders relax,

and he returned to his normally happy and relaxed self.

"It seems that I blinked and missed a lot of what was going on in your life while I was in New York. When you came back here for good, I guess I never thought much about what you'd been up to. I didn't realize you and Mara had become quite so… familial."

"I found the woman of my dreams and I don't intend to let her go for anything." He shrugged his shoulders, as this was obvious.

Silence filled the car once more as green pastures whirred past the window.

"Do you ever regret ever moving away?"

"No."

She felt Connor's eyes trying to search her face for any signs that she might be lying. She'd hesitated only slightly before responding. Seemingly satisfied, he put his eyes back on the road.

"Do you regret coming back?"

"No."

This time, she surprised herself. She'd had this compelling feeling that she needed to be here for Dermot's funeral the moment Rory had called her to let her know of his passing. She loved her life in New York, but now she was back here, she found herself re-evaluating how she felt about it. She'd told Bex and Millie that she was eager to leave as soon as possible, but now she wasn't sure that was true anymore.

"Good." He smiled at her. "Because I'm going to put you to work today. Not just on the proposal, but on helping us with Dermot's things. Michael and Mara decided today's the day they'd like to pack things up."

"So, you kidnapped me for physical labour, is that it?" she asked, turning the tone of the conversation playful again.

"You don't mind, and you know it."

She didn't mind; she would rather be here to help the Flanagans sort through Dermot's things rather than being back in New York right now. How could she be both anxious to get away from here, yet feel so at home, almost as if she'd never left in the first place?

She looked out the car window at the green fields dotted with little white sheep and tried to put her feelings aside for the moment. She had bigger things to focus on, like how she was going to deal with seeing Michael for the first time since she'd tried talking to him at the waterfall after Dermot's funeral. Despite her earlier reservations, she knew the two of them needed to have the conversation, the one that would clear the air between them, but it didn't mean that she was looking forward to it anymore than he was.

She took a breath and braced herself for the day's events.

## Chapter Eleven

Michael stood in the doorway of his parent's bedroom, wondering if he was really ready to do this. He heard the stair creak behind him and, glancing over his shoulder, saw Aoife standing beside him.

"You don't have to do this right now, if you're not ready."

After their last run-in, he was surprised to see her back here, but also felt grateful. His father would have wanted her here for this, and he needed her here. It was strange to think about it, but she'd been so close with his family at a time when everything had seemed to go to hell that Aoife knew his father almost as well as he did. Ailish remembered the ailing Dermot; Aoife had been there when he'd still been himself, remembered him as he'd have liked to be remembered.

He gave her a half-smile of gratitude. "No, it's

time."

Sinead had gone away for the weekend; Molly, Karen and Ailish had taken her to Cork for a girls' trip, so she wouldn't have to be here when the rest of them packed up Dermot's things and took out the boxes. Sinead had said she could deal with packing up her late husband's things, but the idea of seeing them being taken away was too much for her. Right now, he couldn't blame her. He didn't know how he was going to feel when it came time to move them out, either.

"Ye didn't have to come all the way down to be here."

He still wasn't entirely comfortable with it just being the two of them alone like this. The little landing was small, and she was standing close enough to him for him to smell the lightly scented floral perfume she was wearing, and the soft cotton of her three-quarter length navy and white-striped shirt rubbed against his bare forearm. She was dressed casually for herself in brand new black jeans and ankle-length boots, but the rest of them were dressed in t-shirts and tattered jeans, knowing they were going to get dirty trying to clear everything out. But then again, that was Aoife: always impeccably dressed, and even more so since returning from New York. Clearly, living in one of the fashion capitals of the world had rubbed off on her.

"I wanted to."

Despite the conviction in her words, Michael doubted Aoife had actually planned on being here today. It was more than likely that Connor had brought her down here on the pretense of something else, but at least she had the decency to sound sincere when she said it.

"Are Colin and Miriam with you?"

"No, they stayed back in Dublin."

Despite himself he'd liked Colin, and wee Miriam was a dear thing, but he would be lying if he'd said that he hadn't found himself just a little pleased to have Aoife here by herself today.

"He doesn't mind ye being down here?"

He remembered her last boyfriend, Danny, and how he hated every second of her being in Ballyclara. That jerk had been so possessive of her, always thinking she was up to no good here.

*Well, it's not like you didn't eventually give him a reason to be concerned.*

Michael couldn't help but give a self-satisfied smirk. Obviously, Aoife had seen the smirk and replied a little snappishly, "He's not my keeper. He doesn't own me. I don't need his permission to do anything."

He glanced over, surprised at her tone.

"Sorry, I didn't mean it like that. It's good that he isn't bothered by you being here. Other men might feel insecure about their girlfriends helping their ex pack up their father's belongings. I'm glad to see Colin's not like that."

"No, he's not. He's not like Danny. He's a good man." Her tone softened. There was also something else in there too… sadness, perhaps?

He searched her face for some clue as to why this would be, but it was clouded with a mix of emotions he wasn't sure how to read. Why was it so difficult for the two of them to talk to one another? Was it just the time that had passed? Or was it that they hadn't really known one another at all?

*Or is it because you won't ask the real question?*

His shoulders stiffened at his subconscious' question. After she'd left, he'd resigned himself to the fact that he'd probably never really know why. He'd thrown himself into his new life, trying to forget about the question, but having her here now made it harder to push it to the back of his mind. Just as he was wondering if he should take advantage of the silence that had fallen between them to try and air things out, he changed his mind. Now wasn't the time.

*When will it be time?*

"How are we getting on in here?" They both turned at the sound of Father Patrick's voice behind them on the stair.

"Aoife, I didn't know you'd be here today." He manoeuvred himself onto the little landing between them. Michael was both annoyed and relieved at the presence of the priest. He could delay the inevitable a little while longer.

"I'll let you two catch up since ye haven't had a proper chance since Da's funeral," Michael said to the two of them. "Take anything you like. Da would want you both to have something to remember him by."

He sidled past the priest and went down the narrow staircase, past Brendan, Connor, Mara, Rory, and Des, who had set upon the little sitting room and kitchen.

"Michael?" he heard his sister call out to him, but he kept walking out the back door, not looking behind him, hoping no one would follow.

※

Michael wandered up to the rock at the base of the waterfall and sat wearily upon it. It was cool and wet beneath him, and he could feel the dampness seeping into the seat of his trousers. He didn't mind it so much; they'd seen worse than a little damp. He reached into his pocket for his packet of smokes only to realize that he didn't have any on him since they were in his jacket pocket back at the cottage and he'd walked out in nothing but his light-grey cotton t-shirt and jeans. He ran his hands through his dark hair and cursed under his breath.

He hadn't been back here since the day of his father's funeral, since Aoife had followed him. He'd been angry and annoyed with her that day, not just for coming to his sacred space where she knew he came to think, but for coming back in general.

He didn't know what to think of her being here anymore. When they'd first met, she'd completely upended his life. As much as he'd tried to resist it, he'd eventually felt safe with her, only to have her upend things once more by leaving. When he'd first seen her at his father's funeral, he was sure that the only reason she could have returned was to torment him. Now, he couldn't begin to guess at her motivation for coming back, let alone staying. He knew his father had been special to her, but she hadn't reached out to Dermot since she'd left. Or, if she had, his father had certainly hid it from him. So why did she feel compelled to come back here and stir up all these old feelings again?

He sat there on the rock, feeling the cool spray of the waterfall against his skin, watching as it crashed to the bottom of the small pool, sending little ripples across the water's edge, gently lapping at it as it ebbed and flowed. His emotions felt much like the waterfall, crashing about inside him. Just when he thought he had a handle on things, like the water reaching the shore, they retreated towards the swirling centre of the pool, sucked in by the water crashing in from above. The weight of all the emotions of the last week, from the death of his father to seeing Aoife again, crashed into him over and over. Even though he'd been living the last couple of weeks without his father, today was the first day that he was faced with the fact that Dermot's steadying presence wouldn't be around anymore. He couldn't help but think how much he could use a little of that fortitude right now. Even knowing he was going to lose his father, nothing could fully have prepared him for it.

Michael put his head in his hands and sighed heavily. Right now, the one thing he wanted most in the world was for Aoife to come here and find him, put her arms around him and hold him. He'd wanted her to do that back at his parent's place, to feel the safety he'd had with her like it was before everything had gone to hell.

"Shit," he cursed, knowing that all the work of trying to forget her over the last three years was completely undone. The feelings he thought he'd pushed aside when she'd left had come back with her, and he was just as much in love with her as he'd been the day he'd first met her, and there was not a damn thing he could do about it, not without seriously wrecking two homes.

"Feck it all to hell."

# ∞☙

Not for the first time that day, Aoife found herself staring out the front window of Sinead and Dermot's cottage. Michael still hadn't returned after leaving her standing on the stairwell landing with Father Patrick. She tried not to worry about where he'd gone or the fact that he hadn't come back yet, but found she couldn't help her mind from drifting to him. Father Patrick had tried valiantly to distract her, engaging her in easy conversation. She was grateful for the elderly priest at that moment.

## Where I'm Home

Although she was no longer a practicing worshipper of any religion, she'd always been fond of Ballyclara's resident priest. Father Patrick, with his kind heart and calm demeanour, seemed able to make friends with just about anybody, and was always there when a bit of advice was needed.

"He'll be alright. He's been out of sorts these last weeks, but anyone would be given the circumstances, wouldn't they? Don't ye worry yerself."

Father Patrick's bushy brows nodded in the direction she'd just been looking, and his soft eyes smiled at her. His lined face was relaxed and confident with the assurance that Michael would be back any moment now.

Aoife put her worry over Michael aside for a moment and placed her hands on her hips, surveying the room around them. She struggled to imagine an entire life contained to just this pile of boxes in front of her. She hadn't really ever put much stock in having many possessions; she'd never found a place to call home before Ballyclara, so she'd never really thought to collect anything that would find a permanent place somewhere. When it really came down to it, she had a few things she owned. She'd sold off most of her stuff from her flat in Dublin before going to America. Even her flat with Colin was more his, since she was the one who'd moved in with him and Miriam. She'd always lived her life with one foot out the door in case she needed to leave, so she'd never put down roots anywhere.

*Except here.*

Anything she did own was currently in storage up at Aldridge Manor, the things she'd bought to make it a home sitting in a house she hadn't lived in for years.

*It could still be home.*

She was just about to start mentally listing all the

reasons this was not true when a flash of movement outside caught her eye and she noticed Michael walking up the path. She gave a sigh of relief, releasing a breath she hadn't realized she'd been holding.

"Uncle Michael's back," she heard Rory call out from the upstairs bedroom.

"Good. We'll put him to work lugging these boxes out to the shed," Mara said. Her tone was annoyed, but her face showed relief at his return. Obviously, Aoife hadn't been the only one worried about him.

"Just in time too. Molly, Karen, and Ailish will be coming back with Sinead in the next couple of hours." Brendan glanced down at the silver-plated watch on his tanned wrist.

"Des! Rory! Lads, come help your Uncle Michael and I take these boxes out back," he called upstairs, and the two boys quickly scampered down at his command. Aoife picked up one box and began to follow them to the back door when Des held out his arms to her.

"Here, I can take that."

She relinquished her box – which had been much heavier than she'd been expecting – to him and watched him follow his father and best friend outside as if the box didn't weigh a quarter of his weight.

Des' hair had gone sandy-blonde like his mother's in the time since Aoife had last seen him, but his twinkling eyes and mischievous grin were all Brendan.

"That one's going to be a heartbreaker for all the girls in the village," she said to Father Patrick, who'd come out to the back to take a seat at the little dining table near the kitchen.

"Oh, I don't know." He paused, watching Rory and Des through the back window. "I think he'll be like his father. It was apparent to anyone who saw Brendan and Molly together that the two of them would end up together, even when they were young. I think it'll be the same for those two."

Aoife was distracted, only half-listening to the priest as she watched Brendan pause to talk to Michael, who waved off any apparent worries his friend had about him. She breathed another sigh of relief, glad that whatever had been going on with him earlier had seemed to pass.

"There are a couple of boxes in the front room that can go out back," Connor said to Michael as he came through the door. He shuffled past him, carrying a couple of boxes himself, the sleeves of his shirt rolled up to reveal his military tattoos.

"Great," he replied to Connor's request.

"Aoife."

Michael nodded to her as he brushed up against her to move out of Connor's way. He placed a hand on both of her shoulders, deftly manoeuvring the two of them out of the doorway. She stood so close to him now that when she looked up into his face, she could see how the irises of his eyes transitioned from dark and stormy blue-grey to sky blue closer to the centre, and how soft his lips looked. She breathed in the woodsy scent from his clothes, mixed in with a bit of damp.

*So, he'd gone back to the waterfall again.*

"Aoife? Can I get you and Father Patrick to help me with getting supper ready?"

Mara's voice behind them made them both jump, and he released her from his grip.

"Of course."

A flush rose in her cheeks as she walked towards the kitchen. She noticed a look flash between the siblings, but it was gone as quickly as it had come, and she wasn't sure exactly what it meant. Whatever it was, clearly Mara had come out the winner, for Michael hung his head and went to the front room to collect some boxes.

"What can I help with?" she asked, her voice a little more breathless than she'd been hoping for. Her cheeks were still flushed, even though she wasn't sure why she should feel any embarrassment. It wasn't like anything had happened, and nothing *could* happen. Not without causing some serious damage, something she wasn't presently willing to do.

Once again, she felt herself oscillating towards being happy that she'd soon be on a plane back to New York. Being back in Ireland was making things far too confusing where Michael was concerned.

Mara nodded to a bowl of carrots on the counter and a peeler. "Can you start with peeling those for me, please?"

Aoife nodded, grabbed the bowl and went to sit at the table with Father Patrick, who was shelling green peas. Mara put an apron over her t-shirt and jeans and began to stuff a couple of chickens, the three of them working in silence. She could feel Father Patrick's eyes gazing at her over his bowl of peas, but she kept her own firmly fixed on the carrots in front of her. She knew he'd seen the exchange between her and Michael, and she really did not want to talk about it right now.

When all the boxes had been taken outside and/or stored away at Michael and Mara's cottages, and the scent of supper cooking was making all of their stomachs grumble, they heard tires in the drive.

"Gran's home," Rory announced, without even needing to look up from the game of chess he and Des had pulled out and had set up at the table. They could hear the women on the back step, and Mara greeted them as they came inside.

Ailish was the first through the door. Michael stood to greet her, kissing her deeply. Aoife couldn't help but feel that this show was more for her benefit than anyone else's, a reminder that he was with someone else now. The strange sensation of jealousy bubbled inside her again.

*It's just because Colin isn't here. You just think you're jealous because you see Michael with someone else, but you're happy with Colin*, she reminded herself.

"Something smells nice." Sinead sniffed the air and noticed the pots bubbling on the stove.

"Oh hello, Aoife. I'm glad you came back down."

"Hi Sinead." She came over to hug the older woman. "I'm glad to be here, even if I was kidnapped under false pretences." She shot Connor another look as he put his hands up, feigning innocence.

"Hey, you're free to leave any time."

"With what car? Or are you willing to let me drive your car back to Dublin?"

"Hell no. After all that time in New York, you don't know how to drive anymore. You're too used to taking the subway everywhere."

Aoife rolled her eyes at him. She was an excellent driver, and they both knew it. He just wanted another excuse to keep her here.

"I hope you are all hungry, because supper's almost ready," Mara announced, breaking up the argument between the cousins before it went anywhere.

"I should go back home," Father Patrick said, rising stiffly with old age from his chair.

"So should we," Brendan said to Molly and Des.

"No, no, please stay. We'd like you all to be here,"

Mara said quickly, putting her arm around Connor's waist and giving everyone an earnest look.

Aoife raised an eyebrow at her cousin in response.

"Just stay," he said to her as the others, not wanting to miss out on a free meal, had all gathered around the dinner table. "You'll be glad you did."

## Chapter Twelve

"Everybody, can we have your attention please?"

Connor rose from the dinner table, clinking his fork against his wine glass. Everyone's conversations came to an abrupt halt, and they sat patiently, waiting for him to speak. "I'll keep this short and sweet because I'm sure you all want to get back to your food. Mara and I wanted all of you here today so that we could make an announcement. We're engaged."

Exclamations of surprise and congratulations exuded from the small group.

"It's about damned time!" Brendan called out, eliciting a few whoops and nods of agreement from the others. Mara and Connor beamed, rightly basking in the glow of love and support from those closest to them. Connor took out a small velvet-lined box from his back pocket and presented it to his fiancée.

"Now I can finally give you this," he said, presenting her with the box.

Turning to the others, he clarified, "I asked permission from both Dermot and Rory a month or so ago, but with everything going on these past weeks, we wanted to wait to tell everyone until it felt like the right time."

Mara opened the box to reveal a simple gold band with a small heart-shaped diamond in the centre. Simple, yet stunning, like the intended wearer. She held a hand up to her chest and beamed up at Connor, taking the ring and putting it on her hand.

"Ok, let's have a look!" Molly exclaimed, rushing over to her best friend's side.

"Congratulations! So, what date should I put in my diary, then? I want to make sure the church is open for you. I assume you'll want to be married here?" Father Patrick asked, bringing out a small, black leather notebook from the breast pocket of his shirt.

"Of course! And well, we were hoping to have it as soon as possible," Connor said, looking hopefully at the priest. "That is, if the church is available, and if Aoife would be willing to extend her stay here by a couple of more weeks."

"Of course!" she agreed immediately, the joy of her cousin's exciting news overcoming her desire to leave Ireland as soon as possible. "I wouldn't miss it for the world."

"Good, I was hoping you would say that, because I was really hoping you would be my best man or, in this case, best woman."

Aoife's mouth hung agape for half a second. "I'd be honoured. I'm so flattered you'd ask, but don't you want one of your guy friends to stand up beside you?"

Connor came around to her side of the table, having mostly been shoved out of the way by Molly, Ailish, and Karen, who were all admiring Mara's ring and enfolded her in a big bear hug. "There's no one else I'd rather have by my side on the most important day of my life than you."

"Congratulations!" Michael and Brendan both came over to the two of them, shaking Connor's hand, breaking up the moment between the cousins.

"Welcome to the family," Michael hugged Connor briefly. Turning to Rory, he said, "You did well keeping this a secret."

"You have no idea the secrets I can keep," Rory replied cryptically, but was interrupted by Father Patrick.

"How does two weeks from today work for you both?" he asked, looking at his diary. Connor and Mara exchanged a worried look for a moment. The sheer weight of all that comes from planning a wedding suddenly dawned on them.

"We'll all pitch in," Aoife said quickly, trying to reassure them.

"Of course! We can plan this, no problem," Ailish replied, excitedly.

Aoife tried not to feel resentful about her enthusiasm and knack for inserting herself into what Aoife was trying to reclaim as *her* friend group. She was just going to have to accept over the next couple of weeks that, as one of Mara's friends and Michael's girlfriend, Ailish was now going to be a part of that group, too.

"Two weeks it is!" Mara said, trying to contain her excitement.

"Oh good; I won't be showing by then." Molly immediately covered her mouth like she wished she could get the words back. Everyone looked between her and

Brendan, who had a sheepish grin on his face. "I'm so sorry. I didn't mean to say anything just yet and take over your big moment."

"What are ye talking about? This is excellent news!" Mara exclaimed and gave her a big hug. "I'm so excited for you both!"

Michael patted Brendan. "It seems like Rory is not the only one who is good at keeping secrets. I thought we were supposed to be best friends," he teased.

"Yeah, I thought we were supposed to tell each other everything!" Rory said to Des, who looked down at his feet and shuffled a bit, embarrassed at suddenly having so much attention placed on him.

"Ye don't know how many times we both nearly told you." Brendan hugged Michael back, looking like the cat who ate the cream.

"Congratulations," Aoife said, hugging him. "It's the most wonderful news."

"Thanks, Aoife," Brendan replied. "I'm so glad you're here to celebrate with us."

It was a simple statement, but one with special meaning. If she hadn't come back to Ireland, she would have missed out on all this, and she would have felt sorry for it. Whatever confusion she'd been feeling all day about coming back, she was glad she was here now.

"We'll need you on godfather duty again." Brendan turned to Michael.

"I'd be thrilled. I think I did an alright job with this one." He nodded to Des, who was still standing there shyly beside Rory.

"Come over here so I can give you a hug, Brendan," Ailish called over to him, pausing her animated conversation with Molly, Mara and Karen.

Rory and Des had begun talking to Father Patrick,

which left Michael and Aoife somewhat alone for a moment. Hating long, awkward silences, she turned to him and said, "I suppose you and Ailish will be the next ones walking down the aisle and having babies."

Michael's face had that same unreadable expression from earlier in the day, right before he'd bolted and left her standing there with Father Patrick. He didn't make a move to get away from her, but said instead, "I'm fairly certain you and Colin will beat us to it."

He seemed to grimace at the prospect, and she wondered – not for the first time since she'd come back – that he would care so much about her life with Colin.

"We haven't even talked about getting married."

This wasn't strictly true. He'd brought it up once about six months ago, asking her how she felt about making that ultimate commitment, but the both of them had agreed that there was no need to rush things. It was just a piece of paper, after all. It didn't mean they didn't love one another just as much as if they were married. Truth be told, the idea of getting married slightly terrified her; the last person she'd imagined herself married to was Michael, and they all knew how well that had worked out.

Michael raised an eyebrow at this comment, his expression now clearly intrigued.

"We're happy as we are," she was quick to clarify, trying to dispel any thoughts of the conflicting emotions she'd been having lately, lest he pick up on them. That was the last thing she needed right now.

"Of course," he said with a smirk, his tone making her feel slightly uncomfortable, like he knew something she didn't.

*Like he'd known how you felt about Danny before you did.*

She tried to put that thought out of her mind. Her relationship with Colin was nothing like what she'd had with Danny. Still, she couldn't deny that Michael had seen where that had been headed long before she had. She was just about to insist once again that everything between her and Colin was fine, when they were distracted by Ailish.

"What are you two talking about so intensely?" she asked.

She wasn't being territorial, merely curious, but Aoife still felt annoyed at her intrusion, rather than relieved at having Michael's inspection into her love life interrupted.

"We're taking bets on how long it'll be before Aoife and Colin will be the next ones to walk down the aisle."

"Wouldn't it be so amazing if you and Colin, and Connor and Mara had a double wedding?!" Ailish exclaimed.

"Yes, wouldn't it just?" Michael said, but this time, the grimace had returned. "Now, why don't we go and have a look at this ring? Brother of the bride coming through!" he said, making his way to his sister before Aoife could say anything further, Ailish trailing along behind him.

She stood there, exasperated as she watched them walk away. Was he truly upset with the idea of her marrying Colin, or just her getting married in general? And why would he care anyways? He had a girlfriend of his own, so why was her love life of so much interest to him all of a sudden?

"Men," she muttered, shaking her head.

ಸಿಂಯ

## Where I'm Home

"You're staying for another *two weeks*?!" Millie's voice sounded practically apoplectic over the speakerphone.

Aoife stole a quick glance over at Miriam, who was sleeping peacefully on the trundle bed on the other side of the room. Her little chest rose and fell with the regular pace of deep sleep, completely undisturbed by the shriek of Millie's tone. She took her friend off speakerphone and held her mobile up to her ear, laying back on the king-sized bed she and Colin were sharing at their Dublin hotel. After Connor's big announcement the day before, she'd stayed over in Ballyclara, returning late today.

"But you already extended for a couple of weeks the last time we were talking, and you said that you were coming straight home as soon as you were done working on that business proposal with Connor."

"Yeah, well, he had another proposal he was keeping secret, apparently," she said, thinking back to his engagement announcement. "It's not like I can say no and go back to New York now; I'm his best person. Besides, I wouldn't miss his wedding for the world. He's like a brother to me."

Millie harrumphed like a spoiled child. Aoife wouldn't be surprised if she'd even crossed her arms across her chest and stamped her foot. She knew it was mostly an act, and that Millie was secretly happy for Connor; she was just put out that Aoife wasn't coming home as soon as she'd promised.

"Which reminds me, if you're going to stay in New York a bit longer, could you and Bex both check in on the office for me? Gina's still new, and I haven't had time to train her entirely. I'm doing what I can over here, but some things need to be handled in person. Do you think you could find it in your heart to help me out?" She hoped her sickly sweet tone might butter Millie up and get her off the hook for not keeping her promise.

"First you don't come home when you say you will, and now you want me to run your business for you while you continue to gallivant all over Ireland?"

"I'm hardly gallivanting, and it's not like I'm not working over here. I'll be here in Dublin most of the time, except for the wedding itself. And you know you loved working with me, and no one knows how to do the job quite like you do."

"Uh-uh."

"And you'd be the bestest best friend in the whole wide world for helping me out."

"Uh-uh."

"Oh, stop, you know you'll do it." Aoife could hear Bex beside Millie. "Just send us what you need us to do, and we'll get it done."

"Thanks, love. You're a gem."

"I thought *I* was the 'bestest best friend' for helping out?" Millie said, her tone pouty again.

"Yeah, well, Bex agreed with no complaints, so she gets bumped up," Aoife teased. Millie harrumphed.

"Speaking of the wedding, I have to make a few calls to help out with arrangements. There's so much to plan! Good thing Michael was entirely wrong about Colin and I; we are definitely not getting married anytime soon if this is everything that needs to get done to plan a small wedding, let alone a big one." Michael's earlier comment had been entirely preposterous; she would need years to plan a wedding. She could never plan something like this so quickly.

At that moment, the hotel door opened, and Colin entered with two brown paper bags with grease stains seeping through. From the scent of fried batter, she reckoned they were having fish and chips for their supper. Her stomach growled. No one did fish and chips quite like they did in Ireland. In New York, it would all be "healthy this" and "low-carb that;" give her a piece of fish fried in juicy greases and wrapped in newspaper like they did in the old days any time, ink and mercury poisoning be damned.

"You and Colin are getting married?!" Millie shouted over the phone, and she had to hold it away from her ear. Millie's voice was loud enough for Colin to hear her. He cocked his head to the side and mouthed, "We are?" to her. She dismissed the notion with a wave of her hand.

"No, Millie, I said Colin and I are *not* getting married," she tried to tell her, but she was entirely sure her friend wasn't paying one bit of attention to her. "Alright, I'm hanging up now." She would text Bex later to clarify any rumours Millie might have started about her non-nuptials.

"Where would she get an idea like that?" Colin asked, laying down on his stomach on the bed beside her. Aoife wasn't sure why, but she was reticent to tell him about Michael's comment about the two of them getting married before him and Ailish. It was such a small thing, and it shouldn't matter to either of them, but since returning to Ireland, she hesitated to even mention his name around Colin, trying not to bring up her past as much as possible. In the safety of New York, with an entire ocean between them and the promise of never having to see Michael again, she'd felt entirely safe telling Colin everything about her relationship with him. Now that she was home again, it felt different. Like she was rubbing it in his face, or something. Michael was no longer this shadowy figure from her past, but this living, breathing person, and even though Colin had seemed fine with meeting him, she still felt uneasy talking about Michael with him.

"Oh, you know Millie; she hears what she wants to hear. I was telling her about Connor and Mara, and she got it into her head that you and I were getting married, too."

He took her left hand in his, examining her ring finger. "Maybe we should revisit that conversation from six months ago."

Her stomach flip-flopped like a fish on dry land at the thought of talking about marriage, especially with all the conflicting feelings she'd been having over the last couple of weeks. She was saved from answering the question by the ringing of her mobile.

"Hello?"

"What are you doing tomorrow night?" Connor didn't bother to greet her; he knew she would know it was him.

"Trying to get you into the tailor's shop for a fitting for your tux," she responded, wondering what he was really calling her for.

"Good, we can do that first, and then you and I are going to dinner."

"Where?"

"Glover's Alley."

Normally, he wasn't this cagey with his plans, unless he was about to spring something on her that he knew she wouldn't want to do. Her suspicions were readily confirmed.

"Why?"

"Ok, so don't be upset, but I made plans for you, Caitlin, and I to get together and go over our proposal before we present it to Gran."

Aoife rolled her eyes, even though she knew he couldn't see her. She'd skillfully avoided seeing anyone in her family thus far, which wasn't really too difficult in a city the size of Dublin. Aoife had also been actively avoiding anything to do with the social scene, keeping to herself with her brief excursions with Colin and Miriam. The rest of the time had been spent working with Connor, and that was precisely how she wanted it. She was perfectly content to completely avoid them until she went back to New York.

"Honestly, you surprise me with your engagement last night, then you spring this on me; what else are you going to throw my way, Connor?" Her tone indicated she wasn't entirely joking.

"Speaking of the engagement, I've arranged for us to have dinner at Gran's on Friday night. You and Colin need to be there."

"No way in hell. That's going too far."

Colin gave her a curious look as he dug into his plate of fish and chips, wondering what the two of them were talking about.

"C'mon, Aoife. I need you there. I can't do these dinners on my own. The business proposal is all your idea and, well, it'll be easier for Mara if both you and Colin are there on Friday, so I can announce the other proposal to the family."

"Nope. Not doing it. You'll do better with getting approval from your sister if I'm not there, and I'm keeping Colin and Miriam both far away from our family."

Colin's face clouded over as he recognized the direction the conversation had gone in, and he put his dinner aside.

"Please? Don't make me beg."

She was annoyed at his attempts to manipulate her,

even more so with herself, because she knew she was going to cave in. She hated the idea of having dinner with her family, let alone twice in one week, but she also wasn't about to send poor Mara into the wolves' den without at least some back up. These things were best survived with your allies.

"Alright. But Miriam is never meeting our family." She would be firm on this one point. Colin was a grown up; there was far less chance of her family scarring him for life, but she would not subject someone as young as Miriam to them.

She looked over at Colin and he gave her a supportive squeeze of her hand. She was so damned lucky to have him. How could she feel so confused being back in Ballyclara when the best thing that had ever happened to her was sitting right there next to her? It was just a reminder that they needed to get back to their lives in New York as soon as Connor and Mara's wedding was over. She needed to get back to her work, to her clients, to the family life she, Colin, and Miriam had. Once there was an ocean between her and Michael again, everything would sort itself out.

"Oh, come on, they raised you and I; they've obviously done something right."

"Yeah, and they also raised Caitlin, and look how she turned out," Aoife retorted peevishly. She immediately regretted it; it *was* his twin sister they were talking about, after all.

Connor didn't immediately say anything, which made her feel all the worse about it. As loyal as Connor was to her, she knew how much he loved his sister. It was a bond that she could never share in, something that was sacred only to siblings. Being an only child, she would always be on the outside of that dynamic, and if

## Where I'm Home

she forced him to choose between her and his sister, she was not entirely sure he would choose her.

"I'm sorry Connor. I didn't mean it."

"Yes, you did," he replied, but there was no hint of resentment or malice in his voice, just resignation and understanding. "But, I get it. Grandda stepped in and played a huge part in how we were raised, but Caitlin was still singled out as Gran's favourite from the start. So, we had an unconventional upbringing from her, which has had its consequences, but also its benefits."

*There's also the fact that we weren't born fully-fledged narcissists like the rest of the family*, Aoife thought to herself.

After Aoife declined to comment further, Connor said, "For what it's worth, Mara didn't feel it was appropriate to introduce Rory to the family just yet either, so we'll bring him and Des up with us, and they can watch Miriam for you. See you tomorrow."

He hung up with the same abrupt manner with which he'd called.

Aoife lay back on the bed and made a garbled noise in her throat. "Feckin' hell."

"I take it I'm going to meet your family after all."

Colin lay down next to her, propping his head up on one hand to look at her.

"You don't have to, if you don't want to. You can stay here with Rory, Des, and Miriam. Actually, that's probably best. You can stay here and watch the kids and –"

"Or I can go with you to meet your family. From what you've told me about them, I don't think you should go there on your own."

She rolled onto her side and kissed him gently, then curled up into the crook of his arm. "How'd I get so lucky to find you?"

"I think I'm the lucky one."

Typical Colin, modest and supportive to a fault. She didn't deserve him.

"You re-booked our tickets to fly out two days after Connor and Mara's wedding, right?"

"Yup. Flights are all arranged, but are you sure you want to leave so soon after the wedding? We can stay longer if you want to spend more time in Ballyclara."

"Yes. I'm sure."

She snuggled in closer to his chest. The sooner she got away from Ireland, the better.

## Chapter Thirteen

The last place Aoife wanted to be right now was sitting across a table at Glover's Alley with Caitlin, but she knew Connor had been right when he'd said he wanted to run the proposal by her first. She, more than anyone, had their grandmother's ear, and was likely to be the best judge of character for whether she would accept or reject it.

As Aoife sat at the table with her cousins, she couldn't help but notice how, in Aoife's absence, Caitlin had only grown closer to their grandmother, and had grown to be more like her. She just wished she could think of this as being a good thing. After all, their grandmother had turned their grandfather's pub into a multi-million euro, worldwide chain; but in the process, had taken away all the things that had made *O'Reillys* what Paddy O'Reilly had envisioned it would be.

To say Aoife and Caitlin didn't get along was an understatement. The two young women could probably only ever agree on the fact that they both loved Connor and that they'd both loved their grandfather. In all other respects, they were entirely different people, and not just in their looks.

Caitlin, blonde-haired and grey-eyed like her twin, with an icy stare to rival their grandmother's, favoured her grandmother's side of the family in both looks and personality. But where Grainne was shrewd and calculating, Caitlin was petulant and spoiled, or at least she had been the last time Aoife had seen her. Now, she'd seemed to grow more into herself over the last three years. It wasn't that she was more confident, per se – she'd always had the air of confidence that comes with a life of wealth and privilege – but she seemed less conflicted or apologetic for being the person she was now. Obviously, the last few years under Grainne's tutelage – and likely, Aoife's disappearance to America – had helped her overcome some of the insecurities she'd had about being their grandmother's favourite. Aoife and Connor had both, in the past, struggled with Grainne's obvious favouritism when it came to her grandchildren, but seeing the person her cousin had become, Aoife was once again grateful that she'd never had her grandmother's attention lavished on her. She hated to think of the person she'd have become had their roles been reversed.

The three of them sat around the table in silence while Caitlin looked over the proposal Connor had given her. The servers had cleared their dinner away, mindfully leaving them to finish their drinks while Caitlin perused the document. She appeared to be deep in thought, but Aoife was entirely certain she was trying to draw out this moment for dramatic effect to make her younger cousin squirm.

"Oh, for the love of Christ, do you think Granny will approve of it, or not?" Aoife demanded testily, flinging her long auburn locks over her shoulders and leaning in towards Caitlin. "You've read the same line three times now. What do you think of it?"

Connor, who was sitting beside his sister, shot her a warning glance, knowing that it was entirely possible for a new world war to begin right here if the two women weren't able to keep their tempers in check. Aoife ignored the warning and raised an eyebrow in Caitlin's direction.

Caitlin put papers down on the table, examining her perfectly manicured hands. "I think you've got a sound business proposal."

Aoife felt her jaw go slightly slack with amazement as Connor grinned. Caitlin smirked upon seeing Aoife's reaction and she immediately composed herself once again.

"You're surprised."

"A bit, yes." There was no denying it.

"Probably no more than I am to find out that you seem to somewhat have a head for this business."

Was that a compliment? From Caitlin, no less? Aoife waited for the knife in her back, the comment that was intended to slice through her and cut her down to her very soul. It was a classic Grainne move – attempt to flatter your opponent with what they might perceive as a compliment, then plunge the knife in swift and deep to throw them off-guard and take them off the board. But curiously, it didn't come.

"I think it's the perfect compromise for everyone involved. We all know that when Grandda left those shares to you and Connor that neither of you had any interest in having a controlling interest in the company, but none of us were willing to go against his wishes either."

Aoife thought back to the reading of their grandfather's will and remembered there being a whole lot of commotion about this very topic. But at Connor's stern glance, she held her tongue.

"I'm happy the both of you came to your senses," Caitlin continued. "I know the two of you are not pleased with the direction Gran has taken the company, but without her vision, none of us would have the life we have now." She waved her hand around the restaurant, gesturing to the kind of decadence they could afford.

There was no denying this point. None of them would have the privileges they currently enjoyed if it were not for Grainne elevating the family business to where it was today. As much as she and Connor liked to think themselves independent of their family's wealth, neither of them would have been given the opportunities they had without it. She certainly may not have gone to Harvard, and Connor would not have enjoyed his playboy lifestyle he'd had before and during his military days. And those perks were just the tip of the proverbial iceberg.

"I think with this proposal, the two of you will have something of Grandda's legacy to call your own, while still affording the lifestyle we're all comfortable with."

Sensing the victory, Connor wanted to quickly wrap things up before either his sister or his cousin had a chance to turn what had been a mostly pleasant dinner into a mud-slinging contest.

"Thanks sis," he said, signalling to the server for

the cheque. "So, you'll present it to Gran tomorrow?"

"Yes. We should discuss it with her tomorrow after dinner."

She turned her attention from her brother back to Aoife. "I think it's best – if you truly want this proposal to succeed – that you leave the discussion to Connor and I."

"Suits me just fine," she said, taking a sip of water. "I'm more than happy to be the silent partner in this venture."

Caitlin nodded, and Aoife felt a weird sense of something she couldn't quite describe. It was weird having the two of them finally agree on something for the first time in a very long time. She wondered what had made her cousin change her attitude towards her. Had she really grown up since she'd last seen her?

"Excellent. I'll see you both tomorrow evening."

Caitlin rose from the table, gave her brother a kiss on the cheek, and departed without another word. Connor grinned broadly at Aoife and raised his glass of wine to her in triumph.

"Don't smile too much," she warned. "We still have tomorrow to get through."

"Oh, come on! This is a triumph! You and my sister sat through an entire meal and managed to not kill one another. That in and of itself is something to celebrate, let alone the fact that she approves of the business proposal and is going to advocate on our behalf with Granny."

Connor downed the rest of his wine and sat back in his chair, clearly pleased with himself. "This is exactly what Grandda wanted from us: something to unite the three of us and to work together."

Aoife couldn't disagree on that point. It had always

been their grandfather's wish that his grandchildren would get on better than they did. She just wished she didn't have the looming sense that the other shoe was about to not just drop but come smashing down on them like an anvil.

## Chapter Fourteen

"Wow!" Colin gaped at Grainne O'Reilly's house. "So, this is where you grew up?"

"More or less." Aoife looked up at the pale red-brick house in front of them with a lot less enthusiasm than Colin. "My mother has a house in Ballsbridge, which is my official childhood home, but this is where I spent most of my time."

She was regretting having brought him to Malahide to meet her family. Having learned from the disastrous family dinner introducing Michael to them, she knew she couldn't simply *not* tell him about her family and how she'd grown up, but Colin had a certain naïveté about this world, and the types of social circles she moved in, and she cared about him too much not to make sure she prepared him for what he could expect from tonight.

They climbed the steps and the front door opened for them.

"Good evening, Miss Aoife," intoned Moore, her grandmother's butler, and only loyal servant. Ever since childhood, she'd always sort of thought of him as the Lurch to her grandmother's Morticia Addams. "And… guest."

His eyes widened at the sight of Colin, and Aoife gave him a smug smile. She'd not told anyone in the family that she was bringing Colin tonight, and had sworn Connor to secrecy. She'd wanted to see the looks on all their faces when she introduced him to them. It was childish, she knew, but there was something about returning to what was essentially her childhood home that brought out the surly, pre-teen attitude in her.

"Colin."

He reached out a hand to introduce himself and Aoife wanted to roll on the floor, laughing at the sight of Moore's expression. She did her best to stifle a snort and removed her jacket, handing it to him, jolting him back to reality and his role. He took the proffered jacket silently and went to hang it up.

"Oh God, I've screwed it up already," Colin fretted adorably, trying to smooth down his dinner jacket that she'd picked up for him the day before when she'd taken Connor to the tailor's shop.

"Don't worry about it," she reassured him. "He's just never had anyone try to shake his hand before. At least, no guest who's ever come here before. Besides, it will do him good to have a few surprises. Things are entirely too predictable around here. It will give him something to gossip about with the maids."

She took Colin's hand and gave it a reassuring squeeze before leading him into the drawing room where her family was gathered, minus Connor and Mara, who'd said that they needed a few more minutes before going over to Grainne's, and that they should go on without them. Sensing her trepidation, Colin squeezed back and smiled at her. He always knew just what to do to make her feel safe again.

At their entrance, her family all turned towards them, and Aoife felt the little ball of ice that had been in the pit of her stomach since earlier grow into an iceberg. She desperately wanted to turn back and run to the car, to take Colin and Miriam and get on the first flight back to New York, but instead, she propelled them both forward with as much confidence as she could muster. To scare off a shark, you had to punch it in the face, right?

"Aoife, so glad to see you, darling."

Maureen, Aoife's mother, came over to her and planted a dutiful kiss on her daughter's cheek.

"Mother," Aoife replied, and returned the quick kiss on her mother's proffered cheek that had definitely seen more Botox in the last three years than Maureen would ever admit to.

She wished desperately that Connor would hurry up and get there, so she wouldn't feel so alone and outnumbered. She hoped this hadn't become one of his little plans where he dropped out at the last second and left her here to deal with them on her own. He knew she'd only agreed to this in the first place because he'd said that he would be here too. This was supposed to be his big debut with Mara, introducing her to the family and having them get to know her.

*More like interrogate her*, Aoife thought. Which was exactly what they were planning to do to poor Colin now that he was standing right in front of them.

No amount of preparation she could have given

him would have made him feel ready for what he was about to face. No one in her family, except Connor, knew he even existed, and while this meant she could spring her relationship on them and give them all a shock, she also knew that Grainne O'Reilly didn't like surprises, and she could easily choose now to take out a churlish revenge on her youngest granddaughter for it.

In the three whole years she had been living in New York, the only contact her family had made was to send her a solitary birthday card, and that had been sent four months late. Her mother had phoned once to say she was coming to New York for work and had left instructions to have Aoife meet her for lunch, but then had had her assistant text to say she was too busy to spend time with her.

She hadn't been upset. In fact, she'd become so used to her mother putting everything and anyone else in the world before her that she couldn't even muster up the energy to feel anything at all towards her. She knew this wasn't how people were supposed to think of their parents, but it was simply that she'd been raised to have no expectations of her family whatsoever.

"You didn't tell us you were bringing a friend." Maureen looked at her daughter expectantly, demanding an answer as to why Colin was here.

"Mother, this is my partner, Colin Lee. He's a poet. Colin, this is my mother, Maureen O'Reilly."

*A self-important narcissist, who's never known what it is like to have to work for anything and has never given a second's thought to anyone else in her life, least of all her own daughter.*

Maureen's mouth hung open at this revelation and Aoife would've been lying if she'd said she wasn't just a little bit thrilled at giving her a good shock. Her mother did not have time to make any kind of response because

Connor and Mara finally appeared.

*Thank God.*

She knew she and Colin would only be temporarily spared the inquisition, but at least they could revel in the spotlight being turned on someone else for a brief time.

"Where have you been?" she hissed at him under her breath, coming over to give him a hug, not even trying to hide how relieved she was that he was there. He merely shrugged and gave her one of those winning smiles that so charmed everyone else. She narrowed her eyes at him, unimpressed, but she didn't have time to take him to task before he was dragged away by the sound of their grandmother's voice.

ജരു

*Earlier that evening*

"We don't have to do this, you know. We can turn this car around right now, pick up Rory and go back to Ballyclara and totally forget this whole thing. We can call Aoife and tell her and Colin to come back to the hotel to be with Miriam. I know she'd love any excuse to get out of this dinner; she didn't even want to come to it in the first place. I had to talk her into it."

Connor's hands gripped the steering wheel of his Jaguar tightly, his knuckles turning white against the dark leather. It was the only sign that he was nervous about her meeting his family. She knew it had nothing to do with her – he was more concerned with how they would come across to her than her to them – but the way he was acting, it would make someone less secure in their relationship a bit concerned about the meeting tonight.

"Yes, that's what we'll do. I'll just call Aoife now –" he moved to use the car's Bluetooth system to call his cousin.

"We are not turning this car around, Connor." Mara's voice was firm as she put a hand over his and squeezed it reassuringly.

His hand stilled in her firm grasp. It amazed her that he'd been overseas with the military and been far less nervous about the thought of being shot at than he was about a dinner party with his own family. She knew his fears weren't entirely unfounded; her brother had recounted his own disastrous experience with the O'Reillys when he and Aoife had been dating. Thanks to this, and Connor's frank honesty about his family, she was under fewer illusions than Michael had been.

"Colin and Aoife will already be there and expecting us. Besides, tonight is as much about us as it is about that business proposal you and Aoife have been working on. And I want to meet your family."

The look of terror that crossed his face made her think that this statement may have scared him more than anything else she could have said. She could have told him she was pregnant, and it would probably have been less terrifying for him.

"Everything will be fine."

This she said more for her own benefit than his. She *did* want to meet his family. She'd been reading about them in the tabloids for years now, and she was curious to see if they were really like how they appeared in the gossip columns. But a bigger part of her wanted to get to know the people who had raised this wonderful man sitting in the car beside her. She didn't doubt for a second that both Aoife and Connor had good reasons for feeling the way they did about their family, but both of them had turned into fantastic people, and Mara couldn't imagine that truly terrible people could raise two people like them.

As the car pulled into the drive of Grainne's house, Mara gazed up at the pale redbrick mansion with much the same look of wonderment Colin had had earlier, although she kept any exclamations of surprise inside.

"Are you sure it's not too late to turn around?" Connor asked her before switching off the ignition.

"Come on, ye big 'fraidy cat," she teased him, hopping out of the car, not waiting for him to come around to open it for her, like he liked to do. He may be a gentleman, but this independent woman still liked to do some things for herself.

She silently marvelled at his grandmother's house, with its immaculate flower beds and perfectly manicured lawn. It was all a little too perfect for her liking; her own tastes as a landscape artist ran a little more to the wild side, letting nature take over and guide her designs, but she could still appreciate their sculpted beauty. He quickly locked the car, causing it to beep and the lights to flash once, and quickly caught up to her on the front path. As soon as their feet touched the front steps, the door opened, a fully uniformed butler standing before them.

"Master Connor," the butler greeted him. "And Miss…?"

"Flanagan," Connor answered for her and handed him the white silk shawl she'd wrapped around her shoulders, otherwise dismissing the other man entirely.

If she hadn't known it before, she knew now with certainty that she'd stepped into a different kind of world, and that she was going to see a side of her fiancée she was not well acquainted with. Connor wasn't the type of person to dismiss someone else so readily; he thoroughly engaged people in conversation, wanting to hear everything they had to say. The Connor she knew would never treat someone like staff just because they were, but now that they were in Grainne O'Reilly's world, she supposed she was going to have to get used to things being different in here than they were in the real world.

Standing inside the foyer of Grainne O'Reilly's Malahide home, Mara couldn't help but feel small and out of place. Her entire cottage could fit inside this one room alone and probably still have room to spare. The walls were lined with imposing portraits of eighteenth-century figures. If Connor hadn't told her that his family was, in fact, not related to a single person in them, she would have wrongly assumed they were images of long-dead ancestors. She supposed this was exactly what Grainne wanted people to think, though. A grand staircase led to the upper floors, a skylight offering a view of the night sky above.

"Where have you been?" Aoife seemed quite annoyed with them for running late. Mara couldn't help but notice she seemed more on edge tonight than usual, which was saying something considering how tense she'd been every time she was down in Ballyclara for the last couple of weeks. She knew it had to do with unresolved feelings between her and Michael, but she hadn't had a chance yet to corner either of them about it.

"Connor!" she heard an elderly voice call from inside the drawing room to the left and assumed that this must be the voice of the woman of the house herself.

"Granny." Connor left her side and went inside to greet her. With more than a little trepidation, Mara followed.

She noted that there were several people

assembled. Although she'd never met them before, she'd seen them enough times in the tabloids to single out Connor's parents, John and Siobhan, and his sister, Caitlin, who had the same blonde-haired good looks as him. Aoife and Colin were standing near a woman who looked like an older version of Aoife. She assumed this was her mother, Maureen. She wasn't entirely sure who the other two men were, but she was fairly certain they were Nate, Caitlin's husband, and Anton Dabrovnic, Aoife's stepfather. She immediately felt the cold eyes of Siobhan, Caitlin, Nate, and Maureen, surveying and dismissing her as being of little importance to them. They weren't even curious as to who she was or why she was there. She thought she'd feel prepared for that kind of reaction, but she realized now that no amount of preparation could ready a person to be dismissed so peremptorily by people who didn't even know her. She felt an indignant anger rising inside of her.

There was one person, however, who seemed to be intensely interested in her, giving her more of a sense of unease than anyone else so far that evening. Grainne's beautiful brow was drawn down into a slight furrow as she stared openly at Mara. She couldn't have felt more exposed and on display than if she were standing naked in front of them. Grainne's steel-grey eyes took in everything from her clothes, her hair, her face; every little detail scrutinized behind that implacable, marble-like face. Maggie Smith's Dowager Countess of Grantham from Downton Abbey had nothing on Grainne O'Reilly.

"Granny, there's someone I'd like you to meet. This is Mara, my fiancée."

There was absolutely no doubt that Connor's grandmother was not at all pleased with this news, nor was she pleased with Mara. Grainne's face took on a dark look, and Mara wondered how the woman could hold such wrath for someone she'd never even met. Almost as quickly as the look came on, it disappeared, and her face relaxed into its normal disposition, a sickly sweet smile upon her lips as she extended a hand in a limp handshake. Mara knew from Aoife that you always had a better idea of where you stood with Grainne if it seemed she was angry or annoyed with you. If she was trying to be nice, Aoife had said, it very rarely meant anything good for you and her earlier indignation had turned to regret for coming tonight.

"It's a pleasure to meet you, Mrs. O'Reilly," Mara said with perfect deference. It would not be said that any daughter of Sinead Flanagan would have anything less than impeccable manners. Based on the snide look in Grainne's eyes, she doubted they would do her much good. It only seemed to further enrage the older woman that someone she so clearly wanted to despise was behaving so properly. She couldn't even pick on her for her attire; Mara had been sure to ask for Aoife's advice on her outfit for tonight the last time she was down. She was wearing a perfectly demure dark blue lace, high-necked dress that fell just to the knee. She had kept her make-up light, only enough to accentuate her red lips, relying on her natural tan from working outside so often to give her colour in her cheeks. She'd scrubbed under her fingernails several times to erase any trace of dirt or potting soil, then put on a clear polish, to make herself feel more elegant. Connor had told her before how she looked stunning with her raven-coloured hair pulled back into a half-up/half-down look, so she had recreated it tonight, the loose curls falling into perfect waves below her shoulders. She was trying so hard to make a good impression for Connor, but she was only beginning to realize how much of an uphill battle this was going to be. She glanced over at Aoife, who smiled warmly at her; at least she had her in her corner. Mara smiled back, grateful.

Before anyone had time to say anything else, they heard Moore announce, "Dinner is ready, ma'am."

"Shall we move to the dining room?"

Grainne posed it as a question, but there was no doubt in anyone's mind that this was a command. Connor, still by her side, led her into the dining room to their pre-assigned seats, their names having been hand-written in Grainne's elegant script in metallic gold ink on cream-coloured stationary and placed over their dinner plates. Aoife followed behind with Colin.

The first thing Mara noticed was that she'd been placed at the far end of the table, as far away from Connor as it was possible for Grainne to place them, making it all the easier to divide and conquer later in the dinner, she supposed. She had the unfortunate luck to be placed on Grainne's right side, giving her no place to hide, and affording Grainne ample opportunity to grill both her and Colin with little interference from their significant others. On her other side was Nate, so there would be no friendly face there either, if his earlier demeanour was anything to go by. Her only saving grace was that Grainne had slightly rearranged the table and seated Colin opposite her since he had been a last-minute addition. At least she'd have one friendly face at this end of the table. He'd been placed on Grainne's left-hand side, with Aoife's mother, Maureen, on his other side. To Maureen's left were John, Siobhan, then Aoife. Opposite Aoife was Connor, Caitlin, Anton, and then Nate, which rounded out the table.

She noticed the seat at the head of the table

remained empty. Presumably, this had been Paddy O'Reilly's place, still left empty after his death, no one brave or willing enough to claim it for themselves in the time since he'd passed. Perhaps no one had felt themselves worthy of the spot, unable to live up to the excellence of the man who had once occupied it. Although an enormous fireplace stood at one end of the room, it was left cold on this summer's eve, the only light coming from two antique chandeliers that hung above the long cherry-wood table, casting a glittering light along the pale, cornflower blue walls.

They'd barely been seated when the first course, a tomato bisque, was served on Delftware pottery. No sooner had she brought her spoon to her mouth than Grainne launched into her inquisition, starting with Colin.

"Tell me, Colin, what do you do for a living? Aoife has told us nothing about you; why, we didn't even know you existed before tonight! She's always been so unnecessarily secretive, as if her life is one great mystery. One would think she's rather someone special, the way she hides things from the rest of us, as if anyone cared to pay her any notice." Grainne laughed at this last statement, eliciting laughter from all but Aoife, Connor, Mara, and Colin.

"I'm a poet, Mrs. O'Reilly, and I do happen to think your granddaughter *is* something really special."

He looked down the long table at Aoife, who was beaming back at him.

Grainne's eyes narrowed. She was unused to anyone sticking up for her youngest granddaughter. Clearly, Colin was going to be a harder nut to crack than she'd anticipated.

Grainne sniffed in response, dismissing Colin for

the moment until she could find another way to drive a wedge between him and Aoife. She chose to momentarily turn her attention to Mara, hoping for easier prey. Mara registered the look of intent in the older woman's eyes and vowed not to give her any ammunition to use against either her or Connor. They were stronger than anything Grainne O'Reilly could throw at them, and she intended to prove it.

"You know, I have the strangest feeling that we've met before, although I'm sure I would remember meeting such an… accomplished person as yourself," she said in as much of a patronizing tone as she could manage.

It wasn't Grainne's tone that made her look over to Aoife, but rather a question of whether she should reveal her connection to Michael. She didn't think that bringing him up would impact Aoife and Colin, but she wasn't sure what information Grainne might twist out of it. By not being careful about what she said, she may very well give Grainne all the ammunition she needed against the two of them.

Aoife shrugged in response. Grainne had probably already surmised the answer; she'd have made an excellent lawyer in that respect, only asking questions she already knew the answer to. She also doubted that Grainne ever forgot a face, and she and Michael did have a striking resemblance.

"You may be thinking of my brother, Michael," she replied cautiously. "I believe you met him a few years ago."

She noticed the puzzle pieces clicking into place in Grainne's mind, confirming what she'd already suspected.

"Michael Flanagan? Didn't you bring someone here by that name, Aoife?" Grainne couldn't bring herself to say that her granddaughter had been dating Michael at the time.

"Yes, Granny."

"Oh, well, isn't that interesting?" Her eyes glinted with a twisted pleasure, and she attempted to take another swing at Colin and Aoife's relationship.

"Such an… industrious young man, he seemed to be," she faltered for a moment, trying to think of something nice to say about a man she'd only paid attention to in order to find some way to turn his relationship with Aoife against her. "Also, so handsome! I can see why my granddaughter might be drawn to someone… like that."

"Yes, I've met Michael. He's a nice guy. He's got a great business going." Colin's tone was neutral, but sincere. The twist of her thin lips was the only indication that Grainne was disappointed again that she couldn't shake his confident attitude.

"And what is it you do for a living, Mara? Didn't your brother own a pub or something in that little village you come from? Is it a family business like ours?"

Bored with not being able to ruffle the unflappable Colin, Grainne seemed to settle her attention fully on Mara.

"Yes, he co-owns *O'Leary's* pub in Ballyclara with his best friend, Brendan, and the two of them also own a contracting company."

"Ah, right, a labourer." No one could fail to miss the derision in her tone.

"And no, I don't work with them, at least not entirely. I'm a landscape artist. I do a lot of work alongside Brendan and Michael through their contracting business, but I don't have anything to do with the pub beyond filling in when they need an extra hand now and then."

Colin an artist, and she, a labourer; exactly the kind

## Where I'm Home

of people Grainne disapproved of her grandchildren choosing for their significant others.

"Oh, well, there can't be too much money in that, can there? I mean, can anyone afford that kind of luxury where you come from?" She made it sound like Mara came from an entirely different continent, instead of the next county. There were a few twitters of amused laughter from her daughters.

"She does quite well enough," Connor defended her. "Besides, with her talent, I'm sure she will be in demand from the entire country soon enough."

Her heart beat a little faster at his unwavering belief in her.

"But the two of you can't possibly hope to afford a decent place in Dublin on a labourer's salary once the two of you are married." The implication was clear in Grainne's tone: if Connor married her, his grandmother would cut him off. She'd never explicitly say it to his face, but there was little doubt in those cold grey eyes that she meant her veiled threat.

"We won't be moving to Dublin when we get married, Granny."

Mara thought Grainne might choke to death on her wine when he revealed this bit of news.

"You can't mean to say that you would stay in that place, would you? And I was only speaking hypothetically about marriage. Of course, you're too young to settle down just yet."

"It *is* our home," Connor replied simply, "And I am marrying Mara. In two weeks' time, in fact, at the church in Ballyclara. You are all welcome to attend, but only so long as you agree to accept Mara into this family and be kind to her."

Both Maureen and Siobhan stared open-mouthed

at Connor's bombshell of an announcement. Caitlin's fork clattered on the table as she dropped it in shock, while John's face went pale at his son's news. Silence fell on the room and all heads turned towards Grainne to see her reaction.

Grainne's face turned a distinct shade of puce, her mouth twisted as if she'd just tasted something sour. She stayed like this for a good few seconds before her face calmed and returned to normal. Grainne carefully picked up her fork and knife and resumed her dinner, as if Connor had been talking about nothing more interesting than the weather.

"That place is not *your* home." On this point, Grainne wanted to be quite clear. "You have your flat here to consider, and you can't live so far away; you would be too far from the office."

It amazed Mara that Grainne could so easily dismiss everything that her grandson had just told her, all because it didn't fit into the vision she had for him. How could she think that in any scenario Connor would be here running the business when his grandmother had all but said moments ago that she would entirely cut him off if he married her? She knew Connor still felt a deep sense of loyalty to his family, no matter how they treated him or Aoife, but she thought even that might be taking it a bit too far.

"Well, Granny, perhaps we should go to the library and discuss exactly what my role within the company would look like in the future? There's an idea I wanted to discuss with you."

"Yes, I'm aware of your business proposal," Grainne promptly cut him off. "And I'm inclined to reject it."

Mara could see that neither Connor nor Aoife

looked surprised at this news. Connor had all but sealed the fate of their proposal by announcing his other one.

"It's shoddy work, and really dear, it shows just how much you still need to do with *O'Reilly's* before you even consider thinking of taking over your grandfather's business. That pub is the lynchpin of this family's entire business, and I won't part with it."

Mara snuck another glance down the table at him and saw a look on Connor's face she hadn't seen on him before. She was reminded once more of how different he was when he was around his family, and it made her uneasy.

"Let's just get right to the point, don't we? There is nothing wrong with that business proposal and we all know that you lot would benefit greatly from it," he said, addressing everyone. "This is because I've chosen to marry Mara. You don't want to sell Grandda's pub so you can punish me for doing something you don't approve of."

Grainne's face took on a "who me?" look of innocence that Mara was amazed she'd had the gall to muster up.

"And don't think I don't see right through your threats about cutting me off. Go ahead and do it. See how far it gets you."

Grainne sniffed at his insolence, but Connor didn't give her the opportunity to speak.

"And you can keep the pub, even though we all know you don't give a damn about it. But don't expect me to stay in this business, or in this family. If you won't accept the person I love, then I don't want to be a part of your family anymore."

He rose from his seat, throwing down his white linen napkin onto his plate, and stormed out of the dining room.

※

"What did you expect, Connor?" Caitlin hissed at him furiously as she, Nate, Mara, Aoife, and Colin followed him into the library. She was trying to keep her voice moderately low, knowing that, at the very least, Moore would be standing outside trying to listen in on them.

"You're supposed to be the heir to all of this, and you choose the very moment that we are delicately trying to get Gran to release you from that obligation to choose to flaunt everything she's given you your whole life by bringing that woman here tonight? How did you think Gran was really going to react to all of this? Did you honestly think she was going to throw her arms around her and welcome her into the family like she was one of us?"

Aoife noticed how Caitlin couldn't even bring herself to use Mara's proper name when talking about her.

"You are such a naïve fool sometimes," Caitlin continued. You've always believed that all you've ever needed to do is flash that charming smile and everything will just work out for you. You've never once given a thought to the people who've sacrificed their whole selves just to get a tiny morsel of the privilege you do nothing to earn."

With this comment, Aoife saw a side of her cousin she hadn't seen before, someone who appeared to feel... what? Remorse? Remorse for becoming someone terrible in order to fit into their twisted family?

Connor leapt to his feet from the chair he'd morosely plunked himself into and came to stand directly in

## Where I'm Home

front of his sister. "That is my fiancée you are talking about, and her name is Mara, so you best get used to using it. And she has every right to be here, just as much as you or I."

"I really don't care who the fuck she is; she doesn't belong in this family, and you know it."

His twin sister matched his stance, boldly choosing to defy his indignation.

This really *was* a whole new side of Caitlin that Aoife was seeing. She was still a bully and a snob, yes, but right now she was demonstrating something resembling a backbone. Aoife didn't know she'd even had one to begin with. She might have been impressed too, had Caitlin ever used it to stand up to their grandmother, even just once.

Connor's face turned the same thunderous shade it had just moments before he'd stormed in here, and for half a second, everyone in the room held their breath, waiting to see how he might explode. Even Nate – who'd always been a tad useless in Aoife's opinion – did nothing to intervene on his wife's behalf. Thankfully, Connor had a much better handle on his temper than any of them expected and composed himself.

"Come on, Mara, we're leaving."

With tears forming at the corners of her eyes, Mara silently took the hand he held out to her and followed him out of the room. As they passed her and Colin, Aoife tried to give her a sympathetic look. None of this was her fault, and she'd deserved none of the ill treatment she'd received tonight. Caitlin may have had a point that bringing her here tonight had not been Connor's best idea, but Mara still hadn't deserved the hurt that had been heaped upon her.

"Maybe you two should both get a reality check

before you step foot in this house again," Caitlin called after them, and Connor slammed the library door behind him, causing a couple of the books on the nearest shelf to fall to the hardwood floor as he and Mara breezed by a shocked Moore, who had indeed been listening in on their conversation.

"And maybe you should check your snobbery at the door," Aoife retorted, picking up the leather-bound books and carefully returning them to the shelf. "Or have you forgotten that a mere two generations ago, our family was in a lower social class than even the Flanagans?"

She stared her cousin in the eye and was disappointed with herself for thinking last night that there might be the tiniest glimmer of hope that deep down, there was a decent human being behind the fake façade. She'd been waiting for the other shoe to drop, for the knife to be plunged into her back then. She guessed she was seeing it now.

"And to think I was willing to believe you might actually have a heart, Caitlin. I guess I've always been right about you all along and you're still just like the rest of this family." Aoife turned on her heel and took Colin's hand, leading him out the same way Connor and Mara had gone.

No one tried to stop them as they exited the house and headed for the car.

## Chapter Fifteen

"I take it back, and I sincerely apologize for not entirely believing you before. I mean, I didn't doubt that they would be a little stuck up, but honestly, I wasn't expecting that!" Colin waved his hand towards Grainne's house as the two of them got into the car. "And that comment about you thinking you're someone important? What the hell was that?"

Aoife merely shrugged off his incredulity. There was a time when her family's opinion of her mattered, when their words hurt. But her time in Ballyclara and New York had taught her that there were people in her life that could love her, and that she didn't need her family's approval, breaking the ability they had to hurt her. Still, there was a part of her that couldn't help but feel a little vindicated.

Her family was the standard by which she'd grown

up, and she hadn't really known any better until she started spending more time around Bex and Millie. It was seeing them with their families that had taught her that the happy families she'd seen on telly were not just made up, as her mother had told her, but based on how families should treat their loved ones. She'd always sort of felt that her family was the odd one out; after all, someone as wonderful as her grandfather couldn't possibly have grown up in a family like hers. He'd spoken up for her enough times for her to know that the way Grainne and the others picked on her wasn't considered normal, but neglect had just become her version of what normal was like until she'd found people who treated her as if she had value, and her perception of normal had inevitably shifted.

"I don't know how you survived growing up in that house; I would have gone insane. And all those comments about Michael; what did she think she was going to do? Get me jealous of an ex-lover you haven't seen or heard from in three years?"

"That's exactly what she was hoping for," Aoife replied, turning the ignition of the car and heading out the drive.

"You know, I find it difficult to imagine the two of you together. I mean, sure, he's reasonably handsome, he's got a stable job, unlike the poor, starving poet you've fallen for…"

She glanced over at him. She knew he was trying to be humorous, but Colin's statement threw her off-kilter.

"I happen to like the poor, starving poet I've fallen for," she replied, being serious. "And you're hardly poor or starving. You make more from publishing one collection of poems than most people make in a year. And do you often find yourself imagining me with my ex-boyfriend? Because if you do, I think you and I need to have an entirely different conversation."

She tried to match his playful tone but couldn't quite manage it. After the night they'd had, Michael was the last thing she wanted to be thinking about. She didn't need any more distractions or confusion from that man. She had to stop thinking of him, but it wasn't so easy with him coming up all the time, either in person or in conversation.

Colin was a good man, everything she deserved. He was good to her, good *for* her. He'd met the worst part of her tonight and had stood up for her, and he wasn't running away scared. He was right here by her side. But that was the kind of the problem, wasn't it? Colin was the man she deserved, but Michael was the one she wanted. She'd never admitted it to herself since coming back to Ireland, but there it was. As it turned out, Grainne's attempts to drive a wedge between her and Colin hadn't been necessary; Aoife was doing that just fine on her own.

*Oh Christ, don't let it be true. Don't let me screw up this relationship, too.*

She'd wanted to believe so badly before coming back here that she'd spent the last three years doing some growing up, and while she had in some ways, when it came to her love life, she was still in just as much a mess as she ever was. If Grainne had wanted to remind her of how much of a screw-up she was, she'd just gotten her wish; just, perhaps, not when she'd been hoping for it.

"Hey, what's wrong? I thought we were just kidding."

She noticed Colin's face was drawn into a worried frown and realized her feelings must be showing on her face again.

"Nothing. I'm fine." She tried to sound more certain than she felt.

"Christ, I'm sorry. Tonight was awful, and I shouldn't have been making bad jokes. You know, we don't have to stay here in Dublin if you don't want to, if it's too close to your family. We can go back to Ballyclara or stay anywhere. Wherever you want."

He was saying all the right things, like he always did, which just made her feel worse.

"At least I'm glad we didn't give your grandmother what she was looking for," he took her hand and kissed it. "We're as solid as a rock, and nothing's going to change that. Man, I thought my parents were hard on me, and that's not to say that they weren't, but your family… At least you had your grandfather and Connor in your life."

She smiled at the few fond memories from her childhood; Connor and Paddy O'Reilly were in every one of them. It wasn't like everything had been smooth sailing between her and Connor all the time; at the end of the day, he had, until right now, always been much higher up the proverbial food chain in their family than her and as children, he'd done his fair share of throwing her to the wolves and not standing up for her when he easily could have said something to make the bullying from their family stop. But that was back when he'd been too young to really understand that the choices we make don't always have consequences for us directly, but instead, hurt the people we care about the most. She'd forgiven him for those slip-ups because he'd learned from them and had done better by her after every one of them.

"Let's go and make sure he's ok. I know this was not how he was expecting tonight to go at all, and I'm worried about him," she admitted.

She knew Connor should've known what Grainne's reaction to his upcoming wedding to Mara was going to be, and yet he had still let his temper get the best of him. There'd been a finality in his tone when he'd told Grainne he no longer wanted to be part of her family that made Aoife concerned for him. It was one thing for her to cut herself off from their family, but it had different consequences for Connor. She was worried about how the ramifications of what he'd done would affect him later.

Taking a deep breath, she sped towards the hotel.

ℬℭ

When they arrived at the hotel, Rory, Des, and Mara were waiting in the little living room of their suite, the telly muted in the background. Aoife could see Miriam fast asleep on the sofa.

"C'mon, monkey. Off to bed," Colin said, sweeping her up into his arms as gently as he could so as not to wake her, and carried her into the spare bedroom of their suite.

"Where's Connor?" she asked.

"He's down in the car park. We were just waiting on the two of ye to come back so we could head out." Mara's eyes were damp, but her voice was steady. Rory and Des kept looking between the two of them, trying to suss out what had happened while the adults had been away. She'd leave it to Mara to explain it to them.

Mara held up her hand to quiet her apology. "It's not your fault, Aoife." Sighing, she then gave her a quick hug and said, "It'll be alright."

"Thanks, lads, for coming up tonight." She handed them each a sizeable amount of money.

"Ah no, we couldn't take all this, Aoife." Rory eyed the cash in his hand. "Sure, and it was no trouble at all to watch Miriam. It's too much."

"Call it making up for missed birthdays and Christmases for the last three years."

Rory looked at his mother, but she didn't seem to be paying attention, anxious to leave and get back to Connor.

"Thanks, Aoife," he said, hugging her. "Come on, Mam. Connor will be wondering where we got to."

"We'll come down in the morning. Tell Connor I'll call him when we're on our way," Aoife told them as she saw them to the door, shutting it softly behind them.

She breathed deeply and kicked off her heels, sending them flying about the room. She didn't care; she'd deal with them in the morning. She padded across the carpeted floor to the bedroom and unzipped the LBD she'd worn tonight, letting it fall in a puddle at her feet, climbed into bed in her underwear. She still had her make-up on and her hair up in bobby pins, but she was too exhausted to deal with them right now. She'd regret it in the morning, but that was tomorrow's problem.

"I'm exhausted," she sighed, cuddling up to Colin.

"Really? That's too bad, because I've been waiting for you to get in here to take in this amazing view." He pulled the sheet back a bit, giving her an ample view of his nakedness. She smiled appreciatively at him. He returned her smile, and she could see what he was thinking. The two of them hadn't made love since leaving New York, and he definitely wanted her. He started kissing her neck, his hand travelling lower and lower beneath the bedsheet. Her brain might be exhausted from tonight's drama, but her body definitely wasn't. Encouraged, he furthered his ministrations. She was giving in to him, her body too determined to have him right *now*.

She put a hand behind his neck and pulled him in, closing her eyes and kissing him deeply. Unfortunately for her, that was exactly when her brain decided to remind her of her earlier doubts about Michael, about Colin, about *everything*. Her body froze.

"What's wrong?" he asked, his voice breathless.

"I…"

How could she explain this to him? She couldn't just tell him in the middle of having sex that her inconvenient brain had decided that right now was the perfect time to make her think about her ex. No, that was just not something you told a guy in a situation like this.

"I'm… I'm just exhausted," she murmured feebly, using her excuse from earlier. Her body was screaming at her, telling her what an eejit she was for doing this at this exact moment.

*Yeah, well, tell it to my brain,* she thought, more than a little resentfully.

"Ok," he said, his voice uncertain, but wanting to be respectful. He shifted off her and scooted back to his side of the bed.

"I'm sorry," she whispered.

"Hey, nothing to be sorry about. It's been a long night. Let's just get some sleep. Come here." He held the blanket up for her and she snuggled in close to his chest, breathing him in. He switched off the bedside lamp and kissed the top of her head, holding her close to him.

She didn't deserve him. No matter what her heart thought it felt for Michael, it was the wrong choice. It was never going to work out between the two of them. She should be happy with the man she had right here in her arms.

So why wasn't she?

※※※

Connor stole another look at Mara as he pulled the car into the drive outside their cottage. She'd been quiet the whole drive down from the hotel, not looking at him, only staring out the passenger side window. He knew she'd been trying not to cry the whole time for Des and Rory's sake, trying not to worry them, which had most definitely had the opposite effect. After leaving the hotel, Rory had leaned forward in his seat, silently placing a hand on his mother's shoulder. She'd patted it reassuringly, grateful for his concern.

For most of the rest of the way home, the lads had sat in the backseat quietly looking out the window into the black night, or occasionally at their phones, but otherwise had been more still than Connor had ever seen them before. They definitely knew something was up; they were just waiting for the right moment to talk about it. He wasn't sure what exactly they were going to tell Rory now they were home. There hadn't been time for him and Mara to talk about it between him choosing to stay in the hotel car park and pace around angrily, trying to blow off some steam, and her waiting upstairs in the room for Aoife to return.

He exhaled. He wished he'd kept his temper in check earlier. He knew he'd frightened Aoife and Mara with his outburst, but he'd just not been able to hold it in anymore. His family could insult him all they liked, his grandmother could turn down his business proposal, but he wasn't going to stand by and watch while they went after his fiancée. He didn't regret standing up for her, even if that meant his grandmother cut him off. The two of them would be alright for money; he still had his grandfather's inheritance, and the money he'd made from his military service, and Mara had her landscaping. They'd be alright financially. He was more concerned about where they stood emotionally.

When they got back to Ballyclara, they dropped Des off before continuing home. When they got into the kitchen, Rory turned to the both of them and asked, "So, are we finally going to talk about what we were not talking about for the last hour?"

Connor and Mara were silent, eyeing each other, trying to figure out how best to explain things to him.

"You come back from dinner early, then Mam looks like she's been crying, and Aoife and Colin look like they've just had the worst night of their lives, and you look like you could murder the life out of someone. What the hell happened at your folks' place?" Rory pressed.

"We'll talk about it in the morning," Mara replied after a second's hesitation. Her voice was weary.

"I'm not a kid anymore, ye know. You can tell me whatever's going on," he said, his tone a bit exasperated.

"It's not that we don't want to talk about it, Rory, it's just that it's been a long night, and we'll talk about it in the morning," Connor reassured him, putting a hand on his shoulder. He knew all too well what it felt like to be at that age when everyone around you forgot you were growing up, and they still wanted to talk to you like you were a little kid. "I promise."

Rory sighed, but didn't put up an argument. "You two aren't going to spend the night coordinating whatever PG version of this you think I can handle?"

"We'll talk about in the morning," Connor reiterated, side-stepping the question.

Knowing full well that this was the only answer he was going to get, Rory turned around and headed upstairs, dragging his feet loudly to make his annoyance known. When Connor heard his bedroom door close, he turned to Mara and asked, "So what PG version of all this *are* we going to tell him?"

Mara sighed and put her face in her hands. "I don't know. How do you tell a kid that a family he's about to become a part of has no interest in getting to know him and will never have an interest in getting to know him, and not have that make him feel like he's lacking in some way?"

Connor pulled her into a hug and kissed the top of her head. "I don't know."

"If you say 'But we'll talk about it in the morning' then I think I might just scream."

He smiled. "C'mon, let's put this all behind us for now and go to bed."

When they'd gotten into the bedroom, she quietly but firmly shut the door behind them. She crossed the room and kissed him deeply, her hands on either side of his face. Her lips tasted like saltwater from crying earlier.

"Take off your clothes," she commanded, when she finally came up for air, taking off her own.

He raised an eyebrow in her direction, surprised at this turn of events.

"What? After the shite day this has been, I want to feel close to the man I love. Now take off your feckin' clothes."

"Yes, ma'am," he replied, flinging his clothes into the corner.

## Where I'm Home

෩෬

As she lay in his arms later, he thought she was dozing quietly until he heard her sharp intake of breath before asking, "Do you have any regrets about getting engaged?"

"No. Why? Do you?" He angled his head so he could see her face.

"No," she said after a pause, and Connor let out a breath he hadn't realized he was holding.

"It's only…" He felt his breath still again. "The things your family said tonight. The threats your grandmother made. I know they're your family and you love them…"

"You're my family. You and Rory," he said, taking her hand and kissing it.

She smiled at him.

"I mean it Mara; I don't care if they cut me off. You and Rory are more important than any inheritance, and I'd rather have just the two of you than a million Grainne O'Reillys. If all I ever have from this point forward is this little cottage, and the two of you, then I'll still be the luckiest man in the world. Oh, and Aoife. I suppose we better not forget about her."

"Yeah, I don't think that would go over well with her," Mara chuckled.

"But seriously, I don't need to keep living the way I grew up. I've got everything I need right here."

She kissed him lightly.

"Speaking of Aoife, I think she and I need to have a bit of a chat about what exactly she means to be doing with my brother."

"What do you mean?" he asked, genuinely

perplexed. "Those two are ancient history. Maybe there was a time when I thought she'd go back to him, but she's happy with Colin now. She and I have both found the families we've always been looking for."

"You didn't see how the two of them were looking at each other right before supper the other night when we announced the engagement. Sure, and there were some definite looks exchanged."

Connor grinned at her. "Some looks, huh?"

"Yes! And you can stop making it sound like I don't know what I'm talking about right now, Connor O'Reilly. I know what I saw. Those feelings they had for each other are far from ancient history."

"And there's not even a little part of you that thinks you might be reading too much into it?"

"No! A woman knows these things. Trust me. There's some definite unresolved feelings there." She punctuated her words by poking at his chest. He took her hand again and held it, then manoeuvred her onto her back.

"What are ye doing?"

"I don't want to talk about my cousin and her love life anymore. I want to focus on my own," he grinned down at her, kissing her and making her squeal with laughter.

## Chapter Sixteen

Aoife stood in what was once the garden of Aldridge Manor, watching Mara pull up weeds with great vigour. She, Colin, and Miriam had checked out of the hotel first thing that morning. She didn't want to spend one more moment in the same city as her family.

"So, any thoughts on where we'll stay in Ballyclara?" Colin had asked her as they turned towards the village.

She wasn't entirely sure, if she was honest. She didn't want to be an imposition on Connor and Mara at this time, but she also wanted to stay near them.

"I was thinking I would ask Brendan and Molly about the flat above the pub," she replied, remembering that it had been offered to them at Dermot's funeral.

"You don't want to stay at Aldridge?"

"It would take too long to get it all cleaned and set

up again. By the time we got things in order, we'd just have to put it all away before we go back to New York."

She also didn't want to stay so close to Michael. She was sort of caught between a rock and a hard place now, unable to stay in Dublin, but uneasy about being back in Ballyclara, too. If only her damned family could have pulled themselves together and been supportive just this once, she wouldn't have to feel like she needed to run away from them again.

Colin pulled into the car park next to the pub and turned off the ignition.

"Why don't you stay here with Miriam while I just check with Molly and Brendan about the flat?" she asked, getting out of the car and heading towards the pub.

It was fairly empty this time of morning, with most people having gone to work by now, and it was too early for the start of the lunch rush. She could see Molly and Ailish in the kitchen through the porthole window, while Brendan was at the bar, idly wiping it down.

"Good mornin' to ye, Aoife," he greeted her, looking a little surprised to see her. She wondered if he and Molly knew about last night's events, but there was no need; of course, Mara would have told Molly everything. They were best friends.

"Hi Brendan," she smiled at him warmly. "I've got a favour to ask of you: I was wondering if the flat upstairs was still open for Colin, Miriam, and I to stay in?"

He looked at her with curiosity but didn't ask questions. He wasn't the nosy type, which was exactly what made people want to confide in him. "Sure is. You three looking to stay awhile?"

"Yeah, until the wedding, if we could."

"Shouldn't be a problem. It's open to ye any time ye like."

"Just let us know how much it is for the rooms and Colin will pay you upfront."

"'Tis no bother," he said humbly, waving away her offer. "You're welcome here any time, for as long as ye like, free of charge."

She knew there was no point arguing with him about it. She'd just quietly slip the money in as a tip when she was paying for dinner some time.

"Anything else I can do for ye?"

"Actually, yes. Do you know where Connor and Mara are?"

"I'm not sure about Connor, but I think Mara's gone to the Old Rectory," he replied, using the name the locals used for Aldridge Manor. "Said she wanted to do some work on the garden. Seemed like she had something on her mind that needed working out through physical labour when she was in talking to Molly this morning."

"Thanks. Colin will get our things and start moving them upstairs."

"I'll lend a hand." He came around the bar and following her outside.

Colin was leaning against the car, talking to Miriam, the two of them basking in the warmth of the fresh air and sunshine after the drive down.

"Brendan says we can stay here."

"Thanks, man," Colin replied, reaching out to shake Brendan's hand in gratitude. "Appreciate it."

"'Tis no trouble at all."

"Listen, babe, can you and Brendan move our things upstairs? I want to go and check in on Mara."

"Of course. We'll see you later." Colin gave her a quick kiss and then went to pop open the trunk.

And so it was that she came to be standing here,

watching Mara hack and pull at the unruly weeds that had taken over the garden in the absence of her pruning. It had gone fallow now, no longer the vibrant, colourful display it had been three years ago. The two of them had once made an extensive plan for the manor grounds, plans that had never been implemented once she left. She knew Karen and Mara had continued to come and look after the place for her, but with no offers on the place coming in, it wasn't like she could expect them to keep it up on the off chance she might return.

She was sad to see the place looking run-down again, but it also reminded her of the first time she'd seen Aldridge Manor, and how she'd fallen so in love with it that she'd bought it on a whim. She'd never expected to be a part of this place when she'd driven down to visit Glendalough only a few miles up the road, but she couldn't say she regretted it; after all, she'd put into this place – and not just the house, but the people as well – it had felt like home. Whatever anyone may think, it had not been easy for her to leave it; she had so many memories here.

She smiled as she remembered the entire Flanagan, McCaffrey, and Connolly families working to restore it when she'd first moved in. How they'd pored over colour tabs for paint and wallpaper, trying to find just the right colours to match what had since faded, all the hours spent stripping everything bare, and putting it all back together brand new. All that hard work had nearly been in vain the day the kitchen had nearly caught fire and Michael had had to come to her rescue. Lord, but he'd been so furious with her that day, and her with him, and the two of them had ended up in one of their famous rows. She chuckled at the thought of the two of them standing there screaming at one another, thinking the other was a complete eejit. Of course, if anyone had been an eejit that day, it had definitely not been her; of that, there was no doubt in her mind.

She glanced behind her towards the kitchen, remembering how she'd met Rory in there for the first time, over there by the kitchen table, him just a small lad then. He'd nearly scared the life out of her, just sitting there quietly doing his homework while his mother had been out here working in the garden. How he'd grown since then, both him and Des. Even back then, you could hardly find one without the other and it seemed the two of them had only grown closer since.

She remembered the first time Bex and Millie had come down here, the wild housewarming party they'd thrown for her. That was the night her relationship with Michael had changed, and she hadn't even known it at the time. They'd rowed that night too. The party had been loud enough to wake him up, and he'd come over, being his high and mighty self as per usual. She, of course, hadn't been much better; she'd been far too drunk, nearly threw up on him, and still he'd carried her inside after she'd passed out, making sure she was alright. He'd been a reluctant gentleman then, just like he'd been during her first Christmas here.

That had been a magical time. She and Michael had most definitely still not admitted their feelings for one another yet, but they'd formed a reluctant friendship. She'd been planning to go up to Dublin to spend time with Connor before he'd shipped out on his last tour, but Mother Nature had intervened and sent a snow and ice storm to prevent her from spending time with her family that Christmas. Instead, she'd spent it with the Flanagans, after Michael found her flat on her back after falling on the ice outside his parents' door. This was the first time she'd seen a bit of the Michael she'd fallen in love with, the family man, the gentleman, the person she thought she wanted to spend forever with.

But then she'd seen the other side of him, the one with the temper, the one who'd gotten into a full-on brawl with Danny outside of the pub. He'd thought he was being a gentleman, fighting the boyfriend who'd cheated on her, but things between them had never been the same afterwards. Dermot had ended up in the hospital and she'd gotten an opportunity to work with a publishing house in New York. From there, it had been all too easy for them to fall apart.

She had so many memories of this place, it hurt. Time had slightly faded them, but they were never gone. They lived on here, in this house, even if she no longer did.

"Hey." Aoife turned around, startled by Michael's voice behind her.

"Sorry, I didn't mean to frighten you." He stepped in closer to her and lightly brushed her cheek with his thumb. Reminiscing about the past must have made her more emotional than she'd realized, and a few tears had escaped.

"It's alright. I'm fine." She glanced down at her boots, trying to hide how uneasy she still felt being this physically close to him, given all the thoughts she'd just been going over in her mind. "Lost in thought is all."

"There are a lot of memories in this place." He looked around the enclosed garden, and she could see all the same memories she'd just been thinking about going through his own mind. The corners of his mouth, so often drawn into a grimace, lifted slightly, and she found a part of her was pleased that the moments they'd shared could still make him smile.

## Where I'm Home

This place held special meaning for Michael, and not just because of their shared experiences here. He'd wanted to buy Aldridge Manor before she'd even arrived in Ballyclara. It had been a point of contention between the two of them at first, with her moving into the home he'd wanted for himself to raise a family. She would gladly have given it to him when she'd left for New York, or at least sold it to him at a much more reasonable price, but she knew he'd never have accepted what he would have thought of as a handout. When she'd first left Ireland, she'd thought about contacting him and proposing an offer, but she'd figured that he probably wouldn't have taken her calls, anyway. Damn his male stubbornness and pride.

She wondered now if maybe she'd made a mistake in not trying to contact him, not trying to fix things between them when she'd still had the chance. Maybe he'd felt the same way Brendan and Molly had, and he'd wanted her to reach out to him. In any case, it was too late now.

"Yes, there sure are a lot of memories here." She brushed away the wetness from her cheeks and cleared her throat. "Is there anything I can do for you?"

"Actually, I was coming over to see if there was anything I could do for you," he replied, putting his hands in his jeans pockets. "Brendan mentioned you were back and looking to stay until the wedding. I thought you might want to open the house up again and stay here."

He smiled shyly at her. "I know Mam and Da said they'd keep up the place for you until it was sold…"

Was she just imagining it, or did he seem happy she was staying? But that couldn't be, given how surly he'd been since she'd come back.

"Oh, that's alright. Brendan said we could stay in the rooms above the pub until the wedding."

Aoife noticed two things then: a remarkably disappointed look in his eyes that he tried to conceal, and how he never really seemed to mention Colin by name around her, like he was almost hoping that it would just be her staying. She wondered if this was really the case, or just her mind toying with her again.

"And I understand about not keeping the place up. You've done the best you can with it." It hadn't escaped her that it would have been Michael, in fact, that had done most of the work maintaining this place while she was gone, what with Dermot unable to do any of the physical work in the last years of his life. It couldn't have been easy for him to look after the house of the woman who'd left him behind, especially when he didn't know if she'd ever return or not.

"It's a lot of work to keep up such a big place. It's still in better shape than when I first bought it. You've taken great care of it for me, Michael. Although, if your sister keeps pulling up the garden like that, I'm not sure we're going to have much of it left."

They both watched Mara as she pulled ferociously at some weeds that seemed to have deep roots and were refusing to come up easily.

*Just like a certain Flanagan I know*, she thought, almost giggling at the comparison to Michael.

"I'm reliably informed that she was highly motivated to commit murder after meeting your family last night. I can't say I blame her."

The sour look that came over his face betrayed the light mood he was trying to convey. Apparently, the sting of his own encounter with her family still hurt. She couldn't blame him; the O'Reillys had certainly not been kind to any of the Flanagans. "At least she's only committing murder on the weeds."

"I feel terrible about how things went…"

"Oh, I wouldn't worry too much about it. As ye know, we Flanagans get our dander all up about something, then we storm about and get it out of our systems, and it's like nothing ever happened. Mara will be fine when it comes time to focus on the wedding plans. Besides, it's not like it's your fault and it didn't all turn out to be awful. It brought ye back down here again."

He leaned casually against the doorframe behind her. With an instinct that only comes from being in such physical proximity of someone you were once so comfortable, she turned slightly towards him, her shoulder and upper arm resting lightly against his chest. Neither of them moved.

"I meant for Connor's sake," he clarified. "He's so excited to have ye back here again."

The way Michael stared down at her with those intense blue eyes, the ones that always seemed to stare directly into her innermost thoughts, she wasn't sure at all that it wasn't him who was happy to have her back in Ballyclara again. Maybe she hadn't just been imagining things earlier.

"Of course." She wasn't sure how to respond just now; being so close to him was making it difficult to think clearly.

"Well, don't just stand around watching me work. Lend us a hand, will ye?"

Both of them jumped nearly out of their skin, completely unaware that Mara had finally noticed them standing there.

How long had she been standing there, watching the two of them? Had she noticed whatever it was that was going on between them? She tried to search Mara's face for some clue, but she was as implacable as ever. If she had noticed something between her and her brother, she wasn't letting on.

"Yes, ma'am," Michael replied to his sister, moving away from her and taking the pile of weeds she was holding out and throwing them into a nearby wheelbarrow. Feeling colder without Michael's warmth beside her, Aoife walked over to Mara, trying to act like her legs did not feel like a bowl of jelly and like her heart wasn't about to beat itself out of her chest. She took the pair of gloves she held out to her. As she was putting them on, she caught Michael staring at her, the faintest smirk on his lips.

*Bastard!* He'd done that on purpose, standing so close to her, knowing how she'd react. Despite herself, she found she was staring back at him, watching as he worked.

*Girl, what are you doing with yourself? Stop staring at him!*

She didn't know how to answer her own question, but whatever she was doing, she knew she was wading into dangerous waters where Michael was concerned.

## Chapter Seventeen

After the incident in the garden earlier that day, Aoife vowed to avoid being alone with Michael as much as possible. Unfortunately for her, this was a nearly impossible task. Not only was she sleeping in the rooms above his place of work, but when she wasn't there, she was helping his sister to plan her wedding. It also didn't help that his girlfriend seemed more excited than ever to hang out with her.

"I'm so glad you've decided to stay for the wedding!" Ailish had practically squealed with delight, seeing her and Colin later that night for supper in the pub. "You and I are going to have *so* much fun helping to plan the wedding together! Now, here's a list of everything Molly's given me of what Mara's mentioned she wants so far…"

Aoife's mind trailed off, not listening to a word

Ailish was saying. Michael was over at the bar, talking to some of the regulars, but she could've sworn that she felt him trying to steal glances at her when he thought she wasn't looking. Even surrounded by other people, the two of them were keenly aware of the other's presence.

Why, oh why, couldn't she focus on the Michael she'd first met when she'd come to Ballyclara? The one who was surly and stubborn, and downright annoying instead of being all sexy and charming.

*Just a few more days and you'll never have to see him again*, she kept reminding herself.

She was thankful that tonight, at least, she would have a few Michael-free hours. Mara had asked her, Molly, Ailish, and Karen to come over to help her try on wedding dresses. It was firmly a "no guys allowed" night. It sounded perfect, exactly what she needed.

Molly and Aoife set out from the pub just after dinner, intending to meet Karen and Ailish at Mara's place. She and Molly settled into an easy stroll, the two of them not in any rush. The last rays of sunshine cast a golden glow over the fields along the lane that led to the cottages where Michael, Mara, and Sinead lived, the sheep lowing quietly as they passed. She and Molly were engrossed in a conversation about what they had left to do for the wedding, which accounted for the fact that neither of them noticed the unfamiliar vehicle in the drive. As it was, they passed by on their way to the cottage, oblivious to its presence.

"Hello," Aoife called out as she stepped into the kitchen. "Mara? Ok, let's see these dresses!"

The excitement in her voice trailed off as she surveyed the room and immediately knew that something was wrong.

# Where I'm Home

## ೞාCಜ

*Earlier that evening*

"Out with ye! You're not supposed to see the dress!"

Ailish stood in front of Connor and Rory, hands on her hips. The two of them were stretched out on the sofa, watching the telly.

"I'm fairly certain that only applies to him." Rory pointed to Connor with his thumb, apparently determined not to move.

"C'mon lad, you don't want to be here either, staring at dresses all night. Let's leave the ladies to gawk at themselves in the mirror," Michael said to him, entering the sitting room.

Ailish narrowed her eyes at him, but then her face lit up, and she turned to Mara. "Oh! I knew I was forgetting something when we were walking over here. You mentioned you might want to borrow some pieces of my jewellery to wear with your dress. I've left them back at Michael's. I'll just nip home and get them and be right back."

"You don't need to go through all that bother. We can look through them another time," Mara reassured her.

"No, no. It's no bother. Besides, you'll want to see how they look with the dresses. I'll not be long." She hurried out the door, not taking no for an answer.

A few minutes later, they all paused as they saw headlights through the front window.

"Who could that be?" Mara peered through the curtain but couldn't make out who was there in the dark.

"Maybe Ailish drove up?" Connor asked, his eyes still trained on the football match on the telly.

"Doubt it," Michael replied, equally engrossed in the match. He'd joined him and his nephew on the sofa after Ailish had left. "She wouldn't drive up for such a short distance."

"Maybe Brendan drove Aoife and Molly up?"

"No, that doesn't look like Brendan's car. I don't think I've seen it before..." Mara's voice trailed off. Curiosity taking over, they moved towards the kitchen.

"Mara?" Karen's voice called out as she came through the door.

Immediately, Mara knew something was wrong. Her junior assistant looked flustered, her movements bordering on frantic.

"We tried to keep him from coming over here, but he insisted..."

Mara wasn't listening anymore, staring instead at the person who walked in behind Karen's husband, Jimmy Connolly.

"Jesus Christ, what the feckin' hell are *you* doing here?"

ଗଡ଼

The first thing Aoife noticed was that there were too many people in the cottage. It was just supposed to be a girls' night, but for some reason, Jimmy, Connor, Michael, and Rory were there, along with Karen and Mara. Ailish, it seemed, hadn't shown up yet. Out of the corner of her eye, she noticed there was someone else there as well, a man she didn't know, but who somehow seemed familiar.

## Where I'm Home

Was he someone from the village she hadn't met yet? Was that even possible? In a place as small as Ballyclara, there were only so many people, and she was pretty sure she'd met them all. This man was tall, about Michael's height and around the same age. He had the same reddish hair and fair skin as Karen, as if they might be related in some way.

"You've got some nerve," Molly said, her tone low and threatening.

She crossed the room to stand beside her best friend, instinctively putting distance between Mara and the stranger. And then Aoife knew exactly who the man was, for despite the difference in hair and eye colour, Rory was the spit of him. This was Alistair Byrne, Rory's father, and Karen's older brother.

"Jaysus, Mary and Joseph!" she muttered under her breath, using one of Michael's favourite catchphrases. She understood immediately why there was tension in the room; it was a miracle there hadn't been a great bloody explosion already.

She first checked on Connor. This situation was nothing like Colin meeting Michael for the first time; this was a whole other kettle of fish entirely and she needed to see how he was coping with meeting Mara's ex for the first time. For Alistair had abandoned Mara when she was pregnant with Rory and, as far as Aoife knew, had never been seen or heard from again. Aoife knew how Connor felt not only about parents abandoning their children, but about this one in particular, and she knew that it greatly increased Alistair's odds of getting punched in the face tonight.

Connor was leaning against the doorframe connecting the kitchen and the front sitting room. Despite his casual stance, his face was unreadable, blue-grey eyes hard and fixed on Alistair. His arms were crossed tight against his chest, seemingly in an effort to have something to do with them that didn't involve hitting anyone, for the moment.

Next, she glanced furtively at Michael. He stood completely still, but he radiated energy from the effort it was taking for him not to launch himself across the room and punch the hell out of Alistair. Every muscle in his body was taut, his hands balled into fists so tight that his knuckles showed white against his skin. Jimmy stood beside him, his body coiled tight as well, ready to hold Michael back, or maybe to join him in pummeling Alistair. It was a genuine concern: the last time Alistair and Michael had been in the same vicinity as one another had been the last day that Alistair had set foot in Ballyclara.

Everyone in the village knew about *that* confrontation. It had been the day a nineteen-year-old Mara had told Alistair she was pregnant with Rory and he'd refused to take responsibility. He'd even had the gall to try and pressure her into taking "a trip to London" – since abortions were still illegal in Ireland at the time – even though she'd been firm with him about wanting to keep their son. When Michael had heard about this, everyone was certain he'd have beaten Alistair to within an inch of his life, if Dermot and Brendan hadn't pulled him off him before Alistair could get more than a little roughed up.

It seemed to be a common theme in Michael's life, she mused, solving things with his fists rather than with his words. However, it seemed that Michael wasn't the Flanagan they had to worry about flying off the handle tonight.

"What the hell are ye still doing here? I told ye to get out!"

She was surprised to find the outburst had come

from Rory. He'd always been a mild-tempered and easy-going sort, much like his grandfather, Dermot, had been. So, it seemed even more out of character for him to shout at someone like that.

"Go on! Get out and stay gone! You're good at that," Rory spat out, shoving Alistair.

"Now son, that's no way to…"

"I'm not your son," Rory snapped at him.

Alistair looked at Mara. If he'd been expecting to get support from her, he was sorely disappointed.

"I'm not going to disagree with him." Mara stood firm with her son, placing her hands on her hips. "You can't blame him for being furious with ye, Alistair. You haven't once been here since he was born."

Alistair threw up his hands, apparently frustrated no one was siding with him. "And who's fault is that?"

"Yours!" she snapped at him.

"Oh, come on, Mara. It's not like you didn't make it perfectly clear you didn't want me around to raise our son. You sent your little dog to make that point for ye." He pointed at Michael.

"I barely touched you," Michael retorted. "You deserved a helluva lot worse."

"And it's not like you've made any room for me in our son's life since," Alistair spat back, ignoring Michael's threat. "I've not heard once from you. And it's not like our son has been particularly welcoming tonight; that's something he could only have picked up from his mother. Whatever happened to giving someone a second chance?"

Everyone looked at each other, wondering at how he had the audacity to play the victim in this situation.

"And where the hell would I have sent anything to? No one knows where you've been this whole time, not even your own sister!"

"You could have sent word through my mam, but then again, you've always hated her."

Mara rolled her eyes at this. Mrs. Byrne wasn't exactly the most well-liked woman in Ballyclara, but it's not like anyone really hated her. They just resented how she had the tendency to judge everyone else when it was hardly like her own family wasn't just as much a mess as the rest of them.

"I was off trying to make a better life for my family."

Alistair's tone took on a distinct tone of victimhood. Aoife noticed that his accent was smoothed out in a way that only came from living outside of Ireland for years. The kind of accent she and Connor had. Wherever he'd been living the last twelve years or so, it hadn't been anywhere in Ireland.

"Oh, you were, were ye? Well, that's funny because your son and I have never once seen a child support cheque, or a postcard, or even a damn letter to let us know where you were, let alone that you were alive.

"And tell me something: what is *my* son's name? You've never once said it tonight. You don't even know what it is, do you? Because you've never given a damn about him until someone else came along who actually wanted him and wanted to make him his family, and you got all possessive like you always do, and felt the need to come here and stake your territory, even though you've no right to anything."

Alistair looked like he was trying to come up with some kind of retort, but was finding it difficult to think of a way to refute the truth.

"Where the hell have ye been all these years, anyway?" Mara asked him. "You know what? Never mind, I don't care. I just want ye to leave. Right now."

Mara went over to the door and held it open, letting in the cool night air, making Aoife shiver as it brushed the skin on her forearms.

Alistair rolled his eyes at her request, clearly not taking her seriously. Aoife imagined he was the kind of man who'd always found that flashing a girl a smarmy smile had usually gotten him what he wanted in life. She was proud of Mara for standing her ground and showing him that kind of arrogant attitude wouldn't work here. When he was clearly not going to get his way with her, he shifted his eyes to his younger sister.

"Don't look at me. I don't want ye here anymore than Rory or Mara do." Karen's normally cheerful smile was replaced with a thin-lipped grimace, her lively green eyes locked in a glare.

Alistair glared back for a second before finally seeming to get the hint.

"Fine," he snapped angrily. "We'll talk again tomorrow, when the whole village isn't here to gawk," he told Mara.

"Like hell ye will," Molly threatened again. "Ye can just get back in your fancy car and drive yerself back to whatever hole ye crawled out of. There's no one here who wants to see your ugly mug again."

"Where do ye think you'd stay anyways? No one here's going to put ye up. And don't ye say Mam and Da's place. You've put them through quite enough, don't ye think?" Karen asked boldly.

"*I've* put them through a lot? Seems to me *you've* been the one to place a burden on them, little sis. Who's looking after your wee daughter right now, after all? You've become quite the talk of the town since getting pregnant and then marrying this one," he gestured at

Jimmy. "Our poor mother, breaking her heart like that."

"Do you dare judge us for something you've done yerself?" Jimmy finally spoke up, gallantly defending his wife.

"Ah, the noble Jimmy Connolly, thinking he's so superior because he saddled himself with a wife and child at eighteen, and you think I abandoned mine? Well, now's your time to prove how noble ye are in front of your wife, Jim. What are you going to do about it? C'mon, be a man," Alistair challenged.

"Leave it, Jimmy. He's not worth it," Molly commanded.

"And at least Jimmy had the balls to stick around and raise his kid, unlike you, who couldn't get out of Ballyclara fast enough when ye heard about Rory," she spat at Alistair.

He turned towards Molly, obviously perturbed by her statement, but Molly McCaffrey was a force to be reckoned with on a good day, let alone when she felt her friend and godson were being threatened. He seethed for a moment, but then shrugged, as if this whole thing was all of no consequence to him and everything up to this point had just been him having a lark. But there was still one person in the room who was not about to let Alistair off so easily. As he made to leave, Aoife could see in Michael's eyes that he was still looking for a fight. If someone didn't do something right now, he was likely to explode.

Having seen what happened the last time he'd been in a brawl in front of her, Aoife made a split-second decision. Moving out of Alistair's way as he went for the door, she stepped in-between him and Michael, and took both sides of his face into her hands, trying to force him to put his gaze on her. She could tell by the way his body tensed from her touch that he was caught off-guard by her action.

"Michael, look at me. He's not worth it." She shook him a bit, trying to force him to look at her, to take his eyes off Alistair's retreating back.

He stared at Alistair, then down at her, letting his body relax into hers, sighing reluctantly. She'd taken the chance that his feelings for her were stronger than his hatred of Alistair, and that if she was between the two of them, he wouldn't put her in harm's way. It had paid off this time, avoiding an altercation no one needed to see happen right now. Michael rested his forehead against hers and she could see both the betrayal in his eyes that she'd robbed him of the opportunity to punch Alistair, but also understanding about why she'd done it.

"What did I miss?"

Aoife and Michael both sprang apart at the sound of Ailish's voice from the doorway Alistair had just stormed out of. She glanced around at everyone, but her eyes settled on Aoife, whose cheeks burned bright red. In one of the rare moments since she'd met her, Ailish was not being bubbly or excited to see Aoife. In fact, she had the same look of distrust on her face that she'd had the day after Dermot's funeral when Ailish hadn't wanted to admit in front of Aoife that Michael had seemed much more bothered by her return than he'd been willing to let on.

"Hi, love," Michael greeted her, walking over to give her a kiss.

She shifted away from him, crossing her arms across her chest, staying just out of his reach. If it was possible for Ailish to get pissed off, Aoife guessed that this was what it looked like.

Michael paused, clearly not hoping for this

reaction from her, but obviously not finding it unexpected. He maintained a respectful distance between them, giving her space.

"I'll tell you all about it on the way home." He held out his hand, gesturing to the open door behind them, indicating it was time to leave.

Ailish hesitated a moment, and Aoife thought she might say something to her, but instead she turned and lead the two of them outside. Aoife moved to the window, watching the two of them as they walked down the lane towards his cottage, engaged in an animated discussion. She felt both guilty for putting Michael in the position of having to explain what just happened between them, and not feeling the need to apologize to anyone for it. If she hadn't stepped in when she had, who knows how things might have turned out?

"Thanks for coming over and sorry about all of this." Mara threw her hands up exasperatedly, obviously frustrated her special night had been ruined, and rightly so.

"This isn't your fault, Mara," Aoife tried to reassure her. She nodded, but she could tell Mara was most certainly blaming herself for Alistair coming home.

"Do you know why Alistair came back, anyways?" she ventured to ask.

Mara and Connor shifted uncomfortably, looking uneasily at each other.

"Let's talk about it in the morning," he told her.

"You know, you say that when you're trying to fob someone off, right?" she replied, but there was no trace of anger or annoyance in her voice; it was just an observation. If they didn't want to tell her now, then she'd leave them to it until they felt like telling her.

"I knew it!" Rory muttered, looking at the two of

them, a slight note of vindication in his voice that Aoife didn't understand.

"Well, if you're not going to say any more, then I suppose we should head out too," she said, turning towards Molly.

"I'm going to stay on a bit. You go ahead," Molly said.

"No, you go on. I don't need a minder. I'll be alright." Mara hugged her. "Thanks, though."

"You let me know if you need anything," Molly instructed her. "I don't care if it's the middle of the night; you call me."

"I will, I promise."

Molly gave her a look.

"I *will*. I promise. I think we just need to talk through some things right now, just the three of us."

"We'll walk back with you." Jimmy put a comforting arm around his wife and ushered her, Molly, and Aoife towards the door.

The four of them walked in silence until they came to where the lane ran parallel to the Byrnes' property. Karen paused, obviously dreading the idea of going back to her parents' place and confronting her brother again, but they needed to pick up Mae.

"Want some company?" Molly asked them.

"I can see myself the rest of the way home." Aoife gave them both a reassuring smile in the moonlight.

"Thanks Aoife, Molly. We'll be alright." Karen gave each of them a hug and then turned to take Jimmy's hand and headed up to her parents' place.

"C'mon, let's get ye back to Colin," Molly said, turning to her and continuing down the lane. Something in Molly's tone seemed odd to her. She knew if something was on her mind that she wouldn't have to wait too long before Molly would let her know.

Sure enough, barely a minute had passed before she asked, "When is it you're planning to leave again?"

"A couple of days after the wedding."

Molly nodded. "Probably the best for everyone."

She was about to ask what exactly this meant when Molly asked, "Does Colin know you're still in love with Michael?"

Aoife was stunned. How did Molly know what had been going through her mind for the last couple of weeks?

"I'm not in love with Michael anymore," she replied, a little too hastily.

Was it really so obvious to everyone else? If so, did that mean Colin knew what had been going through her head?

Colin had always had a way of knowing what she was thinking or feeling without her even needing to say anything. No one had been able to read her quite as well as he did. It was the reason she'd been trying so hard to push away any doubts she had over leaving Ballyclara for New York. No one had been as good to her as he'd been, and she didn't want to screw up what was probably the most stable relationship she'd ever had.

But then again, there was Michael. It was undeniable that there was still something between them, even after three years apart. Colin might have a way of knowing what she was thinking most of the time, but Michael understood what was in her heart and soul in a way no one else had before. It was more than just a romantic attraction between them; Michael challenged her in ways no one else did. It infuriated her, but it also pushed her to be better than who she was. Colin loved her as she was; Michael loved her not just for who she was, but also for who he knew she could be.

"Of course, ye are, Aoife. I can't say I blame you; there's always been something about the two of you when you're in a room together. From the first moment I saw you two together, I knew there was something there."

Molly looked up at the night sky, reminiscing about that first encounter back in the pub on Aoife's first day in Ballyclara.

"I'm *not* in love with Michael Flanagan, of all people," she reiterated, trying to end this conversation before she revealed too much.

"And that little show back there was just, what?"

"I was trying to stop him from trying to throttle Alistair to death. I didn't think Rory needed to see his uncle murder his father. Even if Rory doesn't care about Alistair, he loves Michael like a father, and I was trying to spare him from seeing that darker side of him."

"You mean the side of him that fought that eejit of an ex of yours outside the pub three years ago?"

"Exactly."

"So you were just practically jumping Michael's bones all to protect Rory?"

"I wasn't jumping... That's not what happened... You're just twisting everything I say!" Aoife exclaimed, exasperated.

"He's still in love with you too, ye know," Molly said quietly, reluctantly.

Aoife's heart involuntarily leapt at this thought. Certainly, there had been moments since she'd been back that had made her wonder, but now she had actual proof from someone within Michael's inner circle about his real feelings for her.

"And that's the problem," Molly continued.

*Wait, the problem?*

"Remember when I said it wasn't just Michael you'd hurt when ye left? Well, that was certainly true. Me, Brendan, Mara, Sinead, Dermot, Des, Rory; we were all hurt by you leaving us. But no one was torn up about it more than Michael. He'd never admit to all the times that it was left to us to help pick him up and put him back together after ye swanned off, but there were a lot of them. It was Brendan, Mara, and I who had to watch him spiral and fall apart again and again until one day, something just seemed to change, and that was when he'd introduced us to Ailish."

Molly sighed.

"She's good for him, Aoife, just as Colin is good for you. I know the two of ye have this cosmic attraction thing going on, but at the end of the day, it's not enough to keep the two of ye together. What you have with Colin, and what he has with Ailish, it has the potential to be something great for you both. If you'd only just get out of each other's way. You both deserve to find the kind of happiness that won't just burn bright and then fade out but will last a lifetime."

"Like you and Brendan."

Molly nodded.

Aoife had to admit she was hurt by Molly's words. She wanted her to say that she still believed she and Michael were endgame, like she'd seemed to have done three years ago.

"But you and Brendan were meant to be together from the very start, or so Michael has said. How can you say that cosmic attraction can't keep a couple together when the two of you knew right away you were meant for each other?"

"It's true, we did. But let me ask ye this: did you

think Michael was the one for you the moment ye met him?"

Aoife almost burst out laughing. The first time she'd met him at *O'Leary's*, she'd thought him rude and arrogant, and definitely not someone she'd wanted to see again. But that didn't mean they were doomed from the start, did it? Opposites did attract, and all that. Didn't most romance novels start out that way, with the two main characters not knowing they were madly in love and then ending up happily ever after together? Or was Molly right, and that kind of attraction wasn't enough? After all, most romance novels didn't go beyond happily ever after. They didn't show you what came after, lest it ruin the fairytale.

"That's what I thought," Molly said, when Aoife remained silent. "Now let me ask ye this: when you think of your future, who is there with ye at the end? Colin, or Michael?"

She mulled over the question. Who *did* she want there at the end of her life? She knew who she *should* end up with, but that wasn't what Molly had asked her.

"You know, you and Brendan could really make a killing out of giving people advice," she replied, avoiding the question.

"Don't think we haven't thought of charging a pretty penny every time someone came to us for advice," she said, smiling.

She and Molly continued down the lane until it met the main road and continued through the heart of the village. Stopping where the main road met the lane leading to the pub, Molly stopped and said, "I don't want you to think I don't care, Aoife, or that I'm being cruel. I want to see ye both happy, I do. I just don't want to see you both throw away good relationships for something that might not last."

"Thanks for walking me home, Molly." Aoife hadn't thought that she was being intentionally cruel with her words, but they stung nevertheless, and she wanted some time on her own to think them over.

"Ye don't have to answer my question right now, but you should give it some thought before you do something ye can't take back."

Even though Aoife couldn't see Molly's face in the cold moonlight, she could tell she was being sincere.

"See you tomorrow for the rehearsal," Aoife replied, heading inside and avoiding answering Molly's earlier question.

She was good at this part, the running away from her feelings. She'd been doing it since long before she'd first stepped foot in Ballyclara, and she'd just kept on doing it in New York. Maybe it was time to finally start dealing with them, but not tonight. Tonight, she just wanted to live in denial one more time.

"See ye tomorrow," Molly said to her, before continuing on towards her home with Brendan. "I have a feeling we'll have a lot to deal with."

Chapter Eighteen

Molly had been right, of course.

Before the break of dawn, it was all over the village that Alistair Byrne had come back to Ballyclara. When Aoife, Colin, and Miriam came downstairs for their breakfast, the pub was packed with people eagerly gossiping about last night's events, like they'd been there.

"…Alistair always was a wily one. I knew he'd be back just to cause a stir…"

"…and then he and Michael looked like they were going to get into a right row. I thought there'd be blood all over the place by night's end…"

"…Looks like this'll be the end of that Dublin lad of Mara's now. I imagine we'll be hearing the wedding is off any moment now, if Alistair has anything to say about it…"

"It's a good thing he doesn't then, isn't it?" she

retorted in response to this last comment, annoyed at all the gossip surrounding her cousin and his family. Did people really think Connor would be so easily scared away by the likes of Alistair Byrne?

"People love their gossip. Don't let them get to you," Colin reminded her gently and guided her towards a booth.

As they sat down, the whole pub went quiet. She looked over her shoulder, following everyone else's gaze, and noticed Connor, Mara, and Rory had appeared. Mara's cheeks flushed bright pink at seeing everyone stare at them, and Connor and Rory both distinctly looked like they'd rather be anywhere else right now. Aoife motioned quietly to them and they hurried over to the booth, eager to get away from prying eyes.

"If ye like, you can go upstairs and have your breakfast with Des," Molly said to Rory, coming over to their table. "I'll have Brendan bring ye up something."

Rory looked at her gratefully, not even waiting to see if his mother approved or not. He was just eager to get away from anywhere public right now.

"Would you take Miriam up with you? I'd like to talk to your mam and Connor."

"Wanna come upstairs and hang out with me and Des for a bit?"

Rory did his best to smile at the little girl, trying to pretend like nothing was wrong. Miriam was too smart for that, though. She hopped out of the booth and let Rory pick her up, but whispered loudly in his ear, "Why is everyone staring at us?"

Rory patted her back as he carried her towards the back stairs. "They're just admiring how pretty ye look in that dress today."

Miriam's brow drew into a skeptical frown, but if

she said anything else, Aoife didn't hear it as the two of them went upstairs. With the children now out of earshot, she turned to Connor and Mara.

"Would it be completely callous of me to ask how the two of you are today?"

Mara tried to smile at her. "Oh, ye know, my ex-boyfriend comes back into town the day before my wedding rehearsal after not having seen him for over a decade, completely upends my son's life and makes us all the talk of the town, but ye know, typical Thursday."

She reached across the table and gave Mara's hand a comforting squeeze.

"Why the hell is Alistair back in town, anyways?"

They Mara and Connor both sighed, exchanged looks, and told her and Colin everything.

ಲ⊃ಌ

*Last night*

"Ok, everyone's gone now. Would anyone care to tell me what the hell is going on? And don't ye dare say, 'We'll talk about it in the morning.' I heard what Aoife said about how you use that phrase to fob people off when you don't want to talk about something, but I think I deserve some feckin' answers."

"Rory! Language!" his mother exclaimed, but they both knew he deserved a little leeway tonight.

Rory had the grace to look down at his feet, his cheeks a little flushed, but he did not apologize.

"You're right," Connor said after a tense moment had passed between mother and son. "This is something we should talk about right now. Let's sit down." He gestured to the island in the middle of the kitchen.

When they'd settled themselves on the stools, he looked over at Mara, wondering where the two of them should start. She reached for Rory's hand, and he reluctantly let her hold it.

"Do ye remember when the three of us talked about Connor adopting you when we got married?" She looked at Connor and gave him a small smile.

"Yeah," Rory said, looking between the two of them, connecting the dots.

"Well, we talked it over with the lawyers and drew up the papers. But, because your dad…"

"Don't call him that," Rory snapped. "Sorry… just… he's not my father. Uncle Michael and Grandda raised me, and when Connor adopts me, I want him to be my da."

Connor gave him the most heartbreaking smile.

"Thank you," he murmured, his voice thick with emotion.

"Well, because Alistair is still alive, and he's legally your parent, we had to send papers to him to relinquish his parental rights before Connor can adopt you."

Rory nodded. This all made sense.

"The lawyers tracked him down and sent him the papers. And then, I guess when he saw them, he came here."

Rory grimaced. "Well, if adopting me is going to mean involving him, then let's just not do it. I don't need a piece of paper to say you're my dad. When you marry Mam, you'll be my dad then."

"It might not be that simple." Connor reached for both of Mara's and Rory's free hands. "Alistair might want to have a role in your life."

Rory sat up straight, pulling his hands back. His

nostrils flared and an angry flush rose in his cheeks. "Like hell that's going to happen! You're not going to let him, are ye?"

Connor sighed. He couldn't blame him for feeling that way; Alistair hadn't been a father to him before and showing up here tonight, trying to bully his way into his son's life had just made things worse.

"We might not have much of a choice," he said, tentatively. He noticed the flush in Rory's cheek's deepen.

"No way! No feckin' way!" he screamed, standing up furiously, the stool he'd been sitting on crashing to the ground. "I don't care what legal rights he thinks he has. He's not my dad, and he doesn't have a right to be in my life if I don't want him to be."

He stormed out of the room, and they heard the door to his bedroom slam behind him.

"Well, that went great," Mara said sarcastically, massaging her temples. "Great talk."

༄༅

*Back in the pub*

"Wow."

Aoife wasn't sure what else she could say. It had been gnawing at her since last night, wondering what could have brought Alistair Byrne back to town. Now she knew.

"So, Rory, was what brought him back? But why? It's been my impression he hasn't even seen his son before last night."

"He hasn't," Mara replied. "As soon as he found

out I was pregnant and I was keeping Rory, he couldn't get away from his parental responsibilities fast enough."

"Bastard," Aoife muttered under her breath. "So why does he want to meet him now? Is he dying? Does he need blood or something for some rare condition?"

"No," Mara said quickly. "Or, I don't know. We haven't spoken to him since we last saw you."

"It would not surprise me if Alistair came back now because even though he may not have wanted to see his son before, he'd be damned if he'd let anyone else be Rory's father," Connor finally spoke up, his tone bitter.

Aoife raised an eyebrow at him. The news that he'd wanted to adopt Rory had caught her completely off-guard; she hadn't realized he'd even been considering it. She was reminded yet again of how things had changed so much in his life since she'd been away. Everything was moving at such a break-neck speed, she felt like she was getting whiplash.

"And when exactly *were* you planning on telling me about that?"

He looked at her sheepishly. "I kind of wanted to have the papers signed and ready before announcing it to everyone. We were hoping it would be a nice thing to surprise everyone with when we got married. Of course, we didn't exactly plan to get married so soon; we just kind of got swept up in everything."

Aoife sat back in the booth, taking in the news. Obviously, Connor had been serious about building a life with Rory and Mara – he wouldn't have proposed to her otherwise – and she knew he and Rory had grown close over the last three years, but she hadn't thought that Connor had wanted children. In many ways, she still saw a lot of her own old habits in him: the wanderlust, always looking for ways to stick it to their family, trying to stay in their Peter Pan state of never growing up. She supposed she hadn't thought of either of them as being grown up enough to settle down and start families, but here they were, the both of them in loving, stable relationships, both raising children that weren't theirs by blood. How the hell did that happen?

"I know it all seems kind of sudden to you," he said, reading her mind. "But I've wanted to adopt Rory for awhile now. Before I proposed, I talked it over with him and Mara. I know Michael and Dermot took on the father-figure role in his life before I showed up, and I don't want to interfere with that, but I wanted Rory to know that I was serious about not just marrying his mother, but about he and I being family too. I love the both of them and I wanted us all to officially be family. I just wish we hadn't had to notify Alistair about it all."

Ailish came over then, breaking up the conversation.

"I wasn't sure if you wanted anything, or if you still needed some time to talk, or if you just wanted to be left alone, but I thought I should come over and check on you." Her tone was warm and comforting as she spoke to Connor and Mara.

"Thanks, love." Mara smiled gratefully at her and gave her a breakfast order for her and Connor.

"And what'll you have?"

Although the words themselves held no offense, Ailish's tone when addressing Aoife was markedly different from how she spoke to Connor, Mara, or Colin.

*Fair enough*, she thought. It wasn't like she didn't deserve Ailish's frosty tone. After all, if she found Colin in the arms of one of his ex-lovers, wouldn't she act more than a little frosty towards them?

Or would she? Women fawned over Colin's good

looks on a fairly regular basis, and she'd never felt threatened by it. It was true that she'd never been the jealous type. At least, not until Michael, apparently. She couldn't help but remember those initial pangs of jealousy she'd experienced when she first saw Michael with Ailish and how they were at the root of all her current doubts.

Mara arched an eyebrow in Aoife's direction as she, too, noticed Ailish's tone. Aoife wondered how much of her conversation with Molly last night that Molly had told Mara. Knowing how close they were, Mara probably knew the whole thing, including how Molly thought Aoife was still in love with Michael. In fact, she wouldn't be surprised if part of what Molly had said to her last night about her feelings towards Michael had come from Mara herself. Michael's sister had rarely held back her feelings about how happy she would be about Michael and Aoife ending up together, but that was a different time, and Mara genuinely seemed to like Michael and Ailish together now. At least some part of her must have been worried about Aoife being back in town and what it would mean for Michael.

Aoife gave her order to Ailish and watched as the younger woman walked off towards the kitchen without another word. Connor gave her a "well-what-did-you-expect-after-last-night" look, but before she could give him some snarky reply, the room went silent again.

Everyone stared as the Byrnes stood in the doorway. Mr. and Mrs. Byrne looked entirely uncomfortable about being here today – even for the attention-seeking Mrs. Byrne, this was more than she'd bargained for – and looked to be quietly arguing with their son about leaving. Alistair, completely living up to his reputation as being a total jerk, ignored his parents and sauntered confidently over to where they were sitting, clearly intent on continuing his conversation with Mara from last night. Ailish, who'd been returning with an order for another table, froze as she opened the kitchen door and the plates she was holding crashed onto the floor, bringing Michael and Brendan out to see what had happened, and that's when Aoife knew the proverbial shit was going to hit the fan, and no amount of stepping in-between Michael and Alistair was going to help now.

"If I didn't make things clear last night, I'll sure as hell make 'em clear now. You are not and never will be, welcome to set foot in here again. So, you can get your feckin' arse out of my pub right now, or I'll kick ye out of it."

Alistair didn't budge.

"Michael." Brendan put a hand out in front of his best friend as he took a step forward, his voice low, warning him to think things through.

"Go on! You're not wanted here." Everyone turned to see Rory standing at the bottom of the stairs leading up to the flat above, watching the scene in front of him. He too must have come down when he'd heard the commotion.

Alistair still didn't budge.

"If ye won't leave and Uncle Michael doesn't kick your ass, then I'm more than happy to do it," he said, coming over to the group. Father and son stood locked in a showdown before Michael did something completely unexpected.

"Everybody out!" he shouted at the patrons, taking them all by surprise. Everyone looked at him, stunned for a moment, before he repeated, "Go on, I'm serious. We're closed for the rest of the day."

Never in the time she'd known Michael had he or Brendan closed the pub down early. In fact, even though he'd hated the idea at the time, he'd had to let her help him with running the place when Brendan had taken Molly away for their wedding anniversary three years ago in order to avoid having to close the pub over a busy weekend.

"What about our cheque?" someone asked.

"Just get out. We'll sort it out another time."

Everyone slowly started leaving, obviously reluctant to miss out on the show.

"Go on, ye heard the man," Brendan echoed Michael's command, ushering disgruntled patrons towards the doors, ignoring their grumbling, and trying not to look as surprised as everyone else.

"If ye won't leave of your own free will, I'll have Brendan and Connor here remove ye from the premises," Michael said to Alistair before heading for the bar once everyone else had gone. "So, what'll it be, man?"

For a moment, it looked like he might still try to pick a fight, but as Aoife expected, Alistair lacked the balls to actually initiate a fight. In one of his signature moves, he shrugged off the insult as if it didn't matter to him, and turned towards his parents.

"C'mon Mam, we don't need to stick around this shithole of a pub."

They all watched the Byrnes leave, still keeping one eye on Michael, in case he changed his mind, but he just stood behind the bar, muscular arms crossed over his chest. The only sign of tension in him was the way he clenched his jaw.

"Where'd everyone go?" Aoife and Colin both turned at the sound of Miriam's voice.

"We got worried when Rory didn't come back up," Des said, looking a bit worried at having brought her downstairs. Seeing Alistair's retreating back, and the tense way Rory stood there watching him go, he rushed over to him.

"Hey, is everything alright?" Des searched Rory's face, worry coming over his own.

"Yeah, I'm alright," Rory responded, trying to put on a smile and giving him a reassuring pat on the shoulder.

"C'mon, monkey, let's take you back upstairs," Colin said, scooping Miriam up in his arms.

"Why don't ye bring her home with us? She hasn't had her breakfast yet," Mara suggested, looking like she wanted to be anywhere else but here right now.

"Why don't we all go back to our place?" Connor suggested, giving one last glance at the door to ensure Alistair was gone. "Molly, maybe you could make us all a bite?"

"Sure, I'll just clean up the kitchen…"

"Go on, the lot of ye." Michael shooed at them with his hand. "Expectant mothers should be off their feet anyways. My orders," he said when it looked like Molly might protest. "I'll close up here. You go on up to Mara's. I'll see ye up there in a bit."

"Are ye sure?" Ailish asked him, looking worried.

"I'm alright. You lot go on up and I'll see ye soon."

She nodded, choosing to acknowledge that he wasn't going to let her in right now. She joined Connor, Mara, Molly, the boys, Colin, and Miriam as they made their way out the door.

"Alright, let's get this place cleaned up," Brendan said, picking up some plates of half-eaten food.

"I don't need a minder, Brendan. It won't take long to clean up. I'll be right along." Brendan looked like he might argue with him, but like Ailish, he acquiesced to Michael.

"Right, well, I won't complain if you want to do the work for once." He winked at him, put down the plates, and followed the others.

"Coming?" Colin called to Aoife, and she realized she was still standing there awkwardly.

"Yeah, I'll be right up. I forgot something upstairs. I'll catch up with you."

Colin gazed at her for half a second, then over at Michael, sizing up the situation. He nodded and swung Miriam onto his shoulders, leaving with the rest of their party.

"You don't have to be my minder either, Aoife." Michael gazed at her from behind the bar, his blue eyes seeming to pierce through her white lie.

"I don't know what you're talking about," she pretended like he couldn't see right through her.

He just shrugged and went about cleaning up. She didn't actually have to get anything, and she *was* just sticking around to check on him, but damned if she was going to admit that to him.

"Well, if you're going to keep up with the pretence, then you might as well help, I suppose. But don't screw anything up." He tossed her the towel he usually had slung over his shoulder when he was working.

"What's there to screw up?" she asked, wiping down the bar, leaving him to do the dishes, and the two of them went about their business in a comfortable silence.

When all of the tables had been cleared and wiped down, Michael went to the bar. "Pint?" he asked her.

"It's not even close to noon!"

"You've sure changed your tune from 'it's 4 PM somewhere,'" he said, pouring himself half a pint.

"I'm not the only one who's changed, it would

seem. I could've sworn you were going to beat the shit out of Alistair earlier. Your restraint was a terribly grown-up response from a man who's more used to settling scores with his fists than with his words."

Michael shrugged at her again, but she could see that he was pleased that she thought he'd changed. "I guess I finally decided that I wanted to be a better example for Rory and Des."

That he certainly was. She'd always considered him to be a good father-figure for his nephew and godson, but there was something about him now that was more mature, more aware of how his actions affected those around him.

"Ailish is good for you," she blurted out.

Did she really just say that? It was awkward for her, his ex, to be talking about his current girlfriend, right? So far, every time they'd talked about Ailish or Colin, it had been awkward. So why did she have to bring her up right now?

Michael arched his brow at her comment.

"She's been an excellent influence on you, I mean," she stammered, trying to sound normal. "The Michael I knew would've been the first one to throw a punch at Alistair, or at least would have been quick to retaliate. I mean, just think about the last time you had a fight here."

*Oh good, Aoife, let's just bring up the time Michael beat up your ex-boyfriend…*

She and Michael hadn't broken up because of the fight with Danny, but it had been the start of things going downhill for the two of them, and now she'd reminded him of it. She could tell by the way he winced slightly.

"I seem to remember that it didn't seem to matter

to you who threw the first punch in that fight. You still went running after him," he replied, his voice sounding flat.

"I seem to remember telling him to leave me the hell alone and coming home to you that night," she retorted, reminding him of some important facts he was leaving out.

"So that sexy nurse looking after me was you, then?" he teased.

Aoife felt a blush rising in her cheeks at the memory of that night.

*Oh lordy.*

How did he still have such power over her? She coughed politely, trying to think of a way to change the subject, but Michael seemed to want to pursue the current conversation.

"Tell me, if I'd given Alistair Byrne what he deserved earlier, would you have chosen me first this time?"

She continued to blush under his direct, blue-eyed gaze before finally asking, "So, does this mean you would have preferred I'd sent you packing that night and ended up with Danny instead? Because I think coming in second had some pretty big bonuses for you."

Michael mulled this over a moment, remembering their night together, and a sly smile formed on his lips. "When you put it that way, I suppose not."

"Well, there you go."

"Although, I have to say, if I could go back and change things, I wouldn't have let Danny get in quite so many punches."

"You deserved every single one of those," she reminded him. "Never in the history of this world has fighting with one's fists ever solved a problem."

"Now you sound like Brendan," he chuckled. "He sure likes to get on that real high horse of his sometimes."

"It seems to me he's about the only sensible man in all of Ballyclara, except for Father Patrick, or your father."

Michael gave her a look of mock hurt, making her laugh. "I'm offended."

"Go cry to Ailish then. Get her to kiss your wounds better."

*Shit, Aoife, why do you keep bringing her up?*

A funny look came over his face, the banter over. "At least she'd know what she was doing."

It was her turn to raise her brow at him.

"She worked in the hospital where Da was recovering after his heart attack. It's where we met, after…"

*After I left.*

She sighed, annoyed with herself for always turning their conversation back to the past every time things seemed to be going well. Why did she always have to self-sabotage when it came to him?

"Well, I'm glad things worked out for the two of you," she blurted, trying to mask her disappointment.

"Yeah." A slightly sad look came over his face.

How could he be sad about being with Ailish? She was great, even if Aoife still felt jealous about it.

"Well, we better head up to Mara's. I'm already later than I said I'd be." She looked at her phone and noticed it was now nearing noon. She still hadn't eaten anything and her stomach growled embarrassingly loud.

"Go on. I'll lock up and be right behind you," he told her.

"You sure? If I leave you alone, you promise not to go and find Alistair and tarnish this new-and-improved mature Michael you are trying to be?"

"Don't tempt me," he replied, only semi-jokingly. "Go on. I'm right behind ye. Besides, if we walk up together, it will ruin the pretense that you weren't staying behind to help me."

She nodded, grabbing her purse and headed for the door, excited for some of Molly's cooking.

## Chapter Nineteen

"So, Connor, you'll stand here." Father Patrick positioned Connor on his left, moving him where he wanted. "And Aoife, you'll stand here."

He moved her slightly to the left of Connor until he had them where he wanted.

"Alright, now Rory and Desmond, you two will come down with Mae." He motioned for the two lads to walk down with little Mae toddling between them.

"And then, Karen, yes, yes, you come forward. And then Molly, you will come down and stand here." He placed her on his right, leaving just enough space for the bride.

"And then the music will start, and Michael, you will walk Mara down the aisle and stand here."

Michael linked his arm with his sister and processed down the aisle to the front of the little parish church.

Was that a wink Michael gave her as he handed Mara over to Connor? Before their flirty banter earlier today, Aoife might have doubted it more, but she was pretty certain that Michael Flanagan was flirting with her again. She didn't have time to silently chastise him, for Father Patrick drew her attention back to the task at hand, walking them all through the ceremony.

With the rehearsal done, they all headed down to the pub where Brendan, Ailish, Karen and Jimmy had been working on decorating the place for the rehearsal dinner.

"It's beautiful!" Mara took in the decorated tables set up for their dinner.

"If ye think this is nice, ye should see what we have planned for the reception." Ailish motioned for everyone to take their seats.

"I'm glad ye're home, Aoife," Father Patrick said, taking his seat next to her.

She smiled at the elderly priest sitting on her left.

"I wasn't sure how our man Michael would feel about it all, but I think he's happy now to have ye back, too."

*Funny*, she thought, *because he doesn't seem to even notice I exist anymore.*

She was so confused by him today. First, they were practically flirting with one another earlier, and now they were down here in the pub, it was like he only had eyes for Ailish from the moment they walked in. The two of them were canoodling at the table right across from her, in plain view of everyone.

*And so it should be*, her subconscious reminded her.

She wanted to tell her subconscious right where it could shove its attempts to remind her that she shouldn't be feeling this level of jealousy, considering how it had been toying with her this whole time. She *did* feel jealous, and she wanted to feel justified in sulking about it.

"You think?" she asked, a little more sarcastically than she should have, still watching the happy couple.

"Green might be a beautiful colour on you," he said, nodding at her emerald-green silk peplum dress she'd chosen to wear tonight because she knew it would make her look chic, "but jealousy is not an emotion that looks good on ye, Aoife O'Reilly."

She nearly choked on her sip of wine. She'd forgotten both how observant the old man was, and how forthright he was in relaying his observations. Was Father Patrick really chastising her now, like a child? And how did he know what was going through her mind? Was she walking around with a gigantic neon sign over her head detailing what she was thinking all the time?

She'd always felt she'd been good at hiding her emotions from everyone around her but, since meeting Michael, she'd been feeling that resolve to shut herself off from the rest of the world fading. That's what Michael Flanagan had done to her: made her a less closed-off person, and Colin had only further enabled this behaviour, forcing her to be open and honest with herself. Back in New York, Bex and Millie had been happy at this turn of events, pleased she was becoming "more of a real human being" dealing with her feelings and such, but right now, she wanted just a bit of the old Aoife back, the one who ran from her feelings so she wouldn't have to deal with them. The one who was good at pretending like she never got hurt.

"You might find this difficult to believe, but our Michael was devastated after ye left for New York."

As a priest, he was naturally a keeper of secrets, but

he'd proven in the time she'd known him that he wasn't afraid to give his parishioners a good shove in the right direction – or a knock upside the head – if he felt it was warranted. She'd been sort of avoiding him her whole time back in Ballyclara for this very reason, afraid that he'd give her exactly the advice she needed, even if it wasn't what she wanted to hear.

"Oh, I know."

She looked down at her wine glass, pretending like it was the most interesting thing in the world to look at. It helped distract her from looking at the action going on across the table, at least.

"Molly told me in no uncertain terms how hurt he was and how I should never have waltzed back into his life."

*Bitter much?* she asked herself. Clearly, she was still smarting a bit from that conversation.

"Oh, I don't think she didn't want ye to come back," he replied, trying to be fair. "I think we all understand that ye did what you thought was right at the time. And it seems that decision brought you a lot of happiness."

He watched as Colin helped serve everyone with the delicious coq au vin Molly had left Karen to prepare while they'd been at the rehearsal. Since Ailish seemed to be more preoccupied with staring into Michael's eyes than with serving, he'd obviously stepped in to help.

She sighed. He was too perfect for the likes of her.

"He's a good man, your Colin, and it can't have been easy to come back here, knowing what people might think of ye, and how it might put what you have with your man Colin in jeopardy," Father Patrick pressed on. "I'm proud of you for coming anyways. Even if Michael won't admit it, he needed you here to help him get through Dermot's passing."

She glanced sideways at the priest, wondering what he could possibly know that she didn't. She didn't feel like she'd been helping Michael through anything these past few weeks. Not at all. In fact, she'd mostly felt like she'd just been making everything worse and more confusing for the both of them by being here, but Connor and Mara's continuing family/wedding drama kept forcing her to stick around.

She felt a pang of guilt for how all this drama had gotten in the way of her being there for him when he could've used her here as a friend to talk to. She really should've tried being there more for Michael since coming back. He'd been so close to his father, and with him gone now, at least some small part of him had to be feeling adrift without him. She knew she certainly could use some of Dermot's advice right now. Even if the two of them were no longer together, it didn't mean that they couldn't still be there for each other, right?

She vowed that tonight was the night she would put aside this petty jealousy she felt over his happiness with Ailish and focus on being a friend to Michael. They could do that, right? Just be friends?

"Earth to Aoife!" Connor's voice cut through her musings.

"Hmmm?"

"I was asking you if you had your best man/person speech ready?" He studied her face, looking a bit concerned at seeing her look so introspective.

"Oh, right," she said, remembering she still had to write that. In the hastiness of putting together this wedding at the last minute, she'd forgotten that, as Connor's best person, she still needed to do that.

"Of course! Got it all right here." She tapped her

temple and smiled at him.

"Bullshit."

He knew her all too well.

"It'll be perfect in time for the wedding, I promise."

"It'd better be," he replied, before having his attention taken by something Mara whispered to him on his other side.

She put down "write speech" on her mental list of tasks that still needed to be done before the wedding. She turned to Father Patrick to talk to him more about what he meant about Michael needing her back here, but he'd been pulled into a conversation with Colin, Jimmy, and Karen, who'd sat down on his left.

She added "talk to Michael" to the mental list. It was time she started acting more mature and started putting their past behind them as well.

༺☙❧༻

Figuring that there was no time like the present to begin her journey towards putting the past behind her, she took a moment when Colin was carrying Miriam upstairs, and Ailish was helping Molly finish some things in the kitchen, to corner Michael.

"Can I walk you home?"

"Sure…" He cocked his head to the side, curious about her request. If she were being honest, she was just as surprised at her own forthright behaviour. "Let me just grab my jacket and we can head out."

She fought the urge to cut and run while she waited for him, reminding herself that she was now an adult who dealt with complicated feelings and situations rather than running from them. Besides, she was doing this as much for him as for herself. She wanted him to know she was there for him. As a friend, nothing else. She could be a new-and-improved Aoife too.

"Ready?" he asked, putting his jacket over his arm, and heading for the door.

*No, but this is as ready as I'm going to get.*

She followed him out into the cool summer night air, illuminated by the moon hanging like a great white orb in the sky. An immediate sense of peace and coziness washed over her. It was the first time since coming back that she felt almost serene, like how she used to feel when she was with the Flanagans. The wind rustling through the leaves brushed across her skin, sending up goose pimples. She'd forgotten to bring something warm to put over her dress, momentarily forgetting that summers in Ireland were cooler than in America.

"Here." Michael took his jacket and draped it over her shoulders.

She pulled it closer around her, lost for a moment in the familiar scent of aftershave, cigarettes, and the outdoors: Michael's scent, the one that took her back through so many memories all at once.

The two of them walked along in an old, familiar silence for a bit before she finally spoke up. "I've been meaning to ask you how you've been. Since Dermot's funeral."

He didn't respond right away, looking ahead into the dark night.

"I'm alright," he said, and gave her a small smile. "I miss him all the time, every day. I can't count the number of times I've wanted to walk over to his and Mam's place and just talk to him about nothing… and everything."

Even in the dark, she could see those piercing blue eyes directed at her, and she knew he was talking about her.

"Me too," she admitted. "I know I didn't have near as close a relationship as you did with your father, obviously, but I always found Dermot to be one of the best listeners I've ever met. I'm sorry he's gone."

"You must have felt much the same when you lost your grandda. I know he wasn't your father, but he was near enough to one. I'm sorry I never did get the chance to meet him."

She nodded. She'd dealt with her grandfather's death in a far more destructive manner that Michael was dealing with his father's death, spiralling into depression, anxiety, and a tendency to over drink. It was only when she'd come out of the haze that she'd found her way here, to this place – to Michael – who'd helped get her through the darkest time in her life.

"You'd have liked him, and he would have loved you." She smiled, imagining what it would have been like introducing him to Paddy O'Reilly.

"What?" he asked, curious to know what she was thinking.

"I was just thinking that the two of you aren't so different, really. You're more short-tempered and *way* more stubborn than my grandfather." She looked at him to make her point, and he rolled his eyes at her. "But, in a lot of ways, the two of you aren't so different. You're capable of the same kindness – when you want to be – and you both love deeply and unconditionally."

He smiled at her.

"Now what are *you* thinking about?" she asked, noticing he had the same expression on his face that she'd probably had just a moment ago.

## Where I'm Home

"Nothing. I was just thinking that's probably one of the nicest compliments I've ever gotten. Apart from the 'short-tempered and stubborn' part, which I most certainly am not." He held up a hand to cut off her protest. "But, knowing how much you loved your grandfather, I think it's a great compliment that you think I'm in any way like him."

She blushed under his smile.

"I'm glad, at least, that I got to know your father. I'm sorry I haven't really been there for you since I came back, Michael. Even with everything that's gone on between us, I still want to feel like we can be there for one another when we need it."

He seemed to think about this for a moment and simply nodded, as if he was a little overwhelmed by what she'd said. They slowed and drew to a stop as they reached his cottage.

"Here," she said, handing him back his jacket.

"No, no. Hold on to it for me." He readjusted it on her shoulders. "You'll want it on the walk back."

She paused a moment, not sure what else she should say without making things awkward between them again. She'd taken a step in the right direction tonight; maybe she should just leave it there for the moment.

"Thanks. I'll get it back to you tomorrow."

"It's not like I don't know where you're at, Aoife. And it's just a jacket. I'm not too worried," he said, smiling down at her.

"Well, I'll be seeing you then."

Why was she lingering? She should just leave now before she broke her mature streak and said something stupid to ruin the moment. She needed to leave now and let this moment stay perfect.

"'Night, Michael."

She started back down the path to the village, leaving him standing outside of his place.

"Aoife?" he called out to her.

"Yeah?"

"Thanks. For everything. I know I haven't shown it, but it means a lot to me that you came back."

She could see that he was being sincere. Father Patrick had been right; he was, inexplicably, happy to have her here. She smiled and headed back to the pub, feeling more relaxed than she'd felt since coming back to Ballyclara.

## Chapter Twenty

It was the day before the wedding and there was just one more tradition they needed to do: the stag and hen parties. Since there was only one pub in the village, and they hadn't wanted to do a combined party, Mara had graciously said that Connor and the guys could go to the pub for his stag do, while she had a girls' night in at her place.

"Aoife, I know you're technically part of Connor's groom's party, but if you'd like, I'd love to have you join Mam, Molly, Karen, Ailish, and I at my place for my hen do," Mara had told her when it came time to plan their night in.

"Pizza, wine, ice cream, bad romance films… who could turn that down?" she'd grinned at her.

And so, Michael and Brendan had put themselves in charge of planning Connor's stag do, while she joined

Mara's party.

"You lads bring him home safe and sound," Mara instructed her brother and his friends as she relinquished her husband-to-be into their hands.

"Will do!" Michael replied, crossing his heart in mock seriousness.

"Have a great night." Colin kissed Aoife lightly, leaving her with Mara and the others. Brendan had made sure to include him tonight, for which she was grateful. She knew it meant a lot to him to be included with the other guys.

"C'mon, Colin; it's not like you're not going to see our Aoife in a few hours. Come and have some fun with us." Brendan grabbed him by the shoulders and steered him back towards the pub.

"Behave yourself." Michael winked at her before joining the others.

She looked over her shoulder, sure he must have been talking to Ailish, but she'd already gone inside with the other women.

"Don't worry about me; I'm the one who knows how to hold my liquor, remember?" she called out to his retreating back.

He turned around and grinned devilishly at her, remembering exactly the number of times she'd claimed to be able to hold her alcohol and he'd ended up having to look after her.

A flush rose in her cheeks as she remembered what little she could of those times, and turned to go inside, lest he see what she was thinking.

"Who's ready to get this party started?!" Ailish called out gleefully, pouring the wine.

"I hope you lot know the things I give up for you," Molly grumbled to her pregnant belly and sipped on her water, looking enviously at the others.

"It's worth it, though, right?" Ailish asked.

"Yeah, it is." Molly unconsciously rubbed her belly. "Although, I don't know how we could possibly get as lucky this time around as we did with Des. He was such a delightful baby; hardly fussed, slept through the night earlier than most do… I can't imagine with the twins that we're going to see sleep for a long time."

"Twins?! You're having twins?" Mara exclaimed.

"We just found out this morning." Molly grinned, both pleased and a little sheepish that she hadn't told her best friend right away.

"We have another thing to toast to now!" Ailish exclaimed. "Everyone raise your glasses in honour of our wonderful Mara, the beautiful bride-to-be, and to Molly and Brendan, and the twins!"

They clinked their glasses and took a long sip.

"Well now, when are you and Michael going to be having little ones of your own?" Sinead asked with the abruptness only the elderly can get away with.

Aoife looked up from her glass, finding herself both intrigued by, and dreading, Ailish's answer.

"In the next few years, I imagine. We haven't really talked about it. I'd like to be married first, I think."

"You'd do well to get pregnant now and lock that one down before he knows what's good for him," Molly advised her. "Brendan and I waited until after Des was a bit older to get married, and it hasn't hurt us in the slightest."

"What about you, Aoife? Have you and Colin talked about having more children?"

Aoife could feel everyone's eyes on her as she occupied herself with piling her plate with pizza and re-filling her wine glass. She was going to need a lot of these tonight, if this was the direction the conversation was going to go.

"We haven't really talked about it," she replied cautiously. "We have our hands full enough with Miriam right now."

"I'm sure she must want siblings, though? You might want to get on that, unless you want there to be a huge age gap between them."

"Says the woman who's got a pre-teen and is pregnant with twins!" she retorted gently. She wasn't trying to offend, but she also didn't like all this talk about her uterus and what she was planning to do with it when she hadn't quite figured that all out yet.

"Yes, well, what can I say? Des came along much earlier than we'd planned," Molly shrugged.

"Besides like Ailish says, there's the matter of us getting married first," Aoife pointed out.

Ailish had still been a bit off with her ever since the night Alistair had returned. Maybe if she tried to forge some kind of connection with her now, maybe the two of them could approach something resembling friendship. Yes, that would be a good thing. It would prove she was being a grown-up, and that she and Michael could move past whatever it was between them.

Ailish looked at her, but said nothing.

"Pssshh," Sinead snorted. "It's all very progressive in America these days. Ye don't need to be married in order to have children. Sure, and look at Molly and Brendan, or even our Mara."

"Mam! You've certainly changed your tune!" Mara exclaimed in surprise. "And it's not like I planned on *not* being married when I found out I was pregnant with Rory."

"Yes, well, even I can see that things are more progressive nowadays," Sinead replied, slightly offended by the reproach that she wasn't up to date with the times.

"Considering how my brother turned out, I think

you were lucky he didn't want to get married when he found out about Rory," Karen said, taking a bite of her pizza. They all nodded their approval to this statement.

"And where was this progressive attitude when Rory came along?" Mara still couldn't move past her mother's earlier comment.

Sinead was saved from answering by the sound of the doorbell ringing.

"Who could that be?" she asked, getting up and heading towards the door.

"Don't think you're off the hook just yet!" Mara called out to her.

Sinead opened the door to a deliveryman holding a big white box in his hands.

"I have a delivery for a Mara Flanagan," he said, looking at the slip of paper in his hands. Sinead turned towards her daughter.

"Were you expecting anything to be delivered, dear?"

Mara shook her head. "No, I didn't order anything..."

"I did!" Aoife sprang from the stool she was sitting on and headed for the door excitedly.

The moment she'd heard that Mara and Connor were planning on getting married, she'd phoned Bex in New York and asked her to design a wedding dress. It was a little out of the norm for what she usually designed, but when Aoife had given her the concept, she'd happily acquiesced. Knowing that Mara would think splashing out on a wedding dress would be too much of an expense and would just choose something out of her own closet to wear down the aisle, Aoife had wanted to do something nice for her and buy her a dress of her own, especially after her dress tryouts had been ruined by Alistair showing up. So, she'd put Bex to work and had had her courier it over as soon as she could.

She went over to the deliveryman, signed the form he held out to her, and took the box from him, bringing it back and presenting it to Mara.

"I hope I wasn't being too forward by doing this, but I wanted to get you something special for your wedding. Something I knew you would never get for yourself."

Mara looked at her, intrigued. Taking the box from her, she opened it up to reveal the dress. It was a knee-length white tulle, strapless dress; simple, but stunning. Bex had also designed a short, beaded jacket to go over the top. Mara's face looked at it in wonderment.

"This is too much, Aoife. I can't accept. You've already done so much for us; I couldn't accept something so expensive."

"It's a gift, and I want you to have it," Aoife insisted. "Unless you hate it, of course, in which case I would never want you to feel obligated to wear it."

"Hate it? It's stunning! I just feel bad about you spending so much money on me."

"Pfft, don't worry about it. Call it my wedding gift to you."

"Ok, but I hope this means you didn't also buy us a wedding gift for the reception."

"Umm…" Aoife paused, wondering if she could plausibly deny that she and Colin had also gotten them a proper wedding gift. "Pretend that one's from Colin and Miriam?"

"You're too good to me," Mara said, pulling her into a hug.

"Alright, who's ready now for some pizza and movies?" Karen asked, grabbing some of the wine bottles and leading the way to the sitting room. "It's time to get this hen party started!"

## Where I'm Home

Mara gave Aoife another quick hug before packing up the dress and stowing it away so nothing would get on it.

They all moved to the sitting room, plunking themselves down on the sofa, ready to watch whatever rom-coms Karen had chosen for the night. This wasn't normally Aoife's scene when it came to films, but since she wasn't the bride, she couldn't really say anything.

"Isn't it curious how men in these films always go back to the women who broke their hearts, when the ones who love them the most are standing right there in front of them, and they still pass them up?" Ailish asked, perusing the DVD's Karen had brought with her.

Everyone glanced over at her and Aoife, knowing that she was talking about her.

Aoife silently took a long sip of wine, then reached for the bottle to fill her glass again. Clearly, Ailish was still not ready to let the other night go.

This was going to be one long night.

ೞಠ

By midnight, the pizza had been eaten, sappy love films had been watched, and more alcohol than Aoife's liver cared to think about had been drunk. Sinead, Karen, and Ailish had left an hour ago, all stating that they needed to get their rest for tomorrow. Aoife was pretty sure that, for Ailish's part anyways, she was just trying to get as far away from Aoife as possible.

Not really feeling the need to go home right away, Aoife had lingered on with Mara and Molly. She lounged on Mara's sofa, still feeling zero inclination to walk back down to the pub, especially now that the wine had hit her. She usually wasn't a wine drinker, but it had been what was going around, and there had been no way she was going to face Ailish's snide comments without the fortification of booze. She was going to have one hell of a hangover in the morning.

"I'm just going to sleep right here, ok?" she mumbled, closing her eyes, so close to drifting off.

"Oh no ye don't." Molly's entirely too sober voice cut through the sleepy haze trying to envelop her. "If you sleep there for the night, your back will be killing you tomorrow, and that's the last thing you'll want when you have to be on your feet all day."

Molly poked and prodded her, eliciting a few annoyed groans before Aoife reluctantly found her way to her feet. As she was stumbling slightly towards the door, it opened, revealing Michael and Brendan carrying a clearly drunk Connor between them.

"Well, looks like you lot had fun," Mara said, coming over to help with her inebriated fiancé.

"I'd call it a pretty successful night, if I do say so myself," Brendan replied, clearly pleased with himself for planning the night. "Alright mate, let's get ye upstairs."

Brendan steered Connor towards his and Mara's bedroom.

"Looks like you didn't do so bad yerself." Michael nodded towards the many bottles and pizza boxes strewn about the kitchen.

"We may have had a little fun," Aoife said, trying to stifle a giggle and not quite managing to. She wasn't sure what she found funny, but she found that right now, her brain didn't seem to be working the way it usually did.

"Oh, you did, did ye?" Michael was watching her, a bemused smirk on his lips.

She wanted to smack it right off his handsome face, but she was pretty sure if she tried to move from this spot right now, she would fall into his arms, which would not have quite the effect she was going for.

*Oh God, if I can't stand up now, how will I be in the morning?*

How was she going to stand up in front of a church full of people when she could barely stand upright without the support of the wall behind her right now?

"Just let me die here in peace…"

She didn't realize she'd said it out loud.

"Jaysus, Mary, and Joseph, how much did you let her drink tonight?"

"One, I'm not her minder. She's an adult; she knows her limits. Two, it's not like she can't normally out-drink the best of us."

Mara watched her leaning up against the wall, clearly getting cranky as sleep deprivation and alcohol took their toll on the bride-to-be.

Nope, Mara's statement was false. Aoife definitely didn't remember her limits on alcohol, and the version of Aoife who could out-drink everyone around her had definitely left the building a long time ago.

"Here, take this."

Michael went to the cupboard and brought down a bottle of Paracetamol and poured her a glass of water. Clearly, he could see the beginning stages of Mara's cranky side and wanted to head it off at the pass. He handed her both and kissed her gently on the top of her head.

"Now, off to bed with ye. You have a big day tomorrow. I'll take care of this one." He pointed his thumb in Aoife's direction.

Mara did as she was told and went upstairs to bed.

"You sure ye don't want us to walk her home?" Molly asked.

"I don't think Brendan's going to be going anywhere tonight."

He nodded towards his softly snoring friend who was stretched out on the couch Aoife had recently vacated. After depositing Connor upstairs, he must have gone straight for the sofa and fell asleep.

"You might as well take Rory's bed for the night. Mam's got him and Des staying over with her, so he won't be needing it, and there's no need for you to be walking all the way back home only to come right back here first thing in the morning to get ready."

Molly nodded, agreeing with him. "I'll just tidy this place up then, and head upstairs. Don't you two stay out too late." She gave him a friendly peck on the cheek and motioned for them to get out from under foot while she tidied up Mara's kitchen.

"C'mon you. Let's get you home." Michael indicated for Aoife to head outside.

"I'm perfectly capable of walking myself home, Michael Flanagan," she said with far more certainty than she felt.

Why did the stars above her look like they were all swirling about all of a sudden?

"Sure, ye can," he chuckled, catching her as she stumbled slightly, bumping into him. She brushed away his hand, determined to walk on her own. He put up his hands in surrender, letting her lead the way down the road to the village, always staying just one step behind her, ready to catch her if she happened to stumble again.

Secretly, she was relieved that he was there. She knew she definitely was not going to be able to walk all the way home in these strappy heels she'd worn. Sure, they'd been fine on the walk over, and she knew they looked super cute with the black cocktail dress she'd worn for the hen party, but they were killing her feet now. She stopped in the middle of the road and put a hand out that somehow found its way onto Michael's shoulder, providing her with the perfect balance she needed.

"What are ye doing?" he asked her as she leaned down.

"I can't walk in these," she stated, as if it was completely obvious and kicking off her heels. The pavement felt cool but gravelly beneath her feet.

"Oh no ye don't," he said, turning around so he could scoop her up in his arms and grab her shoes at the same time. "We can't have ye wandering around barefoot out here. God knows what you might step on, and I'm not going to be the one to take you to A&E."

"Put me down!" she demanded, even though the thought of being carried sounded a lot more fun than having to walk all the way by herself. "You can't carry me all the way to the pub. I'm too heavy."

"Heavy? What are ye talking about? You're all skin and bones now. Are the Americans starving you over there? And stop fidgeting!"

He shifted her in his arms to get a better grip on her. She circled her arms around his neck, trying to help him out.

"I'm not skin and bones. By American standards, I'm fat."

She'd never been a particularly athletic person in her life, but she wouldn't have considered herself overweight either, at least, not until moving to America where every woman she met seemed to exist solely for yoga, the gym, flavoured water, and talking about all the things they were *not* eating that week. She tried her best to not buy into this mentality, but it was difficult to not feel pressured to look a certain way when it was around you *all the damn time*.

"Then they've been dropped on their heads more than a few times because you most certainly are not fat. You were perfect the way you were before ye left." He gave her a stern look, as if to emphasize his point.

She turned her face towards his chest, trying to conceal the smile that came across her face as he called her perfect.

They were coming up on Aldridge Manor, and she sighed. "Home."

Michael looked down at her and then followed her gaze, a smile coming across his face. A cool breeze brushed past them, and she snuggled in closer to him, instinctively seeking out his body heat. She yawned sleepily and closed her eyes, feeling cocooned in safety and warmth. She must have dozed off for a bit because the next thing she knew, Michael had stopped, and she saw the back door to the pub.

He gently put her down on the ground and opened the door for her. They walked into the kitchen, and he immediately went for the cupboards, rooting around for something.

"What are you doing?" she asked, standing around, still in a bit of a daze. She stifled a yawn with the back of her hand.

"Ah ha!" he said triumphantly, placing a bottle of Paracetamol on the counter in front of her. Grabbing a glass, he filled it with water and brought it over to her, but did not produce the kiss on the head like he'd done for his sister earlier.

She wasn't sure what had made her do it, whether it was the wine or the fact he'd gallantly carried her all the way home, or that he'd called her "perfect," or just because she wanted to, but she took the glass and set it on the counter beside her and leaned in to kiss him. And not just in the friendly, on-the-cheek kind of kiss either, but the soft, tender kind.

He tasted of beer and cigarettes and crisps, but it was heaven to her. Taken aback by her forwardness, Michael's body tensed at her touch, his hands unsure of where to go. Eventually, he settled into putting a hand gently on one side of her face and another on the small of her back, pulling her closer to him. All too quickly, the moment ended as he pushed himself away from her.

"Aoife…" His voice was rough with conflicting emotions: desire, longing, regret, and so many more. She knew these all too well because she was experiencing them all at this moment, too. She wanted to regret the kiss on account of all the trouble it was going to cause them both, but right in this moment, she couldn't bring herself to do it.

"I know. I'm perfect." She grinned up at him, hoping to break some of the tension in the room.

He smirked and then sighed. "That wasn't what I was going to say…"

She put a finger over his lips. "I know, but let's just leave it there for tonight."

She removed herself from his grasp and headed towards the back steps that led to the flat upstairs, not looking back. If she did, she was afraid she just might do something neither of them could entirely blame on the alcohol.

## Chapter Twenty-One

The women gathered at Mara's cottage the next morning. Still tired and a little hungover from the night before, they were all a little worse for wear. Even though Aoife was technically part of the groom's party, she'd decided the week before that it would be far easier to get ready with Mara and her bridesmaids. After last night's kiss, she was certain that the last place she wanted to be was at Michael's place today.

Thank God for the alcohol, because she was sure if she hadn't fallen asleep in a stupor as soon as her head hit the pillow last night, she'd have been up all night going over every second of that kiss. What the hell had she been thinking?!

Despite the hangover, she'd still woken up quite early, Colin and Miriam still sound asleep beside her. She got up, careful not to wake either of them, and went down to the kitchen, the scene of the crime. Her shoes were on the floor by the counter, the painkillers and water still on the countertop. She emptied the glass and refilled it with fresh water, taking some of the pills. She was going to need a clear head today.

When the sun had crested the hills, she walked up to Mara's place with Miriam. Connor and Rory were still in the kitchen having a bite of toast when she arrived.

"Out with the both of ye," Sinead commanded, coming in behind Aoife, snatching a piece of toast from Rory's hand just as he was about to take a bite.

"Hey!" he protested, but thought better of sassing his grandmother, lest he get boxed 'round the ears.

"Out," Aoife echoed her command, but directed it towards Connor this time. "It's bad luck to see the bride before the wedding. Off to Michael's with the both of you. You're going to be late!"

"We've got ages before you lot are ready. Sure, and you'll take forever to get ready," he teased and laughed as he dodged a slap from his cousin. "C'mon Rory. Let's leave this lot to their beautifying."

The two of them made their way through the throng of clothes bags Molly and Karen were bringing in from the car and headed out towards Michael's place, where the rest of the guys would be getting ready. With them finally out of the way, the women set themselves to the task of getting the bride ready for her big day.

Everything was a flurry of hair, makeup, tulle, heels, fake eyelashes and nail polish, but after a few hours of prep, Mara and her wedding party were all ready to go to the church.

"Don't you look beautiful!" Sinead exclaimed, seeing her daughter standing there in the wedding dress Bex had made her. They'd pulled Mara's dark hair back from her face into a half-up/half-down hairdo, with the ends curling slightly around her face, framing it. They had intertwined little wildflowers throughout her hair, giving her a slightly ethereal look.

Mae gasped. "You look so pretty!"

"Are you a princess?" Miriam asked, making them all laugh.

"See Bex? I told you it would look gorgeous on her! Even the girls agree." Aoife held her phone up to show Bex her creation via video chat. Her stunning Greek-American features drew into an intense stare, examining every piece of her creation, trying to find any potential flaws, like an artist scrutinizes their canvas.

"Thank you so much for the dress, Bex. It's gorgeous. Seriously, you should think of doing a bridal line."

"See? Even Mara agrees with me." Millie's face popped up on the screen beside Bex. She'd dyed her hair an all-too-sensible-looking black since the last time Aoife had seen her, but spiced up her look in typical Millie fashion with a flamboyantly coloured scarf around her neck. "I've been telling her that forever!"

"Only if you agree to be my model," Bex teased.

"Now, Mrs. Flanagan, wipe those tears before you get everyone's make-up running. You have a long day ahead, you all," she instructed, seeing Sinead tearing up at seeing her daughter in her dress.

"I'll do my best!" she said, dabbing at her eyes with a Kleenex.

"Now, show me how yours turned out," Bex commanded.

Aoife handed her phone to Karen and did a bit of a twirl to show off the dress Bex had made her. It was a short, one-shouldered chiffon dress in royal blue to bring out the colour in her eyes. Simple, but elegant.

"You look stunning!"

"Oooh, Colin's not going to know what hit him when he sees you, gorgeous lady!" Millie winked at her appreciatively, making Aoife grin and blush. "Now, where are those boys? Where's the other eye candy?"

"They're over at Michael's getting ready."

Millie pouted. "Well, you're just going to have to send us pics then!"

"Tell Connor that we wish him and Mara all the best. Aoife, I expect to hear all the details tomorrow. Oh, and someone better grab the girls before they get make-up all over themselves."

Bex smiled and waved before signing off. Karen turned around just as Mae was about to put her fingers into some eye shadow and deftly took it away from her before she could get it on her dress.

"You're so pretty, Aoife!" Miriam said, hugging her leg.

"Thank you, sweetie." She knelt down and placed a kiss on top of her head, careful not to mess up the braid Miriam had allowed Molly to make for her because it matched Mae's hair.

"Is it safe to come in?" They could hear Colin's voice coming from the porch step.

"Daddy!" Miriam ran towards the door and jumped up in his arms.

"Well, now, don't you look like the most beautiful girl in the world?" he asked, kissing his daughter's cheek.

Aoife went to the door and opened it up for him. He was dressed in the same smart suit and tie he'd worn the night he'd met her family, looking as impossibly handsome as ever. He'd volunteered to drive the bride and her mother to the church so their dresses wouldn't get dirty by walking up. The bridesmaids had all said they would brave the road and risk a little dirt on their hemlines; after all, no one was really going to be looking at them anyways. Besides, it was a gorgeous day, the road was dry. It was too beautiful not to walk. However, soon after Colin arrived, she noticed another car pull into the drive.

"Couldn't let him be the only gentleman today," Brendan said, hopping out of the car. "What kind of husband would I be if I left my pregnant wife to walk to the church without at least offering to drive?"

"Your gallantry is noted," Molly called to him from behind Aoife. "But don't think it's getting you anything tonight. I may not be able to drink, but I plan to dance the night away and I'm going to be too tired when we get home for anything other than sleeping for the next week."

Brendan feigned disappointment, but kissed his wife's cheek lovingly before he joined her inside. Colin stayed on the step with Aoife, admiring her.

"What?" she asked, feeling self-conscious under his stare.

"She's really pretty, isn't she?" Miriam whispered.

"I think you're right," Colin smiled as he agreed with his daughter. She couldn't help but notice how he sounded a little breathless when he looked at her. A pleasantly warm flush rose in her cheeks.

"Don't ye look so handsome in that suit, Colin!" Sinead exclaimed, coming over to admire him. "The best-looking chauffeur in all of Ballyclara!"

"Sinead! Don't tell me you're also falling for the American's charms? This is what it was like all last night down at the pub: all the women fawning over his pretty face. Don't tell me ye prefer him over me, do ye?"

"You'll always hold a special place in my heart,

Brendan. Ye're like a second son to me. But it's always nice to have a little something to daydream about, ye know?"

"I'm not sure I want to," Brendan replied jokingly.

"Kindly stop objectifying my partner, thank you very much," Aoife replied with mock annoyance.

"At your service, madam," Colin replied gallantly to Sinead, extending his arm to walk her to the car.

"Such a well-raised lad ye are! He's a keeper," she whispered loudly to Aoife as she took Colin's arm and the two of them smiled.

As he escorted Sinead to the car, the rest of them got Mara ready to get into the car.

"Connor is a lucky man," Colin complimented her as he offered her his arm to help her to the car. "You look stunning."

"Oh, you *are* a charmer!" she teased, but smiled proudly at his compliment. "Better watch out, Aoife. I may marry him instead!"

"You can have him," she joked back. "You haven't made it to the church yet; there's still time to change your mind."

Colin gave her a look of mock surprise, but flashed her one of his dashing smiles, the one that made her fall for him in the first place. With the bride, her mother, Mae and Miriam safely in the car, Aoife, Molly, Karen, and Ailish bundled into the other car with Brendan and headed for the church.

૪૭૦૩

It was a rare Irish day, one where not a cloud could be seen in the sky and the late afternoon sun was already quite warm. The little parish church was filled with coloured light as it filtered through the stained-glass windows. Karen and Ailish hadn't done much to decorate the place this morning, other than tying little posies of wildflowers to the end of each pew with yellow ribbons, leaving the natural beauty of the church to speak for itself. Aoife met up with Connor in one of the little rooms off the altar.

"How's it going in here?" she asked. He paced around the room. "Trying to wear a hole through the floor, I see."

"Sorry." He stood still, then smiled at her.

"What?"

"I knew you were going to look beautiful in it."

"Oh, this old thing?" she teased. "Wait, you said that you knew I would look good in it. How'd you know what I'd be wearing today? I had Bex make this especially for me when I had her make Mara's dress, and the only person who knew what it would look like were her and I."

Connor looked down at the ground, caught red-handed. "I was moving the dress boxes this morning, and the cover fell off, and I saw it. I promise I didn't see Mara's."

He crossed his fingers over his heart.

"You better not have! I worked hard on that surprise!" She narrowed her eyes at him.

"Bex is incredibly talented," he said, admiring her dress. "You're going to have all the lads asking you to dance tonight."

"Well, if you think I look pretty, just wait until you see your bride-to-be. I guarantee you are not going to be disappointed. Bex and Millie send all their best to you and Mara, by the way."

A nervous look came over Connor's face again.

"What's wrong? Pre-wedding jitters?"

"Yes. No."

He started pacing again. After a moment, he said, "I'm not worried about Mara. I'm not. I've never loved someone the way I love her, and I know I want to spend the rest of my life with her. And I adore Rory; he's like a son to me. It's just… it's all this stuff with Alistair, and then I got this in the mail yesterday…"

He handed her a crumpled letter he'd been keeping in his jacket pocket. As she took it from him, she noticed it was from their grandmother and she knew that whatever was written in there, it couldn't be good. She sighed.

"Is this why you got pretty drunk last night?" She noticed that he still looked a bit tired, even with a million gallons of coffee probably running through his veins.

"Not entirely, but maybe it was part of it. Aren't you going to read it?"

"Do I need to?"

Her tone was serious.

"Does it go along the lines of trying to make one last attempt to get you to re-think getting married and coming to your senses, and moving back to Dublin, blah, blah, blah? Because that's exactly what it says, doesn't it? She's so predictable."

She handed it back to him.

"You forgot the bit about where she hates me now for converting to Catholicism in order to marry Mara."

Aoife rolled her eyes at this, completely not surprised. Their family was such a bunch of snobs.

"If you really want my advice, you know I'm going to say to just toss that into the trash and never give it another thought. So, what if they don't approve? You made it clear to them the last time we saw them you didn't need their approval; don't lose your nerve now. You've faced down worse than Grainne O'Reilly."

He gave her a small smile. "I don't know about that… you've always been the brave one in this family."

"I'm not brave. I'm just bored of their shit. And I've never had the same expectations placed on me as you've had put on you, so it was easier for me to just walk away from them. I don't miss them, and if they were being truly honest with themselves, they don't miss me either. But you, you're a different story. You matter to them, and they matter to you."

She walked over to him and gave him a hug.

"It's ok for you to be sad they aren't here to share in your happiness today, but don't let their bullshit ruin your big day. Today is about you, not them."

"Thanks," he said, hugging her back. "I'm really glad you're here. I don't think I could've done this without you here."

"I wouldn't have missed this for the world. Even if Dermot hadn't passed, I'd have still flown over from New York just to be here for this. I adore Mara and Rory; you know I do. I still think she's too good for you," she teased, "But I'm so glad they're going to be a part of us now. And I don't care what Grainne says; you, Mara, Rory, you're all family from this day forward."

"Thank you." He cleared his throat. "Now, I guess we better get this thing started."

She poked her head out the door. Rory and Des were helping the last of the guests to their seats; they were getting close to show time. As Rory walked his grandmother to her seat, he gave her a thumbs up to let her know the bridal party was ready. Father Patrick was making his way to the altar.

"Ready?" she asked, making sure he was feeling

calmer.

"Ready."

They walked over to where Father Patrick was standing, taking their places as the pianist switched from light background music to the processional to draw people's attention. First came Rory and Des, holding little Mae's hand. She looked so sweet in her lavender flower girl dress, trying to carry the pillow that held the wedding bands. The four-year-old was clearly enjoying all the attention for, halfway down the aisle, she stopped, took off her headband and stated waving it at the congregation. Little titters of laughter sprang up, further emboldening her. Des tried to convince her to put it back on, but there was no use; she'd gone rogue at this point, distracted by seeing her father and ran straight for Jimmy's arms, leaving the pillow and the rings behind. Rory quickly snatched it up from the floor and continued towards his place.

Next came Karen, which distracted Mae further, and called out "Mam! Mammy! You so pretty!"

Karen blushed all the way to her red-haired roots and came to stand by her daughter, trying to convince Mae to be quiet.

Next, it was Molly's turn. She smiled as Brendan beamed at her, clearly as besotted with her as the day the two of them had gotten married. As she came to stand at the front opposite Aoife and Connor, they all turned their heads towards the aisle. The congregation stood as the pianist began the wedding march.

Connor grinned from ear to ear at seeing Mara standing beside her brother, and her smile matched his. Aoife could see tears at the corners of Sinead, Mara, and Michael's eyes and knew they were all wishing that Dermot was here to share in this moment with them, but

Aoife would bet her life that he was smiling down on them now.

When they reached the front, Michael took his sister's hand, placed it in Connor's and then smiled at Aoife as he went to sit by his mother. She felt her face turning a bright red, wondering if he remembered anything from last night. Of course, he did; she'd never seen him so drunk that he couldn't remember what he'd done the night before. She turned her attention back to the ceremony.

"Dearly beloved, we are gathered here today…"

Father Patrick called everyone to attention, and she put aside her thoughts and feelings about Michael and that kiss for the moment, not wanting to miss a second of Connor's special day.

## Chapter Twenty-Two

The bells of the church rang out as Connor and Mara stepped out into the glorious sunshine. The congregation whooped and hollered, clapping for them as they kissed on the front steps. As the villagers started taking their leave and heading for the pub where the reception would be held, Brendan came up to the couple.

"Jimmy, Colin, Ailish and I are heading down to the pub. We're going to do a few last-minute things and we'll see you down there."

"Oh ok, but make sure you're around later. We want photos with you lot as well!" Mara instructed.

"Will do!" he replied cheerily, heading off with Jimmy.

"I'll see you down there," Colin kissed her, joining the others and leaving her standing next to Michael and Ailish.

"I suppose I should go down and keep an eye on those ones. Make sure they don't mess anything up."

Ailish was clearly reluctant to leave Michael and Aoife on their own, but trying not to show it. "I should also check on Eliza. Karen and I put her and a few of the women in charge of the kitchen tonight, but I know Molly is going to want things done a certain way and if it's not perfect, there'll be hell to pay."

"Everything will be fine, I'm sure." Michael rubbed her upper arms, trying to be reassuring. "We'll see you down there in a bit."

She nodded before joining the crowd, noticeably not saying anything to Aoife. For her part, Aoife would have preferred she was still here, surly attitude or not; anything to avoid being alone with Michael after last night's kiss. She could feel him glancing sideways at her, clearly wondering what he should say to her to break up this silence that had fallen.

"You look beautiful today."

"Thank you."

"You're supposed to say I look handsome," he teased her after she didn't say anything else.

"You look… uh… handsome," she managed, trying not to look directly at him, and certainly not trying to sound like she meant it as much as she did. She tried to focus her attention on Connor and Mara, who were now getting some photos taken outside the church.

"Stop smirking at me, Michael Flanagan."

"Sure, and I don't know what you're talking about," he replied, definitely smirking at her now. "And how would ye know if I was smirking at ye, or not? You've barely looked at me at all today."

She glanced at him now, seeing that there was a little hurt behind the teasing. Had he wanted her to notice him today? She was pretty sure last night that he was going to tell her that the kiss had been a mistake, but had she misjudged what he'd been thinking?

Well, she certainly noticed him now. He looked handsome in his tuxedo, all shaved and his dark hair even look trimmed a bit. He looked about as far from his usually casual, perfunctory look as he could, but she liked it. She was pretty sure he could have worn anything, and she would still have thought him one of the most handsome men she'd ever met.

She also noticed one other detail: he was wearing a tie that exactly matched the shade of her dress. Now, it wasn't like royal blue was an uncommon colour for a tie, but she'd sort of thought he'd have worn a black one like Connor, Rory, and Des had. She was the only person in the bridal party wearing this exact shade; Mara's bridesmaids and flower girl had all worn various shades of purple to suit their skin tones. Even Ailish had worn a light purple tea-length dress today. There was only one other person who could have known what colour dress she was wearing, and he'd been getting ready with Michael this morning… Had Connor told Michael about her dress, and he'd matched his tie to her dress?

No, that was completely ridiculous. She was making too much of it. Surely Michael wouldn't have put that much effort into it. He'd just grabbed the first tie out of the drawer and put it on, and it happened to be the same shade as her dress. Yes, that was the more likely scenario.

"Come over here, you two!" Mara called over to them. "We want photos with the whole bridal party."

Aoife was jolted out of her thoughts. Michael moved towards his sister and the rest of the group, leading the way. Before they reached the others, he turned around.

"Oh, Aoife. Like my tie? Matches your dress."

He smiled at her and then went to stand by his sister, leaving her there with her jaw hanging open.

※

After the photos, they walked down to the pub for the reception.

Because it had turned out to be such a beautiful day, Brendan, Colin, Jimmy, and Ailish had orchestrated moving several tables outside to the back garden and set up a new head table for the main bridal party and some guests. They then opened the doors to the pub, allowing people to move freely between the garden and the pub if they wanted. Fairy lights had been strung up, lending a magical warmth to both the inside and outside spaces. The tables were decorated with floating candles and vases of the same wildflowers that had been at the church.

By the time the wedding party arrived, the sun had sunk below the hills, bathing everything in a golden glow. Music drifted outside from Brendan and some of the lads who had brought out their instruments. Since several of the tables were now outside, it freed up even more space for the dance floor, and by the time the bridal party arrived, most of the village seemed to be making use of it. The band was already well into their first set. When they caught sight of the bride and groom arriving, everyone paused and cheered them on.

"Let's give it up for the new Mr. and Mrs. O'Reilly!" Brendan shouted into the microphone.

Everyone clapped and whistled as the new couple beamed with happiness.

## Where I'm Home

"I'm afraid it's just the same Ms. Flanagan and Mr. O'Reilly," Connor replied.

"If he won't take my last name, I'm not taking his!" Mara said to cheers from most of the women in the crowd.

"Kiss, kiss, kiss!" a chant went up from the crowd and dissolved into more whistles and cheers as the couple obliged.

"Alright you two, keep it PG. We've got young ones here," Brendan joked, making everyone laugh. "We're going to take a wee break here, folks, but don't you worry; we'll be back soon enough to get you on your feet again." He hopped down from the stage and joined the wedding party.

Mara and Connor made their way through the throngs of villagers, thanking everyone for coming. They slowly made their way to the back garden, took a few group photos with Brendan, Jimmy, Ailish, and Colin, and sat down to the feast prepared by Ailish, Eliza, and several other women in Ballyclara who'd taken over culinary duties for Molly, given her role as matron of honour. There was traditional roast beef or chicken, potatoes and garden vegetables, and for the vegetarians, a hearty veggie lasagna.

Aoife took her seat beside Connor at the head table, flanked once again by Father Patrick on her left, as it had been at the rehearsal dinner. Michael still sat at the table opposite her, but this time, he had his mother on one side of him and Brendan on the other. Ailish had taken her place on the other side of Karen, on Mara's side of the head table.

The dinner passed in amiable conversation, everyone simply enjoying the cozy atmosphere, ensconced in the joy of being around friends and family. Aoife was engaged in a conversation with Mara, Connor, Colin, and Father Patrick, who were reminiscing over Dermot, when there was an explosion of laughter from Michael, Brendan, and Jimmy over some joke Brendan had made. She raised her head at the sound of his robust laugh, happy to hear it for the first time in years.

Michael caught her gaze across the table and grinned happily at her.

She couldn't stop herself from smiling back, pleased to see him looking so happy and relaxed for the first time in a long time. There'd certainly been a whole lot of awkwardness between them since her return – last night included – but right in this moment, she was truly glad she'd come back. No place had truly felt like home quite as much as Ballyclara did for her.

"Alright, I think it's time for some speeches!" Brendan commanded, getting up from the table and grabbing a microphone from inside the pub. "Since she's my wife, I'm going to start this off with the beautiful matron of honour, my wonderful Molly."

She stood up, taking the mic from him and launching into a beautiful speech about the long friendship between her and Mara, how honoured she was to have been chosen as her matron of honour, and how happy she was to see Connor joining Mara's family that left everyone with more than a few tears in their eyes. When she'd finished, Brendan took back the mic and handed it to Aoife.

"Oh lord, how do I follow that one up?" she joked, standing up. "I'm regretting now that I didn't request going first."

She took a deep breath and caught Michael's eye as he smiled up at her.

"When I first came to Ballyclara four years ago, I didn't just find a new house; I found a family, an entire village of people who love and care about one another, and I'm truly honoured that you all took me into your hearts the way you did and made me a part of it.

"When Connor told me he'd proposed to Mara, I couldn't have been more thrilled for him, because he's not just gaining a new wife in Mara, or a stepson in Rory. He's not even just gaining a family in the Flanagans; he's gaining an entire village too, a tribe that will love and look out for him forever. I know some of you know about the kind of family we come from, and you'll know that neither of us has had that before, and I'm so happy you all will give him the kind of love and support he deserves.

"Connor, you are one lucky bastard to have found a woman as strong, resilient, brave, kind, and loving as Mara. Don't you dare screw this up."

Connor beamed up at her and then at his bride.

"And Mara, you have found in Connor someone who will love and be loyal to you for the rest of his life. Cherish him and take care of that deep love he has for you; it's rarer than any metal or precious stone on this earth."

Mara smiled up at her, and then at her new husband. "Don't I know it?"

Connor took her hand and kissed it.

"Connor and I are both lucky to have you and Rory joining our family," Aoife continued. "I know that our family couldn't be here today, so it's my great honour to be the one to welcome you both to the O'Reilly clan."

Everyone clapped for her as Connor and Mara both stood up to hug her, tears forming in the corner of Connor's eyes.

"Thank you," he whispered, kissing her on the cheek.

"Well, I don't know about you, but I wouldn't

want to follow that one," Brendan joked, turning the mood humorous again. "Would anyone like to give it a try?"

"Oh, go on, give it here." Michael took the mic from his best friend and stood up. "I know I can't top what Molly and Aoife have said, so I'm not even going to try. I'm just going to keep this short and simple."

He took a breath, glancing down at Aoife before turning his attention to his sister.

"I feel honoured to have been asked to walk you down the aisle today, sis. I know it wasn't supposed to be my job to do it, and that Da was supposed to be here to give you away. I hope you weren't too disappointed being stuck with your little brother."

"Only a little," Mara joked, but she gave him a watery smile, showing him how grateful she was for him.

"I know Da would have wanted to be here today, if he could, to tell you how happy he was for you. But since he can't, I want you to know, Connor, just how much he liked you and how happy he was to have you as part of the Flanagans. If the O'Reillys no longer want you, we're more than happy to have you. You're a good man, O'Reilly, and I'm proud to be able to call you my brother-in-law."

Connor rose and enveloped him in a big bro hug. They both cleared their throats, wiping a few tears away.

"Hey you, O'Reilly," Brendan said, taking back the mic. "I like you, man, I do, but this one here's *my* bromance partner. Go and get yer own. Don't be trying to cut in on our thing just because you're legally brothers now," making everyone roar with laughter.

"I'm free for a bromance buddy!" Jimmy called out.

"There ye go," Brendan said, nodding in his

direction.

Connor stood up, opening his arms wide, inviting Jimmy to hug him. Jimmy obliged, the two of them bro hugging it out until everyone laughed.

Rory stood up next, and they all settled themselves in again.

"I know it's not been easy since ye came into our lives," he started, addressing Connor. "But you've always been there for me in the last four years, Connor. Even when you were overseas, or when you came back and were travelling for work, you always made it known that Mam and I were the most important thing in your life. You've always treated us both with respect, love, and patience, even when our Flanagan tempers flare up."

There were a few titters of laughter; almost everyone here had survived being on the other end of a Flanagan in a fine temper, at least once.

"I can't thank ye enough for that."

Everyone looked at him, tears forming in their eyes.

"I know I'm not your biological son, and I mean no disrespect to Uncle Michael or Brendan, or Grandda when I say that, even if ye can't adopt me, I'd still love it if ye thought of me as your son."

Connor and Mara both got up, pulling him into a hug, and Aoife felt a few tears running down her cheeks as she saw the lovely new family her cousin had made for himself.

"Here." Aoife looked over and saw Michael was handing out a handkerchief to her.

"Thanks," she mouthed, her throat still thick with emotion.

"You guys, I'm going to need to reapply my whole face!" Mara exclaimed, daintily wiping tears from the corners of her eyes with her napkin. When everyone had returned to their seats, Connor continued to stand.

"Mara and I don't want to take up too much more of your time, but we just wanted to take a moment to say a quick thank you to every single person here today. You have all made this day so special for the both of us, and we couldn't imagine sharing such an important day without you all here.

"Thank you so much for doing all of this," he swept his hand around the back garden, "the music, the decorations, the food. Oh my God, the food! Thank you to every single person here for all you have done for us to make this day special for us. It couldn't have been more perfect. There's just one thing that's left: let's get on that dance floor!"

Cheers went up from inside the pub as music started playing.

"Would you girls like to dance?" Aoife asked, coming over to Miriam, who'd been sitting with Mae during the dinner.

"Yes!' they both screamed excitedly and ran into the pub, leaving her to try to catch up to them.

Brendan and the lads played a number of fast songs to get everyone moving. Just as she was feeling like she might need a bit of a breather from letting loose on the dancefloor, Brendan slowed things down. Bored with slower tempo, Mae and Miriam bee-lined it over to where Sinead was now sitting at a table inside the pub with a group of other elderly women. Karen and Jimmy, Connor, and Mara all paired up. Even Ailish had seemed to find a partner, dancing with a relative or a friend who'd come with the O'Sullivans.

She was just about to turn to Colin when Molly proclaimed, "I'm stealing him for this one!"

"Sorry," he mouthed, letting Molly pull him towards the dancefloor.

She dismissed his worries with a wave of her hand. Figuring she would just join Sinead and the girls, she turned around and ran smack into Michael's chest.

"Sorry," she mumbled. He caught her by the elbow, preventing her from falling over.

"Can I have this dance, Dancing Queen?" he asked, holding out his hand.

She looked around, wondering if she could find a way out of this, but knowing she would probably make more of a scene if she refused him than if she just danced with him, she put her hand in his.

"Sure." She put her other hand on his shoulder as he placed his on her waist.

They swayed together to the rhythm, and she was surprised once more at how everything felt so natural between them. They moved together as if they were one person, two halves of the same whole. All the other dancers on the dance floor, the band, and everyone else in the room seemed to fade into the background, and it was if she and Michael were the only two people in the whole world, just like it had been the first time they'd danced together. The rest of the world didn't matter when he was holding her; it was only the two of them.

She breathed in his cologne, felt his body up against hers, and knew with certainty that last night had not just been a fluke, and she *was* falling for him all over again. It was wrong; she should put a stop to things right here, right now, but a part of her was afraid to let go of him again.

She turned her head towards him, and she could have sworn that she saw something of the same reaction in Michael's eyes, that he felt the same longing.

It was the first time she felt a profound sense of regret. She didn't regret going to New York; she'd needed to go for herself and she'd learned so much about herself while she'd been there, but she regretted that she'd left Michael behind.

All too soon for the both of them, the music came to a stop and switched back to a faster tempo.

"Let's take a walk." Michael kept a firm grasp on her hand and led her towards the door, their exit concealed by the throngs of people returning to the dance floor.

## Chapter Twenty-Three

The night air was crisp and cool against her skin, which was still flushed from dancing. She didn't know where he was leading her, but it didn't really matter; she knew she was safe with him.

They walked along in silence, still holding hands, listening to the sounds of the night around them, the sheep lowing in the pasture that ran along the side of the road. Some of them skittered away, annoyed at having their peaceful night intruded upon. They continued along the road until they arrived at Aldridge Manor and stopped outside the front door.

She looked up at the big house, her home. She felt bad that she'd been neglecting it all these years. She hadn't even really been inside since she'd been back here; just that once, back the other week. It just held so many memories she hadn't wanted to deal with at the time, so many memories of a time she'd thought she'd wanted to put behind her.

They stood there in the moonlight, facing one another. He closed the distance between them, tipping her face up towards his with a finger under her chin, and kissed her ever so softly. She felt a shiver run through her, and not from the night air. She leaned into him more, pulling him down into a deeper kiss, only parting when she knew her lungs would explode if she didn't take a breath. She rested her forehead against his.

"That's what I should've done last night," he said, his voice breathless.

"How do we always find ourselves back here, Michael?"

It wasn't entirely a rhetorical question. She needed to know what it was that kept drawing them together. She wasn't sure if he was the one who was going to – or was able to – give her the answer. He was one half of the problem, but she was the other; she couldn't just look to him to solve things for her. She needed to look at her own behaviour, her own actions.

She sighed, sad that this had to happen now. They'd both been putting this fight off for so long and now there really wasn't any avoiding it any longer. She just didn't want to ruin what had otherwise been a perfect night. But they had to clear the air between them before she went back to New York if they were going to move on together.

"Well, it's pretty simple, really. You take the main road, and you continue along it until you get to this lane, and then you just continue up it until you get here." He smiled at her, trying to be playful. He was so happy in this moment; she hated herself for knowing she had to take that away again.

She glared at him. "You know what I mean."

"No, I don't think I really know what you mean, Aoife."

She could see in the moonlight how his face, lit with joy and laughter, twisted into a frown.

He sighed. He knew what was coming too.

"Don't do that. Don't you dare do that."

She turned away from him, frustration in her voice. She felt his eyes following her, still trying to figure out how they'd just gone from the most romantic moment they'd had together since her return to now starting a fight with each other. But that was how it had always been between them, running hot and cold all the time.

"Don't you dare pretend like you don't know what I'm talking about. You know damned well what I mean."

"Oh, yeah?" he asked, folding his arms across his chest, his tone defensive. "Well, let's pretend for a moment that I don't and you spell it out for me."

"Why do we keep coming back to each other? I thought when I left that things were over between the two of us. We just spent three years apart, not talking to one another, not seeing one another, so why are we right back here like we've never been apart?"

"That was your choice," he cut in.

There was an unmistakable edge to his voice this time. "You decided to leave, Aoife. I made it pretty feckin' clear that I wanted to be with you, and you were the one to decide that, that wasn't enough to make you stay. That *I* wasn't enough."

Against her will, tears fell down her cheeks. That wasn't how things had happened at all. It wasn't because he hadn't been enough for her; he *was* enough. But that didn't mean that *she'd* been enough at the time, not for him, but for herself. She'd thought there was still something missing from her life, something she'd needed to find. Had she found it yet?

"That's not true." Her voice caught in her throat. "You were enough. You *are* enough. I didn't leave because of you."

"Then why, Aoife? Why leave, beyond the career dreams, I mean. Because if it was just about your career and pursuing your dreams, then I wouldn't have held you back. We would have made the distance work somehow. But we both know it wasn't just about your career, so what was it that made you leave?"

She thought about avoiding the question again, but he deserved to know the truth. She gathered all her courage. "Because *I* wasn't enough."

He looked at her, perplexed.

"I wasn't enough for me. I thought something was missing, that I wasn't enough as I was. I thought I needed to find some missing piece in order to be someone who was enough by my own standards."

"And have you done that? Found what was missing? Is that why ye came back here, now?" He searched her face, looking for answers.

Why *did* she come back to Ballyclara for Dermot's funeral? It was the question she'd been asking herself the whole time she'd been back. She could have easily stayed in New York with Colin and Miriam. She would be on her way to being engaged to Colin, the three of them forming this ready-made family track they'd been on since the day she'd met him. She could simply have told Rory on the phone that she was sorry for losing his grandfather, that he'd been an amazing person and one whose memory she would cherish forever, but it wasn't like she'd been back to Ireland in the last three years to see him or anything. She could simply have stayed in New York with her family, running her publishing house and moving on with her life.

She was sure she would have been sad for a few days, maybe even a few weeks, after Dermot's passing. Maybe she would have gone to a pub and had a drink for him in his memory, to honour him. But that would have been that, and everyone would have moved on with their lives. She could have let herself get swept up in the swiftly moving current that was New York society and given Ireland only a passing thought every now and then.

But no, she'd not done that. She'd chosen to come back here because the truth was, she felt like she owed Dermot and Sinead Flanagan everything for helping her through one of the hardest years of her life and seeing her through to the other side. She'd wanted to honour the memory of the man who'd reminded her of her own grandfather, one of the kindest people she'd ever known, because the Flanagans had become the family she'd always wanted growing up. She had wanted that closeness and that love, the knowledge that nothing the world threw at them could tear them apart. But she'd gotten scared at the last moment of committing herself to that kind of love, afraid that because she didn't feel like she was entirely whole again after her grandfather's death that she would somehow screw things up. So, she'd chosen instead to put her career dreams ahead of her personal dreams, searching for what she thought was missing.

She didn't regret New York, but she did regret the

way she had left things with the Flanagans. All of them, not only Michael. She regretted not giving them a proper goodbye, not letting them know how much of an impact they'd had on making her the person she was today: someone who could now see herself getting married and having a family, someone who believed that she *was* worthy of having all of those things and not simply settling for what was expected of her. That's what the Flanagans had done for her; they'd made her into the kind of person who could love Colin and Miriam.

Except, it wasn't Colin and Miriam she wanted to build a family with, but Michael that she wanted to do those things with now. She wanted all the things with him she'd never had before: the love, the security, the contentment of being who she was with him and not worrying about whether she was going to mess things up again. She wished she could say that she wished she'd never left him in the first place, but then, she wouldn't be the woman standing in front of him right now, the one who was ready to love him.

Everything came back to him, all the soul-searching she'd done in the last three years. She hadn't been able to move on from him because everything she'd done, even when she was in New York, came back to changing herself into the person who could be with him. It was terrifying to her that she'd put so much effort into wanting to be with just this one person; she'd always been so independent, solitary, even; the depth of feeling she had for him terrified her. Even now, she was afraid of losing herself to him, looking for a way to pick a fight, finding another excuse to run away again.

"I don't know," she lied. "Besides, it's not like I'm the only one who caused all this. You made it clear that you were only willing to be with me if it was on your terms. You only wanted me so long as I stayed here. You made it pretty fucking clear you weren't coming to New York, and if I wasn't going to stay here with you, you didn't want me. I don't care what you said earlier; you weren't willing to give this place up for me to pursue what I needed to."

A passing ray of moonlight showed that Michael's face was now thunderous, and she knew she hadn't been entirely fair to him. It may have been true what he'd said earlier: that he would have supported her going away if it had just been about her career, and that the two of them would have found a way to make it work. She hadn't thought he'd have done those things for her when she'd left, but maybe she'd been wrong this whole time and she didn't really know him as well as she thought she did.

"For feck's sake, Aoife, my father had just nearly died of a heart attack and you wanted to go all the way across the Atlantic Ocean for something you didn't even know ye were looking for, and you expected me to be in the right frame of mind to say, 'Yes, dear, of course I'll chase ye around the world while ye figure out how to act like a feckin' grown-up like the rest of us!' Meanwhile, my father is back here living out the last few years of his life, and you'd have wanted me to miss that, because why? Because ye needed someone around to call ye out on your bullshit and tell ye how to grow the fuck up? God, you can be such a self-absorbed bitch sometimes."

He ran a hand through his dark hair furiously, angry with her.

More tears slid down her face, making tiny rivulets through her make-up. She swiped at them, annoyed that, by falling for someone like Michael, she'd let herself open up and now she had to feel things. Where was the old Aoife who found it so easy to pretend not to care because she didn't let herself dive too deep into her feelings? Right now, she wished she could have a bit of that version of herself back, but she couldn't. The person she was before meeting him was gone, and now she was left with this person who felt everything but was still afraid of opening up all the way to someone else.

"I'm sorry, Aoife," he replied, his voice calmer now, but still tinged with hurt and anger. "I don't know what keeps bringing us together. But I do know that I *was* willing to make things work before ye left. I even went to the airport to get on that plane and tell you that, but I was too late."

"What?!"

No one had ever told her he'd gone to the airport the day she'd left. Not Mara, or Connor, or Molly or Brendan. They must have known; *someone* must have known. Why hadn't they told her?

"Brendan drove me to Dublin Airport, and I was there, not to hold ye back or convince ye to stay here. I was going to tell you I'd support you no matter what you'd decided. I was even prepared to get on the next flight out to New York as soon as I saw your plane leave, but I didn't."

*Brendan, that bastard! Why hadn't he told her any of this?*

"Why? Why didn't you?" she blurted out.

"Because I'm not some hero in a romance novel, Aoife."

Michael threw his hands up in frustration.

"I wasn't just going to sit around and wait for you to figure out that you were in love with me. I loved you,

I still do, and I put my whole heart out there for you, and I wasn't going to let you continue to smash it all to bits while ye figured yourself out."

He put his hands on his hips, then folded them across his chest again, clearly not sure what to do with his body.

"And because I was sad and angry, and I knew you hadn't left simply because of the writing opportunity. I knew that something else was happening, and I was afraid that I couldn't overcome whatever fear it was that was driving you away. I thought it was better to let ye sort it out on your own."

"I was scared," she admitted, her voice shaky, tears still falling down her cheeks. "I was scared of what we were, of what we were becoming, and I didn't know how to make things work. I was so afraid that I would mess it all up if things were good between us, and I didn't want that to happen. So, I sabotaged things in the beginning before I could get hurt later."

"Like you're doing now."

"Like I'm doing now," she admitted, feeling an odd sense of relief as she spoke the truth.

He walked over to her and placed a hand on either side of her shoulders, looking down at her until she looked up at him.

"I meant what I said earlier. I'm not some hero who chases the damsel in distress all over the world like a lost puppy dog. If that's what you're looking for, then stay with Colin. He's a good man, and he'd take care of you until the end of his days. Ye might even be very happy together. But I don't think you're a damsel, and I don't think ye need someone to rescue you, much as you try to get in your own way."

Despite herself, she smiled at this. He smiled back, but then his face turned serious again.

"I'm not going to put my life on hold for ye, Aoife, but neither do I want to go through it without you in it. If ye want to be a part of my life, I'm willing to put my heart out there for ye again, but not if you're not willing to do the same."

She stared into those intense blue eyes, thinking about what he'd said. Trying to be braver, she reached up and put a hand behind his neck and drew him down towards her, kissing him deeply.

## Chapter Twenty-Four

"No, no. I'm sorry, no."

Aoife suddenly pulled back and turned away from him, putting a hand to her lips. They'd been soft when she'd kissed him and had tasted of peppermint lip balm. There'd been an urgency and determination behind the kiss, almost a resolve that he could now feel slipping away with every passing second.

"Aoife…"

"No, stop talking. If you say one more thing, then we're going to end up doing something we're not going to be able to come back from."

He watched her pace back and forth, hands waving about wildly as she seemed to argue with herself. Pebbles skittered along the drive whenever she turned on her heel to tread the same path over and over. She was muttering something, but it was too fast and quiet for him to catch anything but a word here and there. It bothered him to see her conflicted like this, especially knowing that he was the reason for it.

"Aoife, stop."

He stood in front of her, catching one of her hands and holding it against his chest, hoping to get her to stay still for a moment. It seemed to work.

She took a deep breath and looked up at him.

"Look, Michael, maybe tonight was a mistake. We couldn't make things work three years ago, so what business do we have thinking we could make things work now? Maybe we just need to forget this thing between us and move on. We have great lives; we should be happy with what we have right in front of us."

"I am happy with what I have right in front of me," he said, boldly.

She sighed and tried to take back her hand, but he held on to it half a second longer before relinquishing it. She folded her arms across her chest, looking away from him, and he could see she was closing herself off from him again.

"You're the one who admitted that you got scared last time, when we were just figuring things out. You got scared of what all of this could mean, of what the two of us could be together, and you're the one who ran away from it in the end because you knew I wouldn't follow you to New York, not when my father was in the hospital. You knew I would stay here in Ballyclara, so by leaving, you made damned sure that our relationship would end.

"You came here when you were afraid of making a commitment to Danny, and now you're doing the same with Colin. You run away when things get complicated, and you're doing it again."

Her mouth worked to find some snappy retort before finally settling on, "You know what? I'm not the only one who self-sabotages my relationships, Michael, so don't you dare stand there on your soapbox and preach down to me. You are just as stuck in your same old patterns as you ever were."

She pointed her finger right at his chest, punctuating every word with a sharp jab. He batted it away, another verbal spar between them looming.

"Oh really? And how do ye figure that?"

"You stubbornly stick with the same person, even if you don't love them anymore, even if they will ruin your life, because that's what you do, Michael. You stay and you try to make it work, even if it doesn't make you happy. Well, maybe I don't want to just be the next Eliza Kennedy you end up settling for."

"What's that supposed to mean?" He gazed at her.

She sighed, like she was angry with herself for saying more than she'd intended to.

"Molly said you and I were cosmically attracted to one another, but that we weren't going to work out. That I'd only end up breaking your heart. Maybe she's right. Maybe I'll just end up ruining your life."

She stood there with her arms still folded across her chest, biting her lower lip, looking forlorn.

*Dammit, Molly! What right did she have to weigh in on his relationship with Aoife?*

He knew his friend was only trying to be loyal to him, but dammit, it was ruining any potential he had with Aoife before they could even try to figure out what they still were to each other. He took a moment to mull over exactly how he could convince her that Molly was wrong, but impatient as ever, Aoife had already decided to bolt.

After he didn't say anything, she said, "We should

be heading back," and turned on her heel to leave.

He sighed and moved to cut her off. "Where are ye going?"

"Back to the pub. Someone has undoubtedly noticed by now that we've been gone all this time."

Her voice was steady, calm even, but he knew her too well. This was her practiced tone, the one she'd perfected over the years to make it seem like she didn't care. The way she used to do when she didn't want him to see how she really felt.

"So that's just it, then?" He threw his hands up, exasperated. "Molly chimes in about something when she doesn't know the half of it, and that's the end of it?"

Her nostrils flared in annoyance.

"What more do you want from me, Michael?" she snapped.

"I want ye stay so that we can talk about this."

"I need to go."

She tried to push past him, but he cradled her shoulders, keeping her in place.

"Aoife, stay, please." He didn't care that his voice was pleading; he was more scared of seeing the only thing he'd ever been sure he'd ever wanted walking away from him again. "Please stay."

She looked up at him, internal conflict written all over her expression. She took in a ragged breath, her shoulders shaking slightly in the cool air.

"We really need to get back. People will come looking for us."

Her eyes were pleading with him too, begging him not to make her choose between Colin down at the pub, and him.

"And what are ye going to say to him, Aoife? What are you going to tell Colin when you see him, and he asks where you've been tonight? Are ye going to tell him the truth?"

"Are you going to tell Ailish you were with me when she asks you the same question?" she countered, and he dropped his head, cheeks burning red.

It wasn't like he'd been planning this whole night out, but he'd felt what he'd had with Ailish slipping away the moment Aoife came back to Ballyclara. He knew that no matter what, he would have to end things with her; it just wasn't fair to her otherwise. It was just the thought of hurting her that made him pause for a moment.

"You know, for someone who says that they aren't the hero who runs after the girl, that seems to be exactly what you're doing, Michael."

"Then stop running away."

He stared into her eyes intensely, until she finally looked away, clearing her throat in embarrassment.

"Look, Michael, maybe tonight was a mistake. We couldn't make things work three years ago. What business do we have thinking we could make things work now? You are as much of a commitment-phobe as I am, and you damn well know it. Maybe we just need to forget this thing between us and move on."

She stared down at her feet, avoiding looking at him.

"Then let's change that," Michael said to her, surprising them both.

Her eyes widened, and she cocked her head to the side. "What the hell are you talking about?"

Without knowing what he was really doing, Michael got down on one knee and reached out, taking her hand in his. "Marry me."

"What?!"

Admittedly, it was not the reaction he'd been

hoping for, but he *had* just sprung this on her, so he couldn't really blame her.

"You're right." He looked up at her, showing her the God's honest truth in his eyes. "You're right about everything. The both of us are the same; we get into these relationships we know won't work out in the end because we're both afraid of being hurt, so we hurt ourselves first and that way we don't have to feel the pain of someone else hurting us. But Aoife, that's no way to live. And I've known deep inside of me since the day I met you I was meant to be with you. I tried fighting that feeling the whole year you lived here, and for the three years since you've been in New York. I've tried to move on from ye, but the truth is that I can't."

He could see she was at least a little pleased at this last statement, but he could also see in her eyes that this was not going to go the way he wanted it to. He could feel the sorrow creeping over him and settling into his soul.

"Michael, we've been here before. You left Eliza for me, and I left Danny, and look how that all worked out for us. The only thing that's changed is we're with different people this time. *Good* people. People who are going to be really hurt by all of this."

He paused a moment, trying to search for the right words to make her stay.

"We've changed. *We're* different too."

"Are we really, though?" she searched his face, looking for the answer she wanted, but not finding it. "That's what I thought."

She put a hand on his shoulder and turned back towards the road.

"Aoife…" He rose from the ground, brushing dirt off his trousers.

## Where I'm Home

"What else do you want me to do, Michael? I'm in an impossible situation. No matter what I do, or don't do, I'm hurting someone."

Her face took on the saddest of looks, and as much as he was stinging from her rejection, it broke his heart more to see her looking that sad. But, as usual, the anger inside of him won over.

"Fine," he snarled, and he could see her flinch at his tone. "But don't expect me to wait around for you this time. I won't do that again."

He knew as soon as he'd said the words that they weren't true. He knew he would wait for her forever if he had to, but he was too stubborn to take the words back now.

Aoife's own face clouded over in anger. Everything he'd meant to say to her tonight when he'd led her out of the pub and brought her up here escaped him, and the old wound of her leaving that had been re-opened since she'd come back gushed forth with emotion once again.

They were at an impasse once again, and he wondered if one of them didn't do something about it now, would they find themselves in the same place in another three years? Or would this time be the end of things for good?

Could he live with that?

"Goodbye Michael." Her voice sounded rueful as she turned and headed back down the road to the pub.

He simply stood there, not moving. Unlike three years ago when he'd followed her to the airport, it had been within his power this time to make her stay and yet, he'd still ended up just watching her walk away again.

## Chapter Twenty-Five

The reception was still in full swing when she got back to the pub.

What the hell had he been thinking, proposing to her like that? Had he really expected her to accept when the two of them were still just trying to figure out what the hell they were to each other? When she was still trying to figure out how she still felt about all of this? She marched furiously into the pub, trying to put thoughts of what had just happened behind her. She needed to pretend, at least for a little while longer, like nothing had happened. She would *not* ruin Connor's big day with her own drama.

As it turned out, her own drama was going to be the least of Connor and Mara's worries.

She slipped in as inconspicuously as she could, trying to draw the least amount of attention to herself. She noticed several people were still on the dance floor and she tried to skirt the main crowd, sticking to the shadows along the wall. The door opened behind her and Michael appeared, searching for her. She kept moving, not wanting to have another confrontation with him in front of everyone.

"There you are!" Colin came up to her, beaming at her, and her heart wanted to break. She wasn't prepared to see him right now. She needed an out, some way to avoid him without looking like that was exactly what she was doing. She looked back the way she'd come, but Michael was moving towards her, so there was no escape that way.

Thankfully, she was saved by Alistair Byrne, of all people.

In the time she'd been at Aldridge with Michael, Alistair had snuck into the reception. This in and of itself would have been bad enough, certainly enough to warrant a fight breaking out, given Michael's earlier warning to him about what would happen if he ever set foot in his pub again. However, this was the least of it.

She watched as Alistair marched up to Connor and Mara, who'd been dancing. She was too far away, and the music too loud, for her to hear exactly what was going on, but she could tell from the way he gestured that he was upset and he definitely wanted Connor and Mara to come with him somewhere. She noticed two things then: one, Michael had frozen in his tracks upon seeing Alistair, and then started moving swiftly in his direction and two; Rory and Des moving towards the group from the same direction Alistair had come, the two of them looking visibly upset about something. She took the opportunity to avoid Colin by heading straight into this fresh new drama.

He might be a quiet man who tried his best to stay out of everyone's business, but there was very little that happened in Ballyclara that escaped Brendan McCaffrey's notice. Especially when it pertained to his best friend.

He'd seen the way Michael and Aoife had been dancing earlier, and he'd seen the two of them as they'd tried to sneak out when they thought no one was looking. He also couldn't help but notice how long the two of them had been gone before he saw Aoife trying to sneak in, looking guilty as hell. He had a fairly good idea from her smudged make-up and tousled hair what she and Michael had been up to. Either the two of them had fought and made up, or they'd finally ended this dance they'd been doing for the last four years. He was equal parts relieved and worried to find out the final result.

He and Michael had been the best of friends since primary school, but there had been plenty of times in their thirty-odd years of friendship when he'd have liked nothing more than to smack him upside the head.

Tonight was no exception.

He and Aoife had finally seemed to be in a good place in their lives, and now the two of them had likely gone and done something to mess that up. He cared deeply about them both, but he hated to see the trail of broken hearts they left in their wake.

He was distracted from his musings about what advice he was going to impart on Michael later, by the appearance of Alistair Byrne. Who the fuck had let him in? Probably his parents. Connor and Mara had felt obliged to invite them, hoping after the incident in the pub a few days ago, they'd have the sense to stay away. But no, of course they'd shown up.

*Feckin' hell.* If things had been going along a little too perfectly tonight, he now knew the other shoe was definitely about to drop.

"Lads, keep on playing. I'm taking a wee break," he said, hopping off the stage.

They obliged by launching into a new jig.

"Michael."

He tried to step in front of his friend, hoping to get him calm and not have him make a scene at his sister's wedding.

"Get out of my way, Brendan," he growled.

"Come on, mate. Ye don't want to be doin' this here, now." He gestured towards the crowd assembled around them.

"I told him what would happen to him if he set foot in here again. Ye can't say we didn't warn him."

"And I'll take care of it," Brendan tried to reason. "Let me talk to him and get him out of here. You focus on finding your girlfriend. Your absence has been noted."

This got Michael's attention. A flash of surprise and concern crossed his face before it darkened again. Brendan followed his gaze and saw that Alistair had reached Connor and Mara and was now engaged in an animated discussion with them.

"This ends now." Michael pushed past him and headed straight into the crowd.

"Feckin' hell," Brendan muttered, following on his heels.

"Whatever the hell it is ye want, Alistair, my wedding is no fucking time to be talking about it. Now, I suggest you get the hell out of here before my brother finds ye and makes good on his threats and kicks the shit out of you."

Mara was right up in Alistair's face, clearly unamused at him crashing her wedding. Connor looked like if Michael didn't make good on his promise, then he certainly would. They were all momentarily distracted by their sons, who'd followed closely on Alistair's heels.

Rory looked visibly upset, tears at the corners of his eyes and his face flushed red. He was running his long fingers through his hair, tousling it in the same way his uncle did when he was upset about something. Des was close behind him and an icy prickling of fear came over Brendan when he noticed his son's face was white as a sheet, his normally twinkling blue eyes clouded over, his shoulders hunched defensively. He knew without a shadow of a doubt that Alistair was at the centre of this somehow, and nothing in the world was going to save him if he'd messed with Brendan McCaffrey's son. It was usually Brendan who was trying to hold Michael back from getting into a fight, but when it came to his kid, all bets were off.

"Des?" he asked. He put a hand out to his son's shoulder, but Des shrugged it off. This wasn't at all like his normally happy, easy-going son. "Desmond, what is wrong?"

"Rory?" he heard Mara ask, obviously noticing that something was wrong with both their sons. "What's happened?"

"*He* happened," Alistair said, pointing directly at Des, and Brendan's shoulders stiffened, prepared to defend his son against any threat. They were definitely starting to draw attention now, and Molly, Ailish, Karen, Jimmy, and Sinead had joined their group.

## Where I'm Home

"Ye better feckin' watch where you point that finger, Alistair Byrne, unless you want to lose it," Molly threatened, standing with her husband and son. Once Molly McCaffrey had been riled up, there was as much use in trying to stop her as there was in standing in front of a tornado and asking it not to shred you to bits.

"Then maybe you should teach your son to keep his own hands to himself and off my son," Alistair shot back, apparently pleased with himself that he'd finally unveiled what he'd been wanting to tell Connor and Mara earlier.

"And what the feckin' hell does that mean?" Molly asked, now joining Mara in getting up in Alistair's face.

"Mam, can we get out of here?" Rory's eyes were pleading as he saw the way everyone was staring at them now. The music had stopped, and everyone was watching the scene before them with bated breath.

"Sure sweetie, as soon as we sort all this out."

Rory looked like he might start crying.

"Des, what the hell is he talking about? What happened? Des?"

Poor Des was sobbing now at all the attention that was being heaped on them, and Brendan enveloped him into a hug, making soothing noises like he used to do when he was little. "What is it lad? What's Alistair done?"

"What have *I* done? He's the one who's started all of this. My son would never… he's not like that!" Alistair spluttered.

"Like what?" Michael challenged, balling his hand into a fist, and Brendan knew he was just itching to get into a fight.

"Like a –," and then Alistair Byrne said a very derogatory word, one not worth repeating.

"I beg your pardon?!" Mara screamed at him.

"He found me kissing Des," Rory blurted out.

His whole assembled family turned to look at him, shocked by this revelation.

No one said anything for a good, long moment before Michael finally called out to rest of the room, "Alright, everyone out. Reception's over."

Nobody moved, all of them shocked at the scene unfolding before them.

"OUT! I said, get out!"

People scurried away at the anger in his voice, leaving just Aoife, Ailish, the Byrnes, the Flanagans, and the McCaffreys.

"No, son, he's the one who..." Alistair pointed his finger at Des again. "He's the one who's to blame for all of this."

"My wife told you what would happen if you pointed that finger at our son again," Brendan threatened, before launching himself in Alistair's direction. Luckily for Alistair, Michael and Connor were by his side in a flash, holding him back.

"C'mon, Brendan, man; he's not worth it." Connor's voice was trying to sound reasonable, but the look in his eyes said he would love nothing more than to choke Alistair to death with his bare hands. After a bit of a struggle, Brendan put his hands up, reluctantly letting his body relax.

Surprising them all, it was Mr. Byrne, a man who'd never stood up to his wife before, let alone his son, who took the moment now to put a firm grip on Alistair's upper arm.

"I think it's time we be going, son." His tone brooked no argument.

Alistair looked down at his father's hand, his face incredulous that the old man had the guts to take him to task. It was clear that Alistair was used to bullying his parents into doing what he wanted, and he wasn't used to his father talking back to him.

"Get your hands off me," he spat at him, but his father did not let go.

"That's my grandson right there," he said defiantly, nodding to Rory, "And because of you and you," he said, glaring at his wife, who clutched nervously at the necklace at her throat, "I've never gotten to know him. But what I've seen of him tonight shows that he's a brave young man, something he most certainly doesn't get from you or me."

He stared straight into Alistair's eyes. "You've done quite enough damage to this young man, and to this family, and I'm not going to let you do anymore. You're going to leave tonight, and I don't just mean this pub, but this village, and you are not going to set foot in it again while I'm alive."

Alistair glared at his father, unable to form a reply.

"Jimmy, lad, will ye help me escort my son back to his car so he can be on his way?" Mr. Byrne asked of his son-in-law.

"With pleasure," Jimmy said, grabbing hold of Alistair's other arm.

"Wait."

Everyone turned to look at Mara. She marched up to Alistair and looked him straight in the eye.

"I'm proud of who my son is. It doesn't matter to me whom he loves. He is loved, and that's something you'll never feel. And I am not going to let your bigoted, homophobic ass near him ever again. Do you understand me?"

Alistair said nothing, just looked disgustedly down at her.

"Oh, and just one more thing before ye go," Connor said, stepping in and punching Alistair right in the nose, causing blood to gush forth.

"Right, take him away, lads."

And with that, Mr. Byrne and Jimmy steered a bleeding and cursing Alistair out of the pub and into the night.

"He deserved a whole lot more than a broken nose," Sinead said, surprising them all.

"I'm just sorry you beat me to it," Michael said, his tone jealous.

"Thank you, Mam." Rory came up to her, hugged her tightly, and buried his face in her shoulder. "I really just want to go home now."

"Of course, ye do, sweetie." Mara hugged him back fiercely. She looked around at the decorations, the food, all just laying where people had abandoned them.

"Leave it. You've got far more important things to worry about tonight," Ailish told her, guessing what she was thinking.

"C'mon, let's get you home." Connor wrapped an arm around Mara, who was still holding onto Rory, and ushered the two of them to the door.

"Mam, why don't you go with them? I'll be along later to check in," Michael said to Sinead.

"Like Ailish said, we've got bigger things to worry about tonight. You two come along with us and we'll all go up together."

Sinead gave him a look that brooked no argument.

Not wanting to argue with his mother, he nodded and held out his arm to Ailish, linking up with her and walking the two of them out.

"Has anyone seen Colin?" Aoife asked. Brendan had almost forgotten she was there.

"I think he took Miriam upstairs when the shouting started," Molly told her.

"Thanks. And Brendan, Molly, Des? If you need anything tonight, just let me know."

"Thank you, Aoife." Molly kissed her on the cheek and joined her family, walking them outside.

As Michael turned to lock up behind them, he noticed Aoife slowly climbing the stairs to the flat above. He wanted to pick up their conversation from before, to know what she was going to say to Colin. But it didn't really matter what she said to him, did it? He needed to focus on his own relationship now, on what he was going to tell Ailish. If Aoife broke up with Colin tonight or decided to stay with him, it needed to be her decision, and he couldn't interfere in it.

Chapter Twenty-Six

She took a breath before entering the room. This was going to be the hardest thing she'd ever done, and she would need all the strength she could muster if she was going to do this properly.

And it must be done properly. Colin deserved that much, at least.

She wondered for a flicker of a second before entering the room if she could make herself stay, make herself change the way she felt. She'd been asking herself this the whole way down to the pub earlier tonight. She knew she couldn't, and it wasn't fair to either of them. He deserved someone who would love him completely, someone who would put him first.

And so did she.

"Hey."

Colin looked up at her as she walked through the

doorway, that big, happy smile he had every time he saw her, like it was the first time he was ever seeing her. She loved seeing that smile every single time; it never got old. But right now, it wasn't what she needed. It was only going to make this so much more difficult.

"Hey."

He couldn't have helped but hear the difference in the tone of her greeting compared to his own. It would have been impossible not to notice that everything was not alright. He knew her far too well to not know something was up.

"What's wrong?" His voice was calm, for Miriam was right there with them, drawing a picture while the television was playing a kids' show. After the excitement of the events downstairs earlier, Colin had obviously had a difficult time putting her down for bed. "Things downstairs get out of control?"

"You could say that, but that's not what we need to talk about."

"Miriam, sweetie, why don't you take your pencil crayons and your drawing into the bedroom and watch your show in there?" he said to her. He could tell that whatever she wanted to tell him, she did not want to do it in front of his daughter.

Miriam looked up at the two of them.

"You look sad, Aoife."

"It's ok, sweetie. I'm alright." She didn't want her worrying about her.

Miriam paused for a moment, looking like she was trying to assess whether she was lying to her, but eventually said, "Ok."

As she walked past her, she smiled at Aoife and closed the door behind her. She was a smart kid; she knew something was up, but she also seemed to know that this was something she and her dad needed to work out on their own.

"What is it?" he asked her again, after ensuring that the door to the bedroom was fully closed and Miriam had switched on the television.

"Maybe you should sit down," she suggested, pointing to the sofa.

He did as she said, giving her time to formulate her words. She sat down beside him, but realized that being right next to him, feeling the warmth of his body, looking into his eyes was only going to make her lose her nerve. She hastily stood up and started pacing around the room. Colin simply sat there, watching her.

She exhaled, all the way from her toes to her lungs, and decided that the best way to do this was to be as honest with him as possible. It wouldn't do any of them any good to lie about any of it. It would be not only a disservice to him but also to herself.

"The first thing I want you to know is that I love you and Miriam. So much," she said, fighting back tears. She wiped at the sides of her cheeks where the few stray tears she couldn't hold back slipped down her face.

"Oh God. So, this is really happening. You're leaving me for him, aren't you?"

His voice was sorrowful, mournful even. His brown eyes were full of sadness, but also a knowledge she hadn't guessed he'd had about the situation. She could tell by the look on his face this was not a new revelation for him, that he'd been expecting this conversation for awhile now.

This made it so much worse. He'd known she'd break his heart, and yet he'd still stood by her, hoping she'd make a different choice. How had she not seen that he'd been watching what the two of them had together slipping away from him? How could she let herself get so preoccupied with Michael that she hadn't noticed the cracks forming in her relationship with Colin? Had they always been there? Or had they only formed since coming to Ireland?

"You have to believe me when I say that I love you so much, Colin." She needed him to believe her. He was standing now, and she went over to him, pleading with him to believe her. He instinctively moved away, as an animal does when they think a predator is about to hurt them. "And Miriam. I never wanted to hurt you. Either of you."

He took a ragged breath as a couple of tears ran unashamedly down his cheeks. He stared at her for a good, long moment and she wondered if he was about to shout at her, or strike at her, or throw her out of the room. But, in typical Colin fashion, he did none of those things, because that wasn't who he was. He was a good and decent man, and he proved it by doing the most surprising thing of all: he reached out cautiously and pulled her in closer to him, gently enfolding her in his arms, and rested his forehead against hers.

He swallowed hard before saying, "I have never doubted you loved me, Aoife. Only, I could tell, even before meeting Michael, that your love for me was not as strong as your feelings for him."

Tears ran silently down her cheeks as he continued.

"This is as much my fault as it is yours."

"No, that's not true," she choked out, but he put a finger over her lips to stop her from interrupting.

"Let me finish. I knew by the way your face lit up when you talked about this place how special it was to you, and I also knew by how sad you got when you talked about leaving it behind, leaving *him* behind, that you were never going to be entirely happy in New York."

She wanted to refute this, but they both knew it was true.

"I thought by coming back here that maybe you were ready to put whatever the two of you had behind you, and you and I could make our own home here, but I knew as soon as you saw him at the funeral that he still owned the bigger part of your heart, and he always will."

He swallowed again, trying to get out the words through the tears that still fell down his face. "He's a good man, Michael. And I hope he makes you happy."

"Colin... I'm not... He and I aren't..."

She didn't know what she could say to all of that. She could only keep thinking that this might have been so much easier had he been horrible to her. But she was the cruel one, not him.

"Whatever happened between the two of you tonight, even if you're not together now, you know you will be. Somewhere inside of you, you know it's been him all along."

She put a hand up to her mouth, trying to fight back the sob that wanted to escape her throat.

"I think, given everything, you should stay somewhere else tonight."

She nodded. The last place she wanted to be right now was here when he told Miriam that she wasn't going to be seeing her again.

*Miriam*. How was he going to explain all this to her?

"Can I say goodbye...?"

"I think it's best you don't," he said, his voice firmer now, protective. He had a right to be where it concerned his daughter. "I'll arrange for Miriam and I to be out of here and on a flight out of Dublin first thing in the morning."

She nodded again. "Tell her… tell her I love her, at least?"

He paused for a moment, but nodded in acquiescence. With great reluctance, she turned to leave.

"Aoife?" She turned around, a small part of her foolish heart wishing he might call her back to him.

"Be happy."

She could see through all the pain in his eyes that he was being sincere, that he truly did just want her to be happy.

"Goodbye, Colin," she whispered, heading quickly for the door before she broke down completely.

༄༅༄

She stood outside of the pub, not knowing where exactly she should go. She wanted to go to Connor and Mara's, but her cousin and his new wife had plenty of their own drama to deal with tonight, as did Brendan and Molly. They needed to be with their families right now, and she couldn't intrude on that.

She knew Sinead would be with her daughter and grandson tonight, and Karen and Jimmy would likely be dealing with their own drama at the Byrnes' house caused by Alistair, so she couldn't go to them, either. That essentially left Michael, but she was the last person he would want to see right now. Not after she'd turned down his proposal.

God, how did she go from having a great relationship, to getting proposed to by a man she'd been in love with for four years, to losing both men who loved her all in one night? How was this her life right now? She knew she was a disaster when it came to relationships, but this was taking it a step too far, even for her.

She wandered aimlessly. She supposed she could go back to Aldridge Manor, but she didn't feel like returning to the scene of her transgression against Colin, not after what she'd just put him through. It was home, but she wasn't ready to go back there just yet.

Without really thinking about it, she wandered around until she stood in front of the little churchyard. She'd never been a particularly religious person, but she supposed if there was anyone left to put her up for the night, God just might have to be it.

As she walked towards the church, she noticed there was still smoke coming from the chimney of the little stone cottage in the church grounds. Father Patrick had left the reception long before the drama with Alistair had started, but she was surprised to see him still up at this late hour. Feeling lost, cold, tired, and more than a little fragile, she was drawn by the warmth of the cottage and its kindly owner.

She knocked on his door once, twice. She heard some shuffling on the other side and it opened, the soft light from the dying embers illuminating Father Patrick's form. His kind face smiled at seeing her, then quickly turned concerned when he took in her dishevelled appearance.

"I wasn't sure where else to go," she said without explanation, the tears she'd been holding back the whole walk up, suddenly spilling over and she started sobbing, like a total eejit.

"Oh child, come in, come in."

He ushered her inside, guided her to the little settee by the window, and draped a blanket about her

# Where I'm Home

shoulders. She'd forgotten that she was still dressed in her wedding clothes, and they'd not really been designed for wandering around in the cool, Irish night air. She felt half-frozen, grateful for the scratchy wool of the blanket, warming her to her bones.

Without a word, he shuffled his way into the little kitchen, the only other room on the ground floor other than a small bathroom and returned a moment later with a mug of tea, pressing it into her hands. The ceramic mug warmed her fingertips, and she breathed in the black tea's aroma, instantly feeling comforted.

"Now dear, why don't you tell me what's happened?"

She'd stopped sobbing, but as she looked at Father Patrick over her mug of tea, she thought she just might start again. She took a sip of her tea, breathed in unsteadily, and unburdened herself.

## Chapter Twenty-Seven

"You go on inside. I'll meet up with you later," Michael said to Ailish as they approached his cottage. "I want to go to Mara's and check on Rory for a bit. Nothing like having your first kiss broadcast all over the village. Poor lad's not going to get over that one for awhile."

She nodded silently and went inside. She'd been quiet the whole walk up here, unusually quiet for her. He wasn't sure if it was just the night's events, or if it was something more.

He thought back to Brendan's earlier comment about how Ailish had noted he'd been missing for most of the reception. He tried to put aside thoughts of the difficult conversations with her to come and walked towards his sister's place.

He shuffled along the road to Mara's and went in

through the kitchen door. His mother and sister looked up at his arrival. Mara, still dressed in her wedding gown, clutching a mug of tea laced with whisky, nodded towards the back of the house.

"They're out back."

He nodded and headed out to the stone wall separating the Flanagans' property from the O'Brady property next door. As he approached, Connor and Rory looked up expectantly, waiting for him before they had this conversation. When Alistair had left the first time, Michael had stepped in and acted as a father figure to his nephew. He knew that, even though Connor was slowly taking over that role from him, Rory would want them both here tonight.

The three of them stood there, leaning against the cold stone of the wall behind them, when Rory finally said in a very small voice, "I'm sorry."

Michael and Connor both looked at each other over his head, perplexed.

"What are ye talking about, Rory?" he asked him, trying to keep his tone as gentle as possible.

"I'm sorry, about tonight, about ruining the wedding, about... who I am."

Michael felt his heart leap into his throat at this last bit.

"Listen to me, Rory Flanagan," Connor said with all seriousness, beating Michael to the words, "You have *nothing* to be sorry for."

"But I thought... When he called Des and I... And then Uncle Michael yelled at everyone to get out right when I said I'd kissed Des. And it was me who kissed him, not the other way 'round like Alistair said. And then you punched him," Rory spluttered, clearly not expecting this response from either of his father figures.

"Rory, I didn't punch Alistair because of the name he called you or because you kissed Des. I did it because he threatened my family. No one gets to hurt anyone I love like that."

Connor's tone was sincere, his grey-blue eyes seeking out his stepson's, trying to impress upon him how important it was to him that he understood this.

"What he said." Michael said, nodding in Connor's direction. "And I didn't yell at everyone in the village because I was bothered by the fact you kissed Des. I did it because your first kiss isn't something that should be broadcast in front of all of Ballyclara.

"Christ, I remember the first time I kissed Eliza when we were no more than your age, and the whole bloody village knew about it practically before I'd walked home. It was so embarrassing. I didn't want that for you when you had your first kiss. What's between you and Des should be between you and Des, without interference from the rest of the world."

"Thank you," Rory said, his voice full of emotion and his eyes full of happy tears as he looked at the two of them.

"We'll always have your back," Connor said, putting an arm around him and giving him a hug.

"Alright, let me in on this," Michael said, wrapping his arms around both Connor and Rory.

"C'mon guys!" Rory moaned, his voice muffled from being squished between them.

"Oh right; I forgot that it's not cool for pre-teens to be seen giving affection to their parents. I've forgotten what the rules are."

"That's because you're *ancient*, Uncle Michael," Rory teased him.

"Oh, ho ho, you think so, huh? You know that we

just made a promise to always have your back, but there was nothing in that promise that said that you're never too old to still get a good smack upside the head."

Rory laughed at him and the three of them fell into a much more comfortable silence.

"Was it a good first kiss, at least?" Michael asked.

"I mean, it was the first one. I don't have anything to compare it to." Rory shrugged. "But yeah, it was."

He smiled at the memory and Michael was glad at least he still had that moment to hold on to from tonight.

Another silence fell between the three of them, the only sound coming from the sheep lowing in the pasture behind them.

"So, Des, huh? You love him?"

"Yeah… I don't know… maybe? Yeah. I mean, I kind of always have, I think," Rory said, trying to explain it.

"Well, it's a good thing you've got a lot of time to work on figuring that out."

"I promise, for all our sakes, that I'll try not to take as long to figure it out as you have with Aoife."

"Yeah, and what was up with you leaving the party with my cousin earlier?" Connor asked him, arching an eyebrow in his direction.

"Oh, you're so going to get it now," Michael teased Rory, ignoring the question as Rory deftly dodged out his uncle's grasp, laughing.

※

As he drew up in front of his cottage, Michael wished he could be anywhere else but here right now. He did not want to have to do this. Ailish had always been kind and good to him, right from the first moment he'd met her, even when she hadn't known him at all. She was a good woman, and it hurt him to be doing this to her. He took a breath and gathered every last bit of courage he had to do this because it was the right thing to do.

"Ailish?" he called out as he came inside

She didn't answer. He knew she was at home; her car was still in the drive.

He moved swiftly through the small cottage and took the stairs two at a time. The landing to the second floor was small; there was only one of two rooms she could be in. He turned towards the bedroom and saw that she was packing her bags. He leaned against the doorframe, shoving his hands in his pockets, watching her. Although she didn't turn around to face him, he knew that she knew that he was there.

"Did ye sort things with Rory?" she asked finally.

"Yeah. He'll be alright, more or less. Poor lad's going to have a rough go of it for a bit, but he'll weather it."

She nodded. "You Flanagans are a resilient lot."

He finally moved from his post by the doorway and came up behind her. She deftly avoided him, packing a few more things away. Clearly, he hadn't been imagining things earlier and something really was bothering her.

"Ailish, I think we should talk."

"Colin and I aren't stupid, ye know."

Her statement completely threw him off-guard. "I never said ye were."

"When we saw you and Aoife sneak off earlier and then not come back for ages, we knew, more or less, what the two of you were up to."

He sighed and sat down on the bed beside her suitcase.

So, she'd seen that. He shouldn't be surprised; he was sure several people had seen him sneak off with Aoife during the reception. If she hadn't seen it with her own eyes, it would have just been a matter of time before someone had told her. He hadn't been thinking at the time, consumed with Aoife on his mind; he hadn't thought of the repercussions for everyone else until it was much too late.

"Ailish, wait." He put a hand out, trying to still hers. "Don't leave. We can talk this through."

They both knew he didn't really mean it.

"Really, Michael, there's no need."

She zipped up the suitcase and put it on the floor beside her. She came over to stand in front of him and put her hands gently on his shoulders.

"If I thought I was enough for you, I wouldn't be leaving without a fight, believe me. But," she put up a hand to quell any argument from him, "but, if Aoife can swan back into your life and so easily upset the balance of everything we've created here, then I know we aren't right for each other right now. If I was enough for you, Michael, then there wouldn't even be a need for you to question whether you still love her or not."

Michael hung his head, unable to look her in the eye because he knew she was right.

"I remember what you once said about why you didn't go after her three years ago. You said that you weren't going to stick around and wait for her to figure herself out. Well, I'm not going to stick around and wait while you try and fail to convince yourself that you're not still in love with her."

He sighed again, not quite sure what to say. "Ailish... I'm sorry. I never meant..."

She knelt down in front of him now and looked up

at him. "I know. We can't help who we love, Michael."

"For Chrissake, stop being so God-damned mature about all of this. How is it that you, at your age now, are more mature that I will ever be?"

He leaned down and pressed his forehead against hers. "You don't have to go."

He knew it was selfish of him to say it. He knew he couldn't love her the way she needed him to. She owned a part of his heart, but a larger part of his heart belonged to someone else. It was just the part of his heart that still cared for Ailish that didn't want to see her leave.

"You know I do." She looked at him. "I want you to be happy, Michael."

"I *was* happy."

He wanted her to know that. He wanted her to know that she'd made him so happy these past few years. If it hadn't been for her, he might never have known what happiness was again.

"But you're happier with her. Ye know you are. Even if she drives you insane at times, even if you two are a million miles away from each other, you're happier when she's here. And that's why I need to go."

She rose to her feet then and took up her suitcase.

"Where are ye going to go? It's the middle of the night. At least stay until the morning."

He stood up, hoping to convince her to stay at least a little longer.

"It's almost morning."

He looked down at his watch and realized she was right.

She reached up and kissed him gently on the cheek. "Goodbye, Michael."

He wanted to tell her to turn around and come back, but he couldn't do that to her. He knew in his heart that he'd never find someone else like Aoife. Even if she didn't want him, even if they weren't together, it wasn't fair of him to ask Ailish to stick around and be second best.

But as he heard the door to the cottage close behind her, he couldn't help but feel that he'd just witnessed the end of something that could have been truly great, and he might never know something like it again.

## Chapter Twenty-Eight

In the cold, hard light of morning, Michael stared blindly out the kitchen window of his cottage. A mug of lukewarm tea sat on the counter beside him.

He hadn't slept at all after Ailish left, simply changed out of his wedding clothes, took a shower, and made some breakfast for himself. He was too emotionally charged right now to eat anything. Looking at the clock, he figured it was just decent enough for him to wander over to his sister's place to check in on them again. He figured that, like Brendan and Molly, Connor and Mara, hadn't slept last night either. He knew he should probably give everyone some space, but he didn't want to be alone right now.

Brendan had texted while he'd been in the shower to say that he'd seen Colin leave with Miriam, and it looked like they'd packed all of their things with them.

Aoife hadn't been with them when they'd left.

He wondered, then, if he might run into her at Connor's place; if Colin had been at the pub when she'd told him about the night before, then she probably hadn't wanted to stick around in the morning to watch him leave. He'd be lying if he didn't say that the part of his heart that loved her was thrilled at this prospect.

"Anyone up?" he called out, walking in through the kitchen, not knocking. There was no need; Mara and his mother were sitting in pretty much the same spot as he'd left them the night before.

"Did either of ye sleep last night?" he asked, coming over and kissing his mother's cheek.

"About as much as it looks like you've gotten," she responded, running her hand over the stubble on his cheek. The motion made a raspy sound.

"I'm going to go on up and check on Rory. Brendan called 'round to say that he and Molly wanted to bring Des over soon. Hopefully, it will do the boys some good to see one another. I'll see if he's feeling up to having some breakfast."

She got up from the stool she'd been sitting on, groaning slightly, as those with old age did after sitting in one place for too long.

"And how are you doing?" he asked his sister after their mother was out of earshot. She was wrapped up in a fluffy dressing gown, her dark hair damp, and pulled back from her face with a clip. Her make-up had been scrubbed off her pale skin, making the dark circles under her eyes even more visible.

"Oh, ye know; I'm just fine and dandy." She smiled sardonically. "I sure know how to pick 'em, don't I?"

"I think ye have a good one this time around." He

put his arm around her shoulders, trying to be consoling.

"Yeah, me too."

A tiny, genuine smile crossed her lips as she thought of Connor. "I vote we just completely forget about the first one altogether and pretend like he doesn't exist."

"Good plan. It very nearly worked for over a decade. Who's to say we couldn't make it work forever?"

He smiled down at her. "Speaking of he-who-should-not-be-named, do we know what the status of Connor's plan to adopt Rory will be now?"

"Oh, that's all been sorted."

She pulled out an envelope from the pile of mail that sat on the counter near her.

"Connor found this in the mailbox this morning. It would seem that Alistair has no wish to be associated with a gay son."

"Fucking bastard."

There were plenty of other names he wanted to call Alistair Byrne right now, but that about summed up the gist of his feelings.

"Good riddance, I say." Mara looked up at him. "If he can't love my son for who he is, then I don't want that bastard anywhere near him. I just worry about how Rory's taking all this. He's not come down from his room since last night. I imagine he and Des have been up texting, but he's closing himself off from me, and I don't know what's going through his mind."

"He just needs some space," Michael said, sitting down across from her. "Des too. The two of them just need some time to sort out their feelings for one another and what it means for their relationship, or potential relationship. They're almost teenagers now, and that shite ain't easy, let alone when your sexual orientation is broadcast in front of the whole feckin' village."

"I just worry about them both and what this means for them." Mara put her hands to her cheeks, looking overwhelmed. "Just because we love them as they are doesn't mean the rest of the world will. It doesn't seem to matter how progressive the world has become; there's still bigots out there."

"Ye can't keep him wrapped up in a bubble his whole life, Mara."

Michael stretched his arm out to her, and she put her hand in his, giving it a gentle squeeze.

"He's growing up and there's nothing ye can do about it. He's going to run into the bigots, yes, but there's also a global community out there ready and waiting to welcome him in. All we can do is love and support him as we've always done."

She gave him a watery smile, tears forming in her eyes. Not sure what else to say, he changed the subject as tactfully as he could.

"Is Aoife here?"

He was trying to look inconspicuous as he searched his sister's cottage for signs that she'd come here last night.

"No, why?" she asked, wiping away the tears. "I figured she'd stayed at your place last night, since the two of ye are apparently back together again."

He turned towards her, his mouth agape, trying to formulate some sort of explanation.

"Yeah, ye failed to mention that last night."

She raised an eyebrow at him and took a sip of her tea.

"Well, it's not like there wasn't a whole feckin' shit storm of issues to deal with last night," he responded, a little too defensively. She may be his older sister, but that didn't mean he had to run all his big life decisions past her. "And we're not back together. At least, I don't think we are. How did you even hear…?"

"Ailish."

His heart sank in his chest.

"She texted to say that she was sorry that she wouldn't be here to help take down decorations at the church and pub today. When I asked her what was wrong, she didn't respond right away, but I eventually got it out of her."

She looked triumphant at her skills of interrogation.

"What the hell is going through your mind, Michael?"

It was not a rhetorical question. She stared at him, expecting an answer to a question he wasn't sure how to respond to. He thought that, after thirty-odd years on this planet, he would have figured out what the hell he was doing by now. Maybe it had simply been a hope or a prayer he'd had that things would work themselves out.

He sort of felt like he was going insane. Wasn't the definition of insanity doing the same thing over and over again, and expecting a different result? Then that certainly made him and Aoife insane right now. They'd expected a different result to the same problems they'd had before she'd left for New York, but maybe that was never going to happen. Maybe the two of them were never going to move on from this.

"I don't know," he groaned, rubbing his rough hand against the stubble on his cheek. The sound of calloused palm meeting five am shadow made a bristling sound. "I don't know, Mara. I really don't."

She sighed, a look of frustration and compassion coming over her face as she hopped off her stool and came around to him. He thought she may be coming over to slap him on the back of the head, but instead, she put her arms around him.

"I know," she whispered. "I'm not upset that you want to be with Aoife. She's family, and not simply because I'm married to Connor now. That girl has been a part of this family ever since she stepped foot in this village and there's no getting rid of her, even if we wanted to."

Michael smiled at that.

"It's that... I know you were happy with Ailish the last few years. *Truly* happy. Not just the kind of happy that is a placement holder until something better comes along, but the kind of forever happy. And I want you to have that, little brother. I want you to find your forever happy, whomever that may be with. As your big sister, that's all I've ever wanted for you."

"Thanks sis." He pulled back a bit from her embrace, gave her a little smile, and kissed her forehead. "Thanks for always looking out for me, even when I'm sometimes too pig-headed to do it myself."

"Sometimes?" She rolled her eyes at him, and they both laughed.

"Ok. All the time, then."

"Do you think she will make you happy, Michael? Aoife?"

A look of concern and worry crossed her face.

"Yes." The certainty in his voice shocked even him. Internally, he'd been wavering on this very subject since the moment Aoife stepped foot in Ballyclara for the first time. "Yes, she will."

"Then what are you still doing here, standing around in my kitchen? Go and find her!" she smiled at him.

"It's not that easy, and you know it."

"Colin?"

A knowing look came over her face.

"Yes, and Miriam, and Ailish, and the fact that she always runs away every time things seem to get even a little difficult or complicated."

"Oh well, she'll have you for company on that one."

Mara gave him a stern look, her eyes calling him out on his own faults. He was too tired to argue with her about it.

"I need to think about things," he pivoted, deflecting the comment.

"Ye need to think," she snapped at him, putting her hands on her hips and then throwing them up in the air. "Ye always feckin' need to think. That's all ye do! But ye never do enough of the doing!"

Michael got up from his stool, not wanting to hear another lecture from his big sister right now. He meant it when he'd said he needed to think about things. It was a big decision, and he needed to know he was making the right one.

"That doesn't even make any sense!" he shouted back over his shoulder as he left her kitchen, annoyed.

Of course, it made sense; he just wasn't about to let her know that.

༺༻

The little stone church stood in the midst of the churchyard as it had done for centuries, long before even the oldest person in the village could remember. He found it to be a comforting place; he'd been baptized here, he'd been confirmed here, he'd buried his children here along with the ancestors of his family. He hoped to be married here one day, and he knew he would be buried here too.

Michael loved the quiet of the place, loved that he could come here and unburden himself for a short time of all his worries and fears, and keep them in a place where there would be no judgement. The sanctity of this churchyard as was solid as the stone it was built out of.

He also loved that he could come here at any time and usually find Father Patrick either in his little cottage, or tidying up the church, or talking to the headstones in the graveyard, just as he'd been doing since he was a boy. He found comfort in this place, this rock and anchor for him in his life, when everything seemed to be spinning out of control, like it was now.

Aoife had been right, of course. It was difficult for either of them to imagine how they'd ended up back in this same place after all these years. That they'd both given themselves to new relationships, and yet still been drawn to each other enough to put an end to them.

He felt sorry for Colin, knowing that he was part of the reason he'd left, but not quite sorry enough to not feel some bit of hope that his leaving meant that maybe she'd changed her mind about his proposal. He knew he hadn't done it properly, that he'd sprung it on her too quickly and at completely the wrong moment. He'd done it out of fear, so caught up in the thought of her walking away from him again that he'd forced her into doing just that. He only hoped that she hadn't left for America yet.

"Well, Da, it's a fine day for it." Michael sat himself down on the bench beside his father's grave. The entire ancestry of Flanagans stretched out over the churchyard behind him. In front of him lay Ballyclara, nestled amongst the Wicklow Mountains.

"What would you say to all this, eh?"

He hadn't been expecting an answer, of course, so it came as rather a surprise to him when the graveyard answered back.

"Get off that bench and go tell Aoife O'Reilly that you're madly in love with her, and that you'll do anything to get her to marry you."

"Jaysus, Mary, and Joseph! Father Patrick, ye nearly gave me a heart attack!"

He heard the old priest chuckle, and his head popped up from behind a nearby grave. He'd been bending over, replacing some dead flowers by the gravestone, and it had concealed him from Michael's view. Father Patrick groaned as he brought himself to a standing position, walking carefully over the uneven terrain to settle himself on the bench beside Michael.

"I suppose I should feel a bit sorry for that, what with troubled hearts running in your family and all, and I don't just mean troubles of the physical kind like your father had."

Michael knew he wasn't just referring to him, but to Rory as well. Even though he'd left long before the encounter with Alistair, it would not surprise him one bit if gossip had reached the priest, detailing everything that had happened at the reception.

The priest nodded at Dermot's grave, a mischievous smile coming over his face. "Did you really think I was the word of Dermot, Michael? Or perhaps God himself?"

"I don't rightly know, Father," Michael replied honestly. He breathed in deeply, still trying to steady his pounding heart, hoping to calm himself again.

He thought about what his father would have

## Where I'm Home

thought about the situation. He reckoned Dermot would probably be chuckling up in heaven at seeing his son frightened near out of his wits by old Father Patrick. He smiled at the thought.

"Well, I reckon whether it's Dermot or our Heavenly Father, the answer would be the same."

He looked at Michael, raising an eyebrow as if to dare him to challenge his authority on the subject. He had no intention of doing so. He knew he was right, of course, and this was exactly what he should do; he was simply scared of doing it. And that was the problem. He couldn't propose to her again out of fear of losing her, or she'd surely run away for good this time. He needed to be brave and take that leap, prove to her that what they had was more than just fear of losing each other, or of being alone.

"Well," Father Patrick asked after a moment's silence passed between them. "What are ye waiting for?"

"Oh, you meant I should go now?"

"Well, you're not getting anywhere sitting here with the likes of me, now are ye? Go on and find that girl before she flies away to America, or God knows where else again. You've just missed her. She's down at the pub, packing her things. From what I understand, she moved up her flight a day, and Connor's driving her to Dublin in an hour."

Michael sat there, seemingly frozen to the spot. Was he really about to repeat his sprint through Dublin Airport to get the woman he loved? Would he be too late to stop her from leaving again this time?

"How is it that your gay nephew has more courage to go after the boy he loves than you do to go after someone you've been in love with for four years?"

Father Patrick seemed truly perplexed by the

question. "Now, you go and tell her you'll wait for her for as long as it takes for the both of ye to come to your senses."

"Well, go on with ye!" he repeated his order after Michael continued to sit there, unsure of what to do. Spurred on by the priest, he got up from the bench and heard Father Patrick call out as he headed down the road to Ballyclara, "and don't come back without her this time!"

He grumbled about the old priest – and everyone else in the village, for that matter – being in his business, but the truth was, they were right. Aoife was right: they were repeating history all over again.

And the psychologists were right too, because he was going to repeat what he did three years ago, hoping for a different result this time.

୫୬୯୫

Michael was still muttering to himself about how Father Patrick felt he could take his advice and where he could put it, when he found himself at the pub.

"What are ye on about, then?" Brendan asked him from behind the bar, wiping it down. Michael hadn't realized he'd been talking to himself out loud and was startled by his best friend's question.

"Nothing."

He was surprised to find him here, given Sinead had just told him recently that he and Molly would be going over to Mara's with Des. "I thought you were over at Mara's?"

"I was," he replied, picking up some posies that had fallen off the tables and onto the floor. "But the lads needed some space, and this place needed tidying up, so here I am. Molly's up with Mara. I'll go back up in a bit. Just need to keep my hands busy for the moment, ye know?"

He realized this was the first time he'd given a thought to what Brendan was going through, having his son's character attacked in public like that. He looked so much older now than their thirty-four years, weary-worn almost. He wasn't sure if it was the obvious lack of sleep, or everything else or, most likely, both.

"Brendan, I'm a shit friend. I'm so sorry; I haven't asked ye how you, Molly, and Des are doing."

Brendan chuckled. His laugh was without humour, but wasn't tinged with anger either. Just resigned, it seemed. "How long have we been friends, Michael?"

"Well, that depends on whether ye count the first time we became friends as the first day of primary school, or the summer before when we were over at Eliza's house for that big gathering her mam had for everyone our age which, of course, you and I can never seem to agree on."

He tried to infuse a bit of humour into the tension.

It worked: the corners of Brendan's mouth curled into a grin.

"Well, putting that debate aside for another day, and it *was* the first day of primary school, by the way," he interjected, cutting off debate, "it's been about three decades. Do you really think in all that time that I've not become accustomed to your drama taking a front-row seat to everything else? I mean, I love ye dearly, man, as if you were my own brother, but you really do have some strong narcissism running through ye."

Michael could only nod because he knew it was true; when it came down to it, it was usually the Michael and Brendan show, with Michael getting top billing, while Brendan stood by in the wings being the supportive best friend. They very rarely talked about what Brendan was going through, and now he was dearly regretting this.

"I'm a crap friend," he repeated.

"Yes and no," Brendan replied, being fair to him. "You're loyal to a fault, Michael, and I know you'll always be there for me if I just ask you. But, yeah, it's true; unless I ask ye to help with something, ye don't tend to offer."

"Well, I'm here now. I'm ready to listen like you've always done for me. You're never afraid to give me your advice, even when I call ye an eejit and try to do the exact opposite thing, only to find out you were right in the end. I can be the same for you."

Brendan cocked his head in surprise at this comment.

"It's the new and improved Michael," he said in response to his friend's shock. "I can admit when I'm wrong."

"That'll be the day," Brendan chuckled. "Look man, I appreciate you wanting to be here for me today. I really do. But ye do have unresolved drama to figure out before I'm willing to believe you're turning into this new Michael."

He gave him a confused look.

"Aoife. She left just a few moments before ye got here. She was heading to Connor and Mara's – I gather Connor's taking her up to Dublin to catch her flight to America – but she did mention stopping in at the Old Rectory on the way up."

"Are ye sure?" he asked, wondering if it made him a jerk for leaving when his best friend needed him in order to chase after the woman he was in love with. Again.

"Go on," Brendan punched him playfully on the arm. "And for the love of everything holy, and for all our sakes, don't feckin' let her get away this time! If I have to go through another three years of you living without her, I think I really might murder ye this time."

## Chapter Twenty-Nine

Sure enough, he found Aoife in the garden of Aldridge Manor, sitting on a bench near the far side of the garden, under the shade of an oak tree.

Standing in this place, he was reminded of the day he, Mara, Karen, and Aoife had replanted the garden, working together to bring it to life. Mara and Karen had tried to keep it up while she was gone, but she was the lynchpin of this place; the lynchpin of his life. When she wasn't here, nothing worked.

Leaning against the doorframe that was the threshold between the house and the garden, he felt that old familiar longing for her welling up inside of him, along with the fears he hadn't been able to shake: fear of losing her yes, but also, the fear of being happy with her. The fear of giving yourself over to someone else so completely, letting them envelop you into their life, and enveloping them into yours. In all his time with both Ailish and Eliza, he'd never quite let himself become consumed by another person, had never quite given himself over to another person like he had with Aoife, and she with him. It had terrified them both before she'd gone to America, and he knew this same fear of being happy together, of having something to lose, threatened to destroy them once again.

Despite the fear, the worry, the anxiety, he was determined to go all in, even if it meant losing again. It was one thing to lose Aoife; he'd done that and survived. But Michael knew if he didn't at least try to be with her again, to make this all work one last time, he would regret it for the rest of his life. And he didn't think he would survive that.

Hearing him come into the garden, or perhaps simply sensing his presence, she looked up to see him standing there.

"Michael?"

She seemed confused to see him, and he couldn't blame her. Their last time talking in this house hadn't gone so well for either of them. But if he was going to be with her for the rest of his life, he had to change that narrative, right here, right now.

"What do you want from me, Michael?" she asked as he crossed the garden to come sit beside her.

There was pain in her eyes; they were damp from her crying. She'd cleaned up from last night: her make-up had all been washed off, her auburn hair pulled back in a clip. She'd changed out of the dress Bex had designed for her, opting for the navy and white striped shirt and jeans she'd worn the day she'd helped him pack up his father's things. Even dressed casually like this, even without a stitch of make-up on, her eyes sad and tired as they were, she was still a beautiful sight to behold in his eyes.

"I want all the things that we never had," he blurted, eager to get the words out.

It all came out in a rush, and he wasn't sure that he was entirely making any sense, but suddenly everything seemed possible again, and he wanted so badly to make this work.

"What are you talking about?"

He took a breath, trying to collect his thoughts.

"I want all that we could have had before New York. I want the life we should have had back then, back when I should have gotten on the next plane out of Dublin and gone to your flat and told you how much I love you and how we can make this work. I know we can."

He added this last bit on at the last moment, hoping it sounded as sincere as he felt.

"Wherever you are, that's home for me. I don't care if that's here or in America, or in Timbuktu; I want to build a life with you wherever you are."

She eyed him suspiciously for a moment.

"You're lying, Michael; I know you too well. I know you'd rather be here in Ballyclara."

"I mean, I'm not going to lie; I'm kind of hoping it means we stay in Ireland, preferably in Ballyclara."

The corners of her mouth turned up slightly in a sad smile.

"But if that isn't to be, it's not to be. I'd rather live a lifetime away from this village than to go another three years, or thirty, or whatever, without you."

She didn't speak for a good, long moment, and he was terrified he may have scared her off again.

Finally, she took a breath and said, "I asked you before why you thought things would work out this time and you couldn't give me an answer."

He looked down at her and put a finger under her chin, turning her face up towards his.

"Because this time we can learn from our mistakes. This time we're all in. I mean it this time. I'm all in."

She breathed in sharply and he wasn't entirely sure if this was a good sign or not, but then he saw her face change, and a small smile formed on her lips. She leaned into him and kissed him ever so gently at first, and then more deeply. He reached around her waist and pulled her in closer to him, and he knew that every word he'd said was true, that he would roam the world with her if it meant the two of them could be together.

She pulled away slightly, trying to catch her breath, and looked up at him, smiling.

"I've been waiting so long for you to say that. Why didn't you say that to me three years ago?"

"Oh well, ye know, I hear I can be rather stubborn at times, but I wouldn't know anything about that. I think it's completely made up."

He grinned at her.

"At times? More like all the time," she retorted, but it was softened by the amused smirk on her face.

"Ok, you and my sister need to stop talking to one another about me."

She gave him a quizzical look.

"She may have said something very similar to me earlier, before practically shoving me out the door and telling me not to come back home without ye."

"I always knew there was a reason why I liked your sister," she said, smiling.

"And Father Patrick nearly scared me out of my wits, telling me the same."

She gave him a confused look.

"I'll tell ye another time. You'll get quite the laugh out of it, I'm sure. Oh, and then Brendan also told me not to come back to the pub without ye, or I'm pretty sure he's going to murder me, so I really hope this means that you're going to be staying, if for no other reason than it means I get to stay alive."

"I always knew Brendan and Father Patrick were the smartest men in this village."

She smiled at him.

He leaned his head against hers, breathing in the fresh air around them, surveying the house, the garden: everything he'd ever wanted with her suddenly seemed to unfold before him in his imagination. He could picture the two of them living in this house together, raising a family, growing old together. It was all there, right in front of them, if only they reached out and grabbed this opportunity.

"No more running this time?" he asked her, staring deep into her eyes, wanting the unvarnished truth from her.

"No more running," she promised. "I'm home now."

## Epilogue

*One Year Later (or thereabouts)*

It was a bright and sunny spring day, the clouds fluffy and lazy as they floated by on the warm breeze. Amidst this beautiful day, the little parish church in Ballyclara was abuzz with activity like a beehive. The entire village had somehow squeezed itself into the church pews until it was overflowing and there was standing room only.

"Is that everyone, then?" Molly asked the boys, adjusting Des' tie and licking her thumb to wipe away a smudge of lipstick on Rory's cheek from some old auntie who'd gotten to him before he could politely duck out of the way. The boys protested at the preening but were duly ignored in Molly's no-nonsense fashion. She would not have the two of them looking anything other than their best today.

"I sure hope so, else the fire marshal is like to kick us all out. We're full to the rafters." Rory nodded to the door leading to the sanctuary.

"Right, I'll go and let them know we can start, then?" she turned to ask Aoife who gave a small, nervous smile before nodding in agreement.

"You've got nothing to be nervous about. Everything is going to be perfect today."

Molly gave her a quick hug and then turned towards the sanctuary. As she cracked open the door, the buzz of conversation from the excited guests permeated the room.

"You two go and take your places now." Connor nodded to Des and Rory, indicating for them to follow Molly outside.

Before leaving, Rory turned to Aoife. "You sure you're not going to change your mind now, are ye?"

His tone was mostly teasing, but Aoife noticed a slight flash of actual worry in his eyes.

"What kind of question is that, now? Right, out with the both of you. Go on now."

Connor ushered Rory and Des out of the room, smiling the whole way.

"Can you believe the cheek of that one?" he asked Aoife, taking her arm in his as they heard the pianist start up the music on the other side of the door.

"With you helping to raise him, I can, yes," she replied, smirking at him.

Connor narrowed his eyes but didn't give a retort. "You *aren't* planning on bolting, though, right?"

Aoife elbowed him sharply in the ribs.

"Ow!"

"Serves you right," Millie said, watching Bex fix

the train of Aoife's dress, an impossible feat given how much she was nervously fidgeting with her train. No sooner had Bex gotten it where she wanted and then Aoife would move and undo the effort.

"I just had to be sure." Connor smiled cheekily at the both of them.

"Now, why are you playing with her train? She's just going to be walking again in two seconds and it's going to be all moved around again."

"Because for one second, it's going to be perfect and we're going to get a photo to capture it."

"Here, let me."

Karen, who had been standing by with Mae and making sure she looked perfect in her flower girl dress, held her hand out to Bex for her mobile. "Ok, Millie, Bex, you two squeeze in there beside Aoife and smile!"

She quickly snapped some pictures and then handed Bex's mobile back to her so they could all look at them.

"Oh, you look stunning!" Bex exclaimed, turning to Aoife.

"Here, let me see." Aoife held out her hand for the mobile and she, Bex, Millie, and Connor crowded around the screen, examining the photo.

"Well, if I look any good at all, it's all down to the two of you."

She motioned to her stunning, custom-made dress Bex had designed just for her. It was an A-line, floor-length chiffon gown with cascading ruffles. The transparent lace panel in front gave it the illusion of a sweetheart neckline. It was modern yet timeless, flirty and delicate, and absolutely stunning. It was everything she could have asked for.

"I couldn't get through today without either of

you."

She could feel the emotions welling up inside of her and tears threatened to spill over her cheeks, not for the first time since she woke up this morning.

"Now look what you've gone and done," Millie chastised Bex. "I spent all morning trying to get that makeup just right and now she's going to go and mess it all up."

"No, I'm fine." Aoife fluttered a hand in front of her face, trying to compose herself.

She never expected to be the kind of bride who got nerves or got all emotional on her wedding day. Then again, she didn't really think she'd ever be a bride in the first place.

She took a steadying breath and squared her shoulders, reminding herself of all the excitement she felt at the life that waited for her on the other side of that door. "Ok, let's get this thing started."

"Right, now just let me go and get my place before you go anywhere. Mae, you'll go out first and then Bex and Millie, you two can make your procession."

Karen turned back and smiled sweetly at Aoife. "Best of luck out there!"

The buzz of chatter on the other side of the door was growing, the crowd getting impatient for the ceremony to begin.

"Just one sec." Millie adjusted one of Aoife's auburn curls that had escaped her chignon.

"Now who's fussing!"

"Sorry. All good now." Millie beamed at her and then turned around and held out her arm to Bex. "Milady."

"Why, thank you." Bex gave a mock curtsy and the two of them proceeded into the sanctuary behind Mae.

## Where I'm Home

As the pianist cued their arrival, Aoife heard the creak of the old pews as the congregation stood to get a glimpse of the wedding party. She heard the crowd make little "awwws" at the sight of Mae in her pale pink, frilly flower dress as she scatted petals down the aisle.

Unsurprisingly, there were exclamations of approval at Bex's beautiful Grecian-style gown she'd designed for herself as she walked down the aisle with Millie, whose custom-made ballgown with its wispy train and the bodice a riot of multi-coloured embroidered flowers drew murmurs of delighted confusion. The two of them couldn't look more different from one another in their unique styles of dress, but they looked perfectly themselves in Aoife's eyes.

Just before the pianist cued the wedding march for Aoife's big arrival, Connor whispered, "Last chance to back out."

She knew he was only teasing, but with all seriousness, she turned to him and said, "Not a chance. I'm right where I want to be."

Looking up the aisle, she could see Rory and Brendan standing beside Michael, who gazed adoringly at her. Aoife felt a happy blush rising in her cheeks and smiled radiantly at him. Barely waiting for the music to begin, Aoife took a confident step forward towards the only home she'd ever wanted.

Read more from Erin Bowlen:

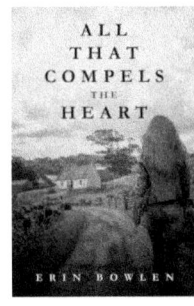

The Aoife O'Reilly series is a collection of bestselling women's fiction novels from Canadian author, Erin Bowlen. With its deeply drawn characters and slow-burn chemistry, you'll love this moving journey. Click the images above to begin reading now!

## About the Author

Erin Bowlen is the author of the best-selling Aoife O'Reilly series.

Erin was born and raised in New Brunswick, Canada. Growing up, she was influenced by her family's artistic roots in both music and storytelling. She began her writing career during her postgraduate studies in Classics at the University of New Brunswick.

In 2018, she published her first novel in the best-selling Aoife O'Reilly series, *All That Compels the Heart*.

In 2020, she published the second novel in the series, *Where I'm Home*, as well as the #1 best-selling prequel novella, *Grainne*.

Erin currently lives in New Brunswick.

Milton Keynes UK
Ingram Content Group UK Ltd.
UKHW051703101123
432260UK00024B/615